Crimson and Cream

In the view of the author, this novel is not suitable for children under 18. It contains some adult material to include adult themes, adult activity, hard language, or other elements.

This novel is a work of fiction. Names, characters, places, businesses, and incidents either are the product of the author's imagination or are used fictitiously. Any resemblance to actual persons, living or dead, events, or locales is entirely coincidental.

If you purchased this book without a cover, you should be aware that this book is stolen property. It was reported as "unsold or destroyed" to the publisher and neither the author nor the publisher has received any payment for this "stripped book".

Crimson and Cream

by
Carmen

A very special thanks to my family. Mom and Dad, Andy, Cissie, Landa, Cyndie, Maggie, Audie, I love each of you and thank you from the core of my being for always supporting me and my dreams. I have the most amazing family!!

Phillip and John, well, there are no words that can define the love I have for you. I am grateful for every smile you give and all the joy you bring. You are my babies and I am so proud of you…Muah!

Ken, you are always there to help and encourage. I love you and thank you so much…you're not only my friend and life-long golf partner, you're my brother.

John, Yvonne, Deidra (Dee-Dee), Tattianna, Skipp, John, Ms. Nik, and Maresa…thanks for the special support you've given to see this dream come true. Thank you!

To all of my supporters, I am so grateful for you.

A special thanks to the MU SIGMA CHAPTER.

A Personal Note:

I'm really excited about the rebirth of Crimson and Cream. It's been 10 years since I first released it and now I can honestly say that I'm ready to enjoy the journey it will take me on.

I've been asked many times why I decided to write a story about a particular Greek organization and repeatedly I've had to answer that the story is not about any organization. Crimson and Cream is a romantic drama that is centered around five men belonging to the same brotherhood. How can I write about an organization I have no knowledge of? Fiction, remember?

I really appreciate each of you and hope we'll one day have the opportunity to chat about what you enjoyed the most about Crimson and Cream, the novel.

God bless you and stay encouraged!

1

Monday night, September 16th

The 72" color monitor was bright. The sound amplified, the drinks, and snacks were in place, and the ladies stood in the corner as they witnessed "their men" prepare for what seemed to be the highlight of their week.

The music and colorful highlights flashed the screen as the opening of prime time football screamed what was known to be the anthem of the NFL. "Are you ready for some football?!" The well known Monday night commercial that shook through the living rooms of many was thundering as the Monday night football ritual for Peter, Marquis, Jamale, Austin and Adrian soon began.

Although most men enjoyed the pleasure of watching a football game with just the fellas and their favorite cocktail, these men took Monday night football to a different level. It was an event, almost celebrated as if it were any holiday. It had been five years of Monday night football, and with the exception of a scheduling dilemma and the lady on their arm, nothing changed.

The TV was loud; the fellas were loud, and they did not seem to care. Monday nights in the fall belonged to them, and the noise level was their furthest concern. It was not like they were in an apartment enjoying the game; they were in the comforts of a well insulated private home of one of the five most eligible bachelors in the city of Dallas.

Adrian's house was the chosen venue, and although he cared about the neighborhood, he certainly did not care about who, what, how, and when his neighbors thought about him having a party or gathering. When the Monday night gatherings first began, it came with snarls and sneers, but that changed when they realized Adrian didn't give a damn about his neighbors opinions. In fact, over time, Adrian had the satisfaction of witnessing the change in his neighbor's attitudes as they enjoyed and expected the four cars to drive up the dead-end-street and park in front of the red bricked house on the cul-de-sac.

In the beginning when the gatherings first began, his neighbors stood out on their lawns and watched the cars as they arrived. For a while, Adrian chalked it up as jealousy, but as he studied their expressions, he came to the conclusion that his neighbors were more confused than jealous. They simply could not fathom how five Black men could be living larger than they were living working a nine to five. Rumor had it that the fellas were either involved in drug sales or were high dollar male escorts.

As the weeks and the football season progressed, Adrian's neighbors found the nerve in their curious and downright nosy minds to stir up frivolous conversations hoping to gain some information about the men. Adrian couldn't walk from his front door to the mailbox without one of his resident snoops interrupting him, but the interruptions didn't faze Adrian one bit. Considering how obvious they were, he knew what was going on and truthfully, Adrian was amused by them.

The conversation always started with the ridiculous, "well, another day at the office." For a while, Adrian would give generic answers such as, "hey, somebody's gotta do it," but deep in his heart, Adrian wanted to get raw and surprise the undercover agent with a bit of urban slang. "Naaw dawg, ain't no office happen'n here. We supplyin' to the dawgs workin' up in them offices...you know, those high dolla pimps." Adrian decided there would be no satisfying point. He worked around enough White folks who wouldn't admit it if their lives depended on it that they controlled the high dollar drugs in corporate America.

Finally, his red headed, freckled faced neighbor across the street couldn't take it any longer, and asked, "So, what is it that you do?" Adrian anticipated the day he'd be able to explain his elaborate position and after several more questions about the four cars that drove up on alternating Mondays, the inquiry was over, and the secret was out. The neighbors learned the men were professionals and probably had a larger net worth than they did. Eventually, the neighbors began walking closer towards Adrian's driveway to speak to the gentlemen and their ladies as they exited their vehicles.

The street began looking like a dealership of luxury cars, and Adrian was digging on how the neighbors were checking the men out and all of their success. The car of choice was the Mercedes convertible SL500; Navy blue, black, red, maroon and forest green, each gleaming with a fresh buff and wheels that grinned of elaborate style.

Adrian's house was the latest and largest house developed on the street. A 4800 Sq Ft, four bedroom split level in the suburbs. The foyer greeted the guests with marble floors and a glass table that occupied a piece of exquisite Italian blown glass. Entering the next room, it enticed you with a crackling fireplace and parquet floor where a black grand piano, adorned with fresh orchids sat. The mantel was decked with fine crystal, and a painting of Ray Charles at the piano decorated the wall. Beveled glass walls surrounded the room making it stunningly elegant, and each room thereafter was as well dressed. Adrian had a house that any woman with good common sense would want to be the lady of.

Adrian had an additional room built off the side of the garage. He called it his "everything" room. A definite man's room with a pool table, large screen TV, mini music studio, small gym, and a bar with beverages of choice. On the wall was a large framed picture of James Brown doing what James Brown did best...breaking it down. The picture was so appropriate for the room. It had a caption from one of his many hits beneath it, "It's a man's world". The room was unquestionably a man's world inside the doors of an "everything" room.

Crimson and Cream

The traditional Monday night football gathering was not just a night of football or a street show for his neighbors. It became a night for the five men to select and exploit a woman and her beauty. Each week the men gave much respect to their contemporaries for the trophy they brought to the house. But it was Peter who started a tradition that was far crazier than anything they did together.

On one hand, consider how a waiter would try to entice you with the restaurants special of the day. And, for example, consider how an attorney presents their case to the Court or stands in front of the jury with the closing argument. Adrian, Marquis, Jamale, Peter and Austin combined the waiter and attorney scenarios and made the women the subject to be enticingly presented. They named the tradition, "Ladies on Trial". Unknowingly to the women that stood proudly beside their men that Monday night, they were being introduced, identified and defined as the men's feast of pleasure. And the men became witness, judge and jury.

The schedule never changed. Arrive one hour before kickoff, get your eat on, mingle and make the ladies feel as though they belonged there, and to be ready for the Ladies on Trial tradition.

Soon after the ladies made themselves comfortable, Adrian asked them to excuse him and the other men for a minute while they met in another room. The excuse they gave would always be to handle some personal business and the women never questioned the nature of the business. Naturally, the women went along with something as small as being excused for a few minutes. Why wouldn't they? The women knew they were spending time with the top choice of men in the city, and to be selected as their dates for a football game around their boys meant there was a good chance if any chance at all at proving they could be the woman who could make them happy. Besides, they also knew if they ever wanted to spend more special time with them, they'd better cooperate.

While Adrian was explaining the need for them to be excused, the other men stood to the side covertly checking out the women to make certain they'd have a vivid mental picture. Had they not, it

4

would leave too much for the imagination as they were being deliciously described.

As they left the room, the men winked at their dates before they headed down the hall. When they entered the den, Peter took his place behind the large desk. Marquis, Adrian, Austin, and Jamale would either find a seat or stand somewhere facing the cherry wood desk near the window.

This was the highlight before kickoff and Adrian was wearing his typical smirk. Marquis and Jamale grinned as they bobbed their heads at one another as if they were rivals. Peter and Austin raised their heads and arms to the side of them as if asking, "So, what you got?" The men were silently announcing that they were ready for whatever the other had to offer.

This was serious men's business that was getting ready to take place. Each of them checked the other out and enjoyed the deviousness that was written across their faces, although, it was always Peter that they got a good laugh from as he got into character. But that laugh was short-lived. They took their tradition serious.

Peter took his place behind the desk that faced the men and then he quietly cleared his throat before he began. He stood with his chest out, and head held high. All he needed was a black robe, a white curly wig pressed to his head, and he would have truly been looking the part. "Here Ye, Here Ye. The court is in session.

Tonight we will determine the entrees of the evening, leaving no room for doubt whether the court is satisfied with the feast." Turning towards Marquis, Peter added, "Brother Marquis, we begin with you."

When the tradition first began, the men used to laugh and be really silly, but soon it became a challenge to see who could describe their woman the best. It was Marquis' turn to finesse his boys.

Marquis was thirty-five and the oldest of the bunch. Although shorter than average, he was 5'6, 165 pounds of faultless sex appeal and with the perfect bald head and tight physique that enabled him to tower above most men. As poised as he could be in his navy blue warm up suit and bottle of imported beer in hand, he stood to the right of the gentlemen as he confidently and arrogantly began his spiel.

"Well gentlemen, today I bring to the table a fine cut of tenderloin. If you'll notice, all of the fat has been trimmed. She is well seasoned and at a medium rare perfection; a fine selection of beef that will satisfy any hungry man's appetite. Thank you, gentlemen." Marquis was equally arrogant and confident as he stepped back to his place in the room to allow Jamale the floor.

Jamale stood at 5'11 and was 200 pounds of pleasure. He was well groomed, clean cut, an athletic build, and an exciting baritone. He was an accounting graduate from Grambling State University and with CPA credentials. It was time for Jamale to put on his most bourgeois tone before he chimed in.

"If it pleases the Court, I have made the decision to reintroduce a fine burgundy dinner wine. One that is very fine to the taste and enough to satisfy the desire. One of which I avoid taking out during the light, keeping it consistent so not to spoil it. And one I keep on its side to keep the cork moist." As Jamale stepped back to his place, Adrian interrupted, "Yeah fine wine my ass. Basically, what you're saying is she's leftovers." Jamale couldn't help his smile and agreed. The other men also knew Adrian had spoken the truth. They laughed a little, but quickly regained their composure to allow Austin the floor.

Austin was 6'1, 210 pounds of absolute muscle and a smile that could dazzle any woman. But it was his sultry voice that mesmerized the women, and when he spoke, he was very direct.

"I offer tonight, delicate but strong asparagus tips that will be firm in the beginning, but very tender once you put them in your mouth. As with anything rich in flavor, the taste is full and succulent and will delight your taste buds." All of the men gave a nod of satisfaction as Austin took his seat allowing Adrian to speak.

Adrian, 6'0 and 215 pounds of excitement, he had this hip-hop flair about him and was open to the taste of life. He was a marketing graduate from Fisk University and the A&R (Artists & repertoire) executive for a major record company.

With a pinch of assurance mixed with a bit of charm, he was very suave when he stood from his chair. "Gentlemen, the evening would not be complete without the flavorful potatoes to go with the beef, asparagus tips and fine wine. They're soft and fluffy and will satisfy your hungriest appetite. As they meet with your tongue, you'll feel their texture as your mouth waters from their creamy fullness and flavor that will have you craving for more in the days to follow." The men couldn't help but nod their heads in agreement and with satisfaction.

Peter was 6'1, 208 pounds of utter efficacy, a well groomed mustache that caressed his savory lips and his hazel eyes that seduced every woman who was within his view. Peter stood like a cool cat knowing he was going to finesse the fellas with his description before they returned to the ladies in the other room.

"Gentlemen, I'd like to end the night with a dessert that will leave you enticingly satisfied. I have with me fresh strawberries; Grand Marnier flavored whipped cream over a crisp orange brandy wafer. When you reach the last bite it will relax you and have your ass knocked out and sleeping like a brand new baby."

The men began to laugh as Peter reached for the red and white cane in the corner of the room and began to twirl it. The other men gave one another palm as they stood in a line and encouraged Peter to do his thing. The men were in their element, and they knew they were trippin', but that didn't stop the tradition.

Meanwhile, the women who were left in the "everything room" were doing their own defining. Marquis' date started with, "Listen, I don't know 'bout y'all, but I can't hold this shit in any longer." Looking over towards the door to make sure the men weren't

7

returning, she continued, "dayum, them some fine brotha's. Five fine ass brotha's who got it goin' on." She glanced over to Austin's date and finished. "Hey, no disrespect to you, but, Austin is fine as hell. Damn he got a sexy ass on him. Gerl, you better work that shit."Except for Tiffany, each of the ladies giggled their approval.

Sipping on her cocktail and feeling the effects of a double Belvedare martini, Adrian's date freely let her words roll off her tongue. "Hell yeah. I'd stay on my back just so I could grab onto his ass. Dayum imagine if the rest of him is as rock hard? Oh, and I ain't talkin' 'bout his arms and legs if you get my drift." These women had learned how to fool people with the way they carried themselves. But even designer clothing, weaved hair and artificial nails couldn't make their expressions of true lust look sophisticated as they nodded in agreement.

Although flattered with the comment, Austin's date thought it was time to set the record straight. She stood almost leaning as her head, and hand moved from side to side, and her lips tightened, and her eyes rolled when she spoke. "Oh, but I do. And the shit is." Turning up her lip a notch more and putting much more attitude into her declaration, she added, "You don't hear me doh. The nigga rocks my ass and trust me, I ain't complainin'."

The ladies started giving one another dap and cheering the other on as if they had just agreed on the final answer on Family Feud.

Marquis' date figured it was her turn to make sure the other women didn't doubt what her man had going on, so she stepped up and took her stance. "Well, I'm here to tell y'all all that shit you hear about short men and what they're working with....well, the shit is true. Mr. Marquis is packin', and he ain't slackin' when it's time to deliver the goods. Damn that negro knows how to work his shit."

They tried not to be too loud, but their shit talk had gotten so good to them they couldn't hold back their roar.

Peter's date was getting ready to start, but she heard the men near the door. The ladies smiled at one another as they checked out the men's "equipment" when they passed.

Returning to the women with a peacocks strut, Adrian's date said at a whisper, "Work it baby." Marquis and Peter's date chuckled loud enough to catch Adrian's attention.

"What's so funny?" Adrian asked.

In unison, the ladies answered, "Nothing." Causing them to giggle.

Each man walked over to their lady and offered a small kiss before finding their place in front of the television. Unknowingly to the women, the men had fully scoped them out and agreed that the description given earlier were right on the money. What a feast to marvel at.

As described as a fine cut of tenderloin, Marquis' lady Camille was much younger than the other ladies. She was pecan brown with a body that she obviously committed to a gym.

Jamale's lady, the reintroduced dinner wine or leftovers as they each agreed, Tiffany was average but satisfying. She was nothing to savor, just a temporary satisfaction.

Adrian's lady, the flavorful soft and fluffy potatoes, Ashley was what men call "thick". She had the hips, ass and tits and appeared to be soft.

Austin's lady, the delicate yet strong asparagus tips, Tabbitha was tall and lean and very feminine; the most feminine of the ladies.

Peter's lady, the fresh strawberries with Grand Marnier whipped cream over a crisp wafer, Jamilla was a caramel brown with hazel eyes and very top heavy. Together, they were these men's feast of pleasure.

Tiffany stood a few steps away from the other ladies. There wasn't any hiding Tiffany's well worn funky attitude and the other women in the room detected it the moment they paid homage. Just like a cheap creamy foundation layered over a bad case of acne, there just wasn't any hiding it.

Tiffany believed her position with her man was substantially different from the other women, and in actuality, it was. She'd been Jamale's guest more than once to one of these weekly gatherings. She figured because she didn't need an introduction to the other male guests in the room, she had an upper edge and was considered to be special.

Women need to stop believing stupid shit like that. A second date does not constitute "special." Chances are you were the last minute option or if you gave "it" to him the first time, he wanted to hit it again, and if you held back the first time, well, he knew he would get it the next time.

The ladies giggled with one another as they fixed cocktails for their men and the fellas relished in it. Like most men, if you give them the upper edge, they're going to allow the woman to believe what she must.

Marquis' date made a few comments about Tiffany such as, "what the hell's up with that bitch?" And, "I know Miss Thang don't think she's all that. Check out her jacked up weave that needs to be re-sewn, glued, velcroed or however she got that shit staying up there."

Tiffany could tell she was being discussed, but she didn't care. She stood with her hand on her hip with a smug expression and humored herself while she mimicked the other ladies under her breath. But Jamale wasn't skipping a beat. He was checking Tiffany's every movement and made a mental note to let her ass go as soon as possible. Ending each thought with an exclamation point, of course. He had no choice but to question himself why he even bothered with Tiffany. She was a trip, to say the least, and there wasn't any room in his life for a controlling, neurotic, and insecure female. Something Jamale had in his favor was his confidence and that he didn't need a woman to make him feel any more a man than he was.

Jamale sat back on the sofa and closed his eyes to reminisce on his earlier years. During his college days, he experienced more than most men did in a life time. Going to school in Louisiana, where the closest town named Ruston seemed to be the capital for the blind, he realized he couldn't survive making minimal wage flipping hamburgers at the Tigers Den. So, being the street savvy Detroit Michigan raised hustler that he was, he did what he did best----- he hustled.

For high school graduation, his moderately well off family came together and contributed to purchase Jamale a new Toyota Camry with all the extras. And because he had run his hustle the last two years of high school, he had a top-of-the-line Movado watch, Hugho Boss suits, alligator shoes and hand woven silk neckties, which, by the way, were purchased at the Back 2 Back Resale store. His uncle Willie, an old school pimp, had introduced him to the marvelously well kept secret world of resale. But, the resale store had to be kept secret because you wouldn't be on top of your game if you let someone know you were a wear another nigga's clothes type playa.

Jamale was driving ten miles west on interstate 20 when he started noticing the billboards that opened his gates to freedom. Isle of Capri. Horseshoe Casino. Bossier City. He had hit the jackpot. Casinos meant many things, but only two mattered to Jamale. Those things were money and desperate women. The way he equated it was if you put a desperate woman and money together with a playa who could give you some northern pleasure, the results would be two things; a satisfied woman who'd give up the dough and he'd be a very happy and paid brotha.

His first year at Grambling, Jamale didn't need any financial help from his family. He had convinced them he had a job near the school and was handling his business; which actually was the truth. Occasionally he'd tell his family it was tough being a college student, but that was just for GP. Jamale was doing fine. He was slingin' dick, male prostituting, running a dick-a-thon, or whatever else it could be called. Regardless, he was averaging $1200.00 a month pimping himself, and that was in cash alone. Not including the clothing and the extras, like jewelry that he was clocking on the side.

On Jamale's first trip to the casino, he wore an olive colored suit with an eggshell shirt, a silk olive and brown necktie, and brown suede shoes. He was debonair and looking years older than he actually was.

He followed the bright red carpet down the stairs into the smoke filled room where the flashing lights from the slot machines seemed to be everywhere. The bleach blond waitress in the skimpy black and white outfit caught Jamale's attention immediately. When she approached him for his drink order, Jamale smiled at the Roulette wheel embroidered across the breast area of her uniform. After declining the drink offer, he walked the room until he found what he had driven the interstate for.

Mission complete. Bingo. Jackpot. Or whatever the appropriate outburst is when you hit it big in a casino. Jamale noticed the woman who would offer big winnings, she stood out like a neon sign that read, "Million dollar winner, come and get me." She had just turned thirty when he met her sitting at the bar alone.

"Hello. Is this seat taken?" Pointing at the empty seat next to her.

"No, actually it's not." Surprised that the handsome young man would be interested in sitting next to her.

"You're looking exceptionally beautiful. May I get you another cocktail?" Lying through his teeth, Jamale knew if he wanted to get anywhere with the plump older woman, he'd have to overlook the three extra roles of fat that hung over her black leather pants. "Damn that shit looks nasty," he thought. A thicker woman was something Jamale commonly ignored, but this time he couldn't. If he wanted to make his plan a success, he would have to indulge in the frequently used saying; a man wants a little meat on her bones.

Hmmm. Young boy fine as hell traveled through her mind more than once. Returning the smile and showing off her gold trimmed front teeth, she accepted Jamale's offer. "Well, yes handsome. What's your name and where have you been the last four hours?"

Jamale could smell the Crown Royal as she spoke, so he used that to his advantage when it was time to impress her with the drink order.

Funky. Funky. Funky. Funky breath female was perhaps the only sufficient description that crossed his mind as he tried to find some fresh air in the smoke infested room. Jamale's head was beginning to feel the wicked effects from the alcohol on her breath, so he stepped back a little to order the drink. Before placing the order, he threw in some art of bullshit he'd learned in his high school years hanging out with his uncle Willie. He looked her up and down as if summing her up and began his performance. "Hmmm, let me see. A classy woman like yourself must be drinking from the top shelf. Only the best for the best. No doubt, you're a Crown lady."

Drunk and dumb, she fell for his pick-up line and Jamale was confident any other fraudulent attempt would be effortless.

"Damn baby you fine." Using her hand to identify herself, she continued, "and you recognize fine when you see it, and you know your liquor." Pointing to the chair she slurred, "Com'on ova here and sit next to your sugga momma."

Jamale sat next to "plump and drunk" and listened as she explained it was her birthday. But though she was drunk and feeling good at the moment, he could see she wasn't happy and felt bad about herself. She was about thirty-five pounds overweight and her weave was something she depended on. At the moment, Jamale didn't care. The only thing Jamale saw were her diamonds. Money bags had diamonds from her ears to her ankle. And let me make a point, the diamonds were full grown rocks.

After pumping three shots of Crown into his system, they left the gamblers behind and went to her room on the third floor of the hotel that the casino was in. As they entered the room, she was trying to figure out how to unlatch her button on her overly tight leather pants when she collapsed onto the bed. Jamale thought he would be sick when he removed her pants for her and saw several rolls that surrounded the tiny black thong that appeared lost in her thickness.

As Jamale began to undress, she was calling out his newly appointed name, "Big Daddy". He was being invited to give her what she needed with explicit instructions. "Hit it from the back, baby. Smack it, flip it and rub it down." The thought of hitting it from the back was making Jamale sick causing "it" not to function. Jamale wasn't getting a rise until his sugga momma helped him along. She began to suck on his soft penis and eventually it came to life after minutes of tongue clucking and lip smacking. Jamale figured out the secret to getting through his night with his future investor. He closed his eyes and never opened them again until it was time to turn over, get dressed, cover her up with anything within reach and get the hell up out of there.

Jeannette was a visitor from Houston and quickly became his number one supplier. She made the trip to Louisiana weekly to spend time with the young man who wasn't sparing the rod; the young man who was taking more than adequate care of her needs.

Jeannette was married to a corporate high roller and a major player in Houston who hadn't played the love game with her for a while. Jeanette was lonely and Jamale being the good business man that he was found nothing but great pleasure in taking care of her and having his financial needs taken care of too.

After pledging into his fraternity, Jamale figured he would share his wealth, so he introduced his successful line of work to his fraternity brothers. With them being the resourceful men that they were, the game was mastered to make enough money to keep them ahead of the game. They kept cash in their pockets. They had all the latest gear. They spent money frivolously without hesitation. Each of them had nice rides, and they made women feel lucky to be with them. It had gotten so good for the men that the women on campus were doing everything to convince them that they were the best thing since sliced bread. The women would cook, clean the men's rooms, wash their clothes and sex them down as often as they were allowed. Between the women on campus and all of Jeanette's friends who needed what she was getting, those men had it going on and they knew it. In a very short time, the Kappa brothers were definitely running things in both Grambling and Shreveport, Louisiana.

Shaking his head back to reality, Jamale sat back on the leather sofa and frowned as he looked at Tiffany. If she only knew; a female like her don't know how to act until she gets messed over and made to feel like shit, he thought. He couldn't stand it any longer. In seconds, Jamale found himself walking over towards Tiffany ready to put her in check and the way he looked, it was obvious he wasn't all that happy. When Tiffany saw his wrinkled forehead and the glare in his eyes as he approached her, she knew that was her cue to change her attitude. Tiffany wasn't about to get played in front of all the women she had been messing with all night. So, before he could reach her, she turned away and started making conversation with the other women. They tried to ignore her but Tiffany kept up with her charade. They smiled at Jamale as he turned around before saying anything to Tiffany. The ladies knew what had just happened, and they loved it. Brother Jamale had put Tiffany's ass in check without saying a word. Jamale had gained the reputation of being fully capable.

Jamale returned to his seat when Marquis stood. Low enough to be heard by the men only, the toast was made. "Brotha's, let the mutha fuckin' game begin." Kick off was only minutes away, so Adrian got the attention of the women and asked them to please be seated. The fellas knew what was about to be said, so they just stood back to observe the expressions of their dates.

"Ladies, here's the deal. I know some of you are new century type women and may know a little something about football, but tonight we don't want to know about it. We're not trying to be rude, but I'm gonna be real with you. As much as we love having you here with us, we really don't wanna know about your football skills. So, what I'm saying is, while the game is on, you gotta give us our space. There's a huge pool table over there in the back of the room, and you're welcome to play, or you can sit and chill and play some cards or do some girl talk. Whatever you decide is on you, but the game is ours, and we need you to respect that." It was unquestionably a strong case of aggressive testosterone and male chauvinism going on.

It was a fact, the women didn't like what they had just been told, but the ladies agreed as they nodded their heads and gave their men a kiss before they walked away. Naturally there always has to be one bad apple in the bunch and that was Tiffany. She was rotten to the core. She had to add some funky shit to the night. Loud enough for everyone to hear, she whispered to Marquis' girl, "Huh, you smilin' and shit, but he's serious. Last week your man had to put the other female he brought to the game in check because she thought they were joking." Tiffany turned her lips up and walked away from the other women thinking, Bitch. Bet she won't be talkin' no shit about me again.

Marquis looked over at Jamale. Without saying a word, Jamale knew what was going on in Marquis' mind. That mess wasn't cool. The fact that Tiffany felt the need and had the audacity to try to mess up his evening was jacked up.

There was no doubt in the room that Marquis was pissed, and Jamale tried to make good of a bad situation. "Man, I'm sorry for her ignorance. Trust me; I'm planning on dismissing her ass real soon."

Jamale looked over at Peter and began giving him props on how he handled women. Jamale commented to Peter, "Man, you never have to deal with lame crap like this. I guess its how much sugar you put in your kool-aid that makes it sweet." Jamale's name for "game" was kool-aid.

"Dawg, it took a lot of tasting and adding before I finally got the shit mastered. But now, my kool-aid will have your ass hooked." They laughed for a minute then shook their heads at Jamale's nuisance of a date and watched Marquis apologizing to Camille for Tiffany's ignorance.

These five brothers loved one another. Jamale, Adrian, Marquis, Austin and Peter had a tremendous amount of respect for one another, and they were bonded forever. Each of them had taken a pledge of brotherhood and became friends in the place they called home, Dallas, Texas. Although different in many ways, they shared one thing in common that would never change. They were Kappa men. Nupes. Men of crimson and cream.

2

$\mathcal{I}$t was six years ago, on an unusually cold October day in Dallas during the State Fair when Grambling State University competed against Prairie View University in the Battle of the Bands/Football game. Marquis and Adrian attended the game together, and because of their credentials, they were able to be guests on the football field. Marquis worked for the NFL, so he earned his football VIP pass and Adrian represented the artists that performed at the fair granting him instant star power.

Marquis' younger brother was PV's starting running back and had been viewed as having a promising future in the NFL. The arena was filled with Black folk of all ages. The crowd was crunk, the bands had just competed at the half time, and the different fraternities and sororities were each representing. The ladies strolled around proudly in the outfits they thought would get them the most attention and the men checked the ladies out as they canvassed the stadium. The Cotton Bowl was at capacity with people from all over, for an event the city prepared for each year. There were no fights, no potential confrontations, well, maybe one or two for someone trying to push up on someone else's "property", but other than that, it was a beautiful day of some good old fashion entertainment. And outside the stadium was just as hyped where K104 pumped up the music in the parking lot.

This has been a long time rivalry game. In the past years, the game would be a blowout, and the crowd would disintegrate after the half time show, but this year the game was better than any of the previous seasons.

This year, the two teams were giving the fans their monies worth. The game wasn't lopsided due to one team being far better than the other, and both teams actually had great potential.

The teams had maintained a tied score throughout the first half of the game, and by the fourth quarter, the score remained even. The bands played their funky tunes and kept the crowd rowdy and the players on the field were doing their jobs, which made this game as good as any other NCAA football game.

It was first, and ten and PV was on their thirty. The ball was snapped and handed to number twenty-one, Marquis' brother, Tyrone. Clutching the ball tightly in his arms, he ran seventeen yards avoiding his defenders when suddenly he was hit and didn't get up. The PV side of the stadium was booing, and the Grambling side was cheering. All at once, PV's staff was running out on the field and the crowd began to silence. After minutes of the coaches and athletic trainers being circled around Tyrone, the emergency medical team was called out. Soon there became a chilling silence at the stadium.

Immediately, Marquis ran onto the field to assist. When he saw his baby brother stretched out and not moving, his heart felt as though it had stopped. He had seen too many football injuries on the field and knew this wasn't good.

Marquis was a kinesiology graduate from Alabama State University with his masters' degree in sports medicine. He was also the youngest athletic trainer on the professional football field. With all of his education and experience, Marquis knew this was beyond his expertise.

The ambulance was called out to the field, and Tyrone was put onto a stretcher and hurried off the field. The people in the stadium could feel it wasn't an ordinary injury. The mood was unnerving, and the sound of the sports announcers' exuberant play by play articulation shifted into a monotone and serious intonation. "Ladies and gentlemen, it appears that Prairie View's top running back, Tyrone Frazier has been seriously injured. We'll keep you updated as we learn any further information on his condition. Let's keep the young brother in our prayers."

The media faced their cameras in every angle to get a glimpse of what had happened. While the emergency team treated Tyrone, the television networks replayed the hit several times for the home viewers. As the radio sportscasters watched, they were on the telephone calling into their stations. This was sports news. One of the top ten potential NFL draft picks had been seriously injured.

Marquis rode in the ambulance with his brother. When Adrian saw them leave the field, he rushed to his car to get to the hospital. Austin, who had been passing the radio station memorabilia out in the parking lot, got the call from his sportscaster from inside the stadium, so he packed up his van. When Austin saw the ambulance leaving the stadium, he rushed to follow it so that he would have an edge on a first hand story for the radio station.

The ambulance seemed to have been traveling slower than any ambulance ever on an emergency call. When they arrived, the hospital's emergency team was waiting. They followed all the procedures to revive Tyrone, but it was too late. Tyrone was gone. He had passed away on the way to the hospital. It was remarkable how one hit and a ruptured spleen could change everyone's life.

Austin rushed into the emergency room doors in time to see Marquis sitting on the orange vinyl seat in the waiting room, rocking back and forth with his head in his hands and almost between his legs. Adrian stood clutching his head in disbelief as the tears streamed down his cheeks. Austin was stunned when he saw the two men. He asked the nurse standing in the doorway to the triage area if she knew where he could find Tyrone Frazier and his family when the nurse glanced over to Adrian and Marquis and informed Austin that Tyrone had passed away. She indicated that Tyrone's brother was one of the men crying.

Austin stood for a moment looking not sure if it would be proper to visit with the men. Suddenly Austin's eyes grew big, and like a magnet, his eyes were focused on the Greek letters on Adrian's gold key chain and then Marquis' tee shirt. Austin was instantly connected to his fraternity brothers and knew he had to visit with them. Austin walked over and kneeled next to the men when he spoke quietly, "Frat. My name is Austin James. I'm with K104. I just heard the news. Man, I am so sorry." Adrian and Marquis looked up at Austin and knew their brother wasn't trying to get a radio scoop. They could see the pain in his eyes. Marquis and Adrian tried to gain their composure for a moment to talk with Austin, but it was impossible. Marquis was in shock as he repeatedly asked, "Why?"

Austin understood his fraternity brother's grief. He sat with them for the next ten minutes watching them mourn. Later a nurse walked over to the men and suggested they spend time in the private waiting room down the hall. Marquis wasn't in any condition to talk, and when he tried to stand, he felt his legs becoming weak. Almost limp, Austin reached to help Marquis. Adrian watched the two men and then invited Austin to join them in the waiting room. Adrian and Austin shared Marquis' pain that afternoon. On such a tragic day, the three men secured their bond.

The funeral was four days later in Atlanta, Georgia. It was a small room at the Resting Place Funeral Home that comfortably sat twenty-five people. Marquis assumed because he didn't have a large family, the room would be large enough for the few people who would come to show their respects. Marquis hadn't figured how popular his brother had become at Prairie View, and he never thought friends would travel from Texas to Georgia. He was wrong. There were bus loads. The football team and three coach buses had traveled the interstate for Tyrone's funeral. People were coming as fast as they were going. Marquis stood at the right corner of the cream casket and watched the people as they stood to pay his brother their final respects.

Most of the people had tears falling from their eyes. But it was the ten men who walked to the casket, who placed a red rose on top of Tyrone's chest that looked the saddest. The men were Tyrone's Line Brothers, or LB's as they're preferred to be called, and they loved him. Tyrone had just pledged the spring before.

Marquis stood watching and feeling their pain as he watched the men mourning for their brother. As the ten men took their seats in the third row, Marquis noticed the other four men seated in the front row with a raised hand to their chest, pointer finger pressed to their thumb, and remaining fingers extended. While Marquis didn't know two of the men, he was happy to have Adrian and Austin there to support him. The two other men were Peter and Jamale. Austin asked them to take the trip to Atlanta with him so they could be there for support. Marquis was pleased they had come. It was a help to have the support of his frat brothers. Marquis knew these men would be men he'd quickly grow to love.

Ironically football brought them together, and tonight the men were following a football tradition that had been going on for years.

SUNDAY MORNING

With the exception of a couple of things, weekdays for Jamale were methodical. Unless the weather didn't permit, he always stood out on his deck in his pajama bottoms and inhaled a deep breath of the fresh morning air before starting his day. He'd go to his handsomely decorated bathroom and perform the typical three "S's", shit, shower and shave; he'd slip into one of his silk bathrobes and go into his well equipped kitchen to prepare a cup of herbal tea. He'd then go out to his sun room that overlooked his in-ground swimming pool to enjoy the Wall Street Journal. Contemplating the rest of his day, he'd find his way to his walk-in closet and select from his diverse and very professional wardrobe. That wardrobe would be the beginning tools that would allow him to blitz the fortune 500 company, Emerson and Harding. His unexpected moves within the brick walls of the company allowed him to receive his lucrative and very substantial paycheck.

Saturday's were always left for chance. However, Sunday mornings were always left for tranquility in every form. Jamale's intake of fresh morning air came when he ran an hour around the manmade lake and, as part of his diet he'd have a hardy and somewhat healthy breakfast at the Original House of Pancakes. It was something about those waffles, fresh strawberries and whipped cream that made Sundays feel special. Feeling refreshed and stomach full, Jamale's next stop would be Sunday school, and as customary, third service at the Bible Fellowship church he'd joined.

Sunday mornings on the lake usually invited new fitness participants, and although Jamale noticed several new runners at the lake, he didn't see the young lady he'd met the weekend before who'd asked him to coach her with her run. He shook his head in regret as he thought about her tight and shapely ass and the missed opportunity.

The air was crisp and was feeling good against Jamale's skin, so he picked up his pace a notch to try to get a good sweat on. An hour later and Jamale was drenched. He pulled two extra thirsty towels from his bag and before sitting, he placed them on the mocha brown leather seat of his car. Unquestionably, Jamale had gone beyond his goal of a good sweat when he turned his head to the left and smelled himself. He was in dire need of a shower.

He only lived two miles from the lake, so the drive home was quick. Jamale entered the house from the garage into the laundry room, undressed fully and put his soiled clothes into the washer. Walking through the house naked after his run was one of Jamale's pleasures. Jamale being the nautilus expert that he was enjoyed the payoffs of his hours pushing up on weights. Before he got into the hot shower, Jamale stood in front of the mirror that stretched from floor to ceiling and almost wall-to-wall and admired himself as he flexed his muscles. He saw exactly what most women enjoyed when they had the occasion to enjoy it. "Dayum. How can a brotha blame a sista for wanting to get with all of this?" He humored himself as he shifted his flexed positions.

Jamale enjoyed the hot water pounding against his skin, and he took great pleasure on how it relaxed his muscles and helped him to think. While showering, so many thoughts ran through his mind, but one in particular made him shake his head in disbelief. Vanity wasn't his distant ally so the thought of his debonair and charming self, and the reaction it caused, specifically at church stimulated him to laugh out loud.

It was common for Jamale's walk from his car and into the sanctuary to have a number of female heads turn. Although, as flattered as Jamale was by his admirers, gaining attention wasn't his purpose for going to church. Besides, Jamale had come to the conclusion day one of visiting the church that the single women had already taken notes of all the single male members, and he was just one more name for the majority of the single women in the church who had made their lists and checked it twice.

When Jamale walked into the church the first day, the women's eyes were on him like lint on black corduroys. But little did they know, Jamale wasn't hoping, wanting, nor needing to be acknowledged. Clearly, Jamale stood out from most of the male attendees, but, looking good and smelling great was just something he did, and he did it better than most with little effort.

Attending church regularly had become something Jamale had committed to six months ago. And although he had met and befriended several women there, he had made a promise to himself that he wouldn't date any of the female attendees. As with most grape vines, rumors from women in church and their gossiping will spread as if they'd been to a Tell It Like It Is Convention. Jamale hadn't planned on getting tangled or strangled in that vine nor had he any intentions on starting any sort of reputation that could potentially end up a bad one, so he kept it safe.

After allowing the pulsating shower to massage his fatigued body, Jamale stood in his bedroom enjoying himself while he air dried. The women of his past had told him how sexy he was and that his glistening body was beautiful. So to take a moment to admire himself in the mirror and to notice how his black curly hair lay wavy and smooth to his head and how his long, damp eyelashes appeared longer, and the hair on his chest and legs lay smooth to his skin, and how his pecks hardened from the cool room. Jamale couldn't help his chuckle as he recalled one woman telling him that his hard ass looked delicious when wet.

In his home, Jamale had the small but powerful Bose speakers built into the walls of each room and on Sunday mornings he enjoyed them to their fullest. Standing in front of the wall-sized mirror as he oiled his skin, the sounds of the jazz saxophonist had Jamale in a zone that almost caused him to miss the ringing telephone. Rushing to answer the telephone, he accidentally kicked the sesame seed oil over onto his carpet. It wasn't very often his phone rang on Sunday mornings because most people who were significant in his life were aware of his routine and didn't interrupt it.

It was Tiffany on the line, and when Jamale heard her voice he was angry with himself that he didn't check the caller ID before picking up the handset. The unexpected phone call from Tiffany kept Jamale on the phone longer than he'd hoped and the unnecessary disagreement with the woman who wasn't worth the aggravation sort of pissed him off. And the fact that he spilled oil on his carpet didn't help the matter.

"Yeah. Hello." Jamale answered with aggitation.

"Hey Boo. What you doing? I hadn't heard from you and wondered why?"

"Why? Tiffany, you know better than to question what and why I do things. Plus, I'm trying to understand why you're even calling today. Tiffany, listen, I don't have time for the asinine BS. It's early, and I am getting ready for church." He'd had enough of Tiffany's drama. But being the compassionate man that he was, Jamale regressed to his charming self and in a low tone, using his sexy baritone voice his next few words calmed his harshness. "You know what, I apologize for saying that. I'm not even going to get into this with you. If you want to talk later, I'll give you a call." Jamale had dealt with many needy women in his past. Needy women came with a lot of twisted mood swings and manipulative and calculable behaviors. And frankly, he wasn't allowing another to take up space in his life.

Tiffany enjoyed how Jamale could be so hard one minute and in a matter of seconds be real charming. It gave her a horny rush that brought out the freak in her. So while he was raising his voice and called himself going off on her, she was sitting on the other end of the line concentrating on her hardened nipples. As long as he flipped his emotional switch, she didn't care what he had to say. What Tiffany hadn't realized was, Jamale had recognized long ago that she was a woman who'd become amused and satisfied by a man's negative response. He was determined not to fall victim to that game with Tiffany a.k.a. Sybil. She just didn't mean enough to give her the satisfaction. But Tiffany was on top of her game, she did what she knew most men expected from women. She became submissive in her own ridiculous way. "Ooooh Baby, don't be mad at me. I'm sorry. Baby, I just wanted to know about tomorrow night. I didn't mean to upset you. I'll wait for your call and talk with you later. I miss you. Talk with you later. Bye." She blew several kisses into the receiver while his eyes rolled as long as the kisses were being blown. Unfortunately, that didn't stop Jamale from ending the conversation with meaningless words that inflated her ego.

"Kisses back at ya. Talk to ya later, Bay."

Jamale was kicking himself for responding as he did.

Like most women, Tiffany heard what she wanted to hear. Jamale spoke the one possessive word that Tiffany zeroed in on; that one word that kept her secure in her position. The word that made her feel like everything was good between them. "Bay." The word "Bay" to Tiffany meant so much more than other pet names. It meant she was his everything and like it or not, in her mind, he had claimed her as just that.

Occasionally Jamale called her "baby", "honey" and other cute names, but when he broke it down to "Bay", in her mind, he took it to another level. Jamale had no idea he'd traveled across and beyond, over and under the boundaries of screw-ups with this woman, and he didn't realize how far and deep he was in the pit of Tiffany hell.

Tiffany had graduated from Texas Southern University with Cum Laude honors, and was popular on campus with everyone but the sorority she'd hoped to pledge. Although most people would have considered her a shoe in, the soror's saw something in her that didn't meet their standards. There was something they saw early on that convinced them she wasn't someone to trust. And they were right.

Tiffany's application to join the sorority was accepted, but her time pledging wasn't something she was ever going to forget. Because of it, she became vengeful. She changed her entire attitude from nice girl to bad ass and became known as the bitch on the campus. Tiffany discarded her old perspective to give everyone respect until they lost it and adopted and lived by the new attitude, "fuck 'em". Tiffany became persistent with everything she did regardless of the expense of others and the words "can't have" was freed from her vocabulary. In fact, she lived by her creed, "you got it and I want it."

In the back of Tiffany's mind, she knew exactly the cause behind her being made the joke of the Delta Sorority. It had been the first day of admissions in her freshman year when Tiffany laid her deep brown eyes onto that fine Puerto Rican brotha standing against the desk whispering into the ears of the woman that appeared to be his girlfriend. Yoli, the golden brown sister had been a soror for three years and watched as Tiffany gave her man a look that clearly said, Forget ol' girl, I got what you been missing. Yoli was pissed. And as she and her boyfriend exited the hall, she made sure Carlos and anyone within a listening range understood her man wouldn't be gettin' with no stank hoe.

The expression was clear, and Tiffany understood the indirect threat to get her ass kicked if she got anywhere near Yoli's man. Tiffany may have played dumb, but she wasn't stupid. She didn't hesitate to give a look that suggested she would stay away. However, it was three days later when Tiffany found Carlos waiting for her in her dorm lobby. And when the bone was thrown, the dog did fetch. Tiffany had no concern letting Carlos know that females got a little dog in them too.

When all was said and done, the rumor hit the campus, and the shit hit the fan. That's the moment Tiffany realized that Yoli was in the sorority she'd hoped to join. Tiffany didn't want or need her reputation tarnished, so she went to Yoli and explained how Carlos had told her that his relationship with Yoli was over. It was an innocent mistake; Tiffany assumed Carlos was open game. She didn't know. A lie no doubt, but so what, this wasn't about Yoli, this was about Tiffany clearing her name. Yoli listened while Tiffany went on, and on with her theatrical plea and when she was finished, Yoli told her everything would be straight. But in the back of Yoli's mind she thought, this bitch is crazy.

Tiffany called herself working Yoli with her ghetto ass charm and thought by ending the conversation with, "Girl, bump that negro. Sista's gotta stick together" that things would be okay, and that would be the end of it. Oh, but Tiffany was not her sister, and it wasn't over for Yoli. Carlos was her man and somehow Tiffany would pay for her mistake. Needless to say, she did. Tiffany had gone through several weeks of pledging. One week before crossing over, the soror's decided to dismiss Tiffany from pledging. Yoli got her ass back and in a painful way.

Jamale had reached the conclusion Tiffany was an idiot and made the decision to end their involvement before the day ended. Jamale wasn't happy with the way Tiffany's uninvited telephone call had him agitated, and he refused to start his day that way. When he looked at the clock and noticed the time, Jamale decided to change his Sunday routine. Instead, he skipped breakfast, went to the early morning service, Sunday school and afterwards had brunch down on McKinney at one of the swanky eateries. Although the area was known to be the homosexual hang-out, Jamale didn't get caught up in the ignorance of most homophobic men. He enjoyed the area of Dallas for its great shops and dining. Masculinity or the lack of issues wasn't Jamale's concern.

Frequenting the third service, Jamale had become well-known with the members. However, the church he attended had a large enough congregation to have three services. Therefore, he hadn't become familiar with the members of the first and second services. And, because Jamale had heard first service was as full as third, he rushed to get ready so he could try to be seated at his usual place.

The drive into Richardson was quiet. Jamale listened to The Oasis, a local jazz station while assuming the few cars on the highway were all church goers. Jamale admired the happy families who passed him; husband, wife, two children in the back seat heading to church to worship together. A wonderful and hopeful lifestyle to have one day, but he didn't see it happening in the near future for himself or any of the other four men.

As he pulled onto Centennial Boulevard, Jamale watched the security officer direct the cars away from the church parking across the street. Just like the third service, the parking lot was full, and the overflow parking across the street was also close to capacity.

As Jamale hurried to cross the street, a white Volvo with two women beeped their horn to get his attention. When he stopped to see the driver, Jamale flashed one of his brilliant smiles. He was flattered but not impressed enough to make him later than he already was. Jamale acknowledged the gesture and kept walking.

When he arrived at the building, Jamale was aware he was a few minutes late. In the foyer was a television that showed what was going on in the sanctuary. All the people in the sanctuary had their heads bowed, and one of the deacons was at the pulpit. In the foyer, Jamale stopped to join the people within the sanctuary to pray.

Waiting to go inside, he smiled at the unfamiliar faces and tried to look occupied by appreciating the Polaroid pictures of the new members framed on the wall. When Jamale heard the doors open, he turned and rushed for his usual seat towards the front, in the middle aisle. Not that it mattered where he sat, it was just a preference.

After being seated in his usual spot, he sat quietly focusing on the royal blue robes above the pulpit. The choir started with a slow and spirit lifting song that had most of the hands in the church raised towards heaven and tears falling from several people's eyes. After the song, the associate pastor, a large man with a West Indian accent asked everyone to reach for the hands of the member to his left and then his right. Just as everyone else, Jamale reached for the hands side of him. Jamale could feel the warmth from the hand to the right, and while praying, something strange was going on inside of him; his mind was racing with loving thoughts. His heart was filled with inscrutable emotions, and his hand was feeling nestled with a woman he felt he knew and cared for. But how could that be? She was a complete stranger. He'd only seen her once before at the singles party months prior and even then he didn't approach her because she was mingling with other members.

Jamale knew he was tripping and surprisingly, he also knew he had no control over his thoughts as his mind wandered into a love story. He tried to focus on the message being taught. He even tried positioning his body so he wouldn't have use of his peripheral vision. Something was going on, and Jamale couldn't make sense of it.

After service, he watched her mingling with other members at the front of the sanctuary. Jamale waited in the foyer trying to look busy. When he thought her conversation would be over, he walked back outside the sanctuary to signal to the woman that he wanted to talk to, but she was gone. Jamale couldn't believe she was gone. He'd hoped she hadn't left the church, so instead of going into the Sunday school classroom he headed onto the front lawn where there was some activity. The youth ministry was having a bake sale. As an alternative to looking obviously disconnected to everyone, Jamale started soliciting members to help the kids. Meanwhile, he found himself having to escape from the annoying woman who made it evident she had her eyes on him and who had followed him most of the morning. As Jamale was sneaking away from his one-woman fan club, and not looking forward, he bumped into the woman who left him confused.

Very surprised when she looked up and saw him, she held onto Jamale. She looked into his eyes and smiled before she spoke her cheerful words, "Hey Brother." Jamale was blown away by this woman and how she had made him feel earlier. Between apologies, he smiled at her when he replied with a flirtatious hello.

Not sure how to react, the woman reached for the door. But Jamale had also studied the art of chivalry, so he stopped her attempt and opened it for her. Jamale had a dark side, however, and he wasn't always a gentleman. From time to time, he'd slip and revert to his old and familiar Northern ways; brash, forward, abrupt, impatient, direct and to the point. But Jamale's attitude was improving since attending church.

Rushing into the kitchen with a foil wrapped plate of food, she asked Jamale to heat her food in the microwave. Surprised by the request, he stared into her eyes as if to say, hold up. But her expression was so inviting, and her eyes were so tempting that he couldn't help himself. He took the plate and went along with the request. They chit chatted a bit and shared a few broad smiles, smirks and laughs when Jamale finally asked her name.

"So lit'l lady, what's your name?"

Looking deeply into his sexy eyes she smiled and answered, "My name is Nikkia, but everyone calls me Cee-Cee."

"Hello Cee-Cee. I'm Jamale LeTreau. Pleasure to meet you, but I must ask, how do you get Cee-Cee from Nikkia?"

Based on the smile she was wearing, the memories of how she got her nickname were fond. "It's a story that perhaps one day I'll share with you." At that moment, the timer on the microwave interrupted their conversation and once more, Cee-Cee was wearing the inviting expression that got him to agree to put the food into the microwave. Before she could ask, Jamale had opened the door and removed the plate. She was quite pleased with his gesture as she thanked him.

His grin made an impact on Miss Cee-Cee, so she finally showed some humility, and in a very coy manner she asked, "Would you like some?"

Jamale was tired of being mister nice guy. He'd forgotten where he was when he asked, "What? The food or you?"

Cee-Cee was shocked for a moment that he would even ask that question, so she continued with what she thought to be the appropriate answer. "O-kaaaay. I'm talking about the food Brother, the food."

It was obvious Cee-Cee was surprised by his question, so Jamale apologized for his foolishness. He smiled and leaned closer and asked if it were at all possible for him to have her telephone number so he could call her and try to make up for his poor judgment. Cee-Cee was satisfied with Jamale's apology and blown away by his interest in her that she agreed to give him her number. Jamale's smile let Cee-Cee know he was happy, but suddenly Jamale looked at his watch and noticed the time. He hadn't eaten all morning when he announced he had to leave. Cee-Cee understood, and their brother to sister hug solidified their acquaintance.

3

$\mathcal{T}$he holidays were near, and the fellas were looking forward to the vacation they had planned a year ago. After a good night of watching the movie Scarface and laughing at the infamous Tony Montana, the fellas decided Cuba would be their vacation destination. Normally they would plan around the first of the year, but this year they chose Thanksgiving weekend. Tax season was quickly approaching, and Jamale knew getting away after November would be too stressful, and besides, Austin and Peter always had a long Thanksgiving weekend. Because the Grammy nominations typically would be in by late October, Adrian would be resting comfortably knowing which of his artists had been selected, and Marquis knew after the Thanksgiving day football game, the 'Boys would be off for a few weeks.

A mild November day and DFW airport was unusually quiet for a holiday. It was probably quiet because most of the holiday travelers had departed earlier in the day or the night before. Most people would want to be sitting at someone's dinner table enjoying the treats that came at a Thanksgiving dinner. For the fellas, they knew dinner meant one of two things; whatever the airline was serving or wait until they reached customs in Cancun and get some Mexican grub there. They had heard the stop at customs would be long.

Most of the evening was spent at one airport or another. It didn't make any damn sense what you had to go through to travel to Cuba. Castro had the shit locked down. He had complete control over who, what, when and whatever else he wanted as it related to Cuba. There were only two choices on how you could enter onto Fidel Castro's island. Either fly out of Miami or fly from outside of America. So you figure, okay, you're in America, you'll fly to Miami and then to Cuba. You would think. But to do that you would be spending almost double the cost than to fly from Cancun. Being so close to Mexico, the fellas opted for the cheaper route. They flew from Dallas to Cancun and from Cancun to Cuba.

Passing through customs lasted over two hours in both Cancun and in Cuba. They couldn't believe it. There were more Americans; White Americans traveling than Cubans; probably because the trip was difficult and disheartening for Cubans. When the aircraft arrived into Cuba, security treated the Cubans like crap. They rummaged through their bags removing whatever they felt should be discarded and to add insult to injury, their luggage was tossed at them as if they were animals. Adrian being the comedian of the group couldn't allow the opportunity to pass. He made several jokes why Tony Montana was getting his butt up out of Cuba and Marquis, Austin, Jamale and Peter cracked up laughing.

It wasn't until the men reached Havana that they understood why Cuba was a great choice for their vacation. It was awesome. It was the most festive and friendly place they had ever visited. If they had to describe it in one word, the best word to describe Cuba would be colorful. The people ranged from all shades and they partied in the streets all night without any confusion. There was no black, white, light skin, dark skin issues. They were Cubans and that was all that mattered. And the Cubans didn't separate the Americans by their skin color either. They were simply Americans.

When the fellas woke the next morning, it was a warm 80 degrees, and the ocean air was fresh. After reading the hotel brochures on the local happenings, they agreed to ride the ferry on the El Malecon, the river that circled Havana.

Leaving the hotel, they flagged down what appeared to be local transportation. The car was without air conditioning but possessed a stereo system that blared salsa music to the point of discomfort.

Arriving at the pier, the men stood in line for what seemed an eternity, but it was worth the wait. As they circled the town, the five men were convinced they'd seen enough when their eyes focused on the bright crystal-like white sand that surrounded the clear blue water on Varadero Beach. The men had reached paradise as far as they were concerned. After the ferry ride, they hailed a cab for a ride back to the hotel. They hurried to their rooms to get into their beach wear and rushed back to the beach.

When they reached the beach, the hunched over older man who was obviously three shades darker from the Cuban sun clung to the men as soon as they stepped onto the sand. He'd made himself their official beach guide informing them that there were separate parts of the beach that offered different things.

He had described so eloquently the area of the beach he felt the five men would enjoy most. The old man was very impressive with how he convinced them to agree to walk down to the far south end of the beach where they'd see nothing but nature at its best... butt naked women. Although his English was limited, his hand gestures earned him five dollars.

Reclined on the wooden chair, Peter enjoyed watching the women who worked the beach. Essentially those women were the only ones who were working and getting over on Castro. The laws on coochie tax had yet to be written. Marquis checked Peter carefully through his dark shades. Peter was hooked on one particular woman so much that Marquis thought Peter was going to run over and lick her dry. Marquis interrupted Peter's stare and asked if he'd planned on getting some Cuban coochie before leaving. Peter sat up in his chair, adjusted his buttocks from side to side and took a long pull from the straw inside his cocktail glass before he spoke. "Hell naw. I could just imagine the crabs on the beach aren't the only crabs that come out at night. Ain't no Cuban ass gonna have me about to scratch my shit off." The other men listened and began laughing at Peter while they sat back and enjoyed the rest of the day at the beach. By nightfall, the fellas had enjoyed a few good Cuban Coriva cigars which cost Adrian 4400 pesos, equal to 200 American dollars. The men accomplished their intent for the vacation. They were relaxed, had gotten their drink on and felt really good enjoying the free peep show. Although some of the women had no business out on the beach butt naked, they were giving them an expose` of their bodies while Marquis, Adrian, and

Austin sat across from one another reciting scenes from Scarface.

One woman went above and beyond trying to impress the American men. She danced in front of them to the Cuban music that blared from her small boom-box. "Ju wont me? Cum an get me if ju wont me", Adrian said to the woman. Marquis was next. "Say hello to my little friend." Although Marquis hadn't done anything to imply what his little friend was, the men knew exactly what he was referring to. Their Cuban accents were funny as hell. The men laughed with great intensity while the non-English speaking woman laughed with them.

Jamale wasn't participating in the fellas jokes. He sipped on a glass of Havana's Rum and felt good. But he wasn't anywhere close to being as drunk as his boys. Jamale had other things on his mind. He missed Cee-Cee, and was happy to get away from Tiffany and Jeannette and all the foolishness that came with them.

The Cuban sun and rum had Jamale reminiscing on some of the crazy things he'd gone through with women. One in particular was with Tiffany. Although Jamale had ended the relationship with Tiffany months prior, she wasn't accepting the decision. She was in total and utter denial. Tiffany called every week trying to see if Jamale had changed his mind. She called so often that Jamale was considering changing his phone number. Caller ID, anonymous block and call block wasn't enough for Tiffany. Her twisted ass would find a way to get through. Jamale would sit on his bed before closing his eyes wondering how long it took a female to understand when it's over, it's over, and what did a man have to do to make her understand he was serious?

It was the day he met Cee-Cee and the same morning Jamale was certain he would put an end to the drama he had experienced in the short period of time messing with Tiffany. As promised by Jamale, that morning when Tiffany called that she would be getting a call back. Only it wasn't for the reasons she'd hoped. Jamale had another agenda.

The phone rang once when Tiffany answered trying to sound

unsuccessfully sexy, "Hey Ba-By." Tiffany had no need to wonder who was calling. She had her phone set with a distinguished ring when Jamale called. She was obsessed with him to no end.

Sighing, Jamale responded, "Listen, could you meet me at Friday's on Beltline Road at 6:00 this evening?" Jamale knew exactly what he was doing when he made the request. He didn't want to be anywhere private with Tiffany. He wanted to be in a public place with people surrounding him when he told her they wouldn't be seeing one another again. In the back of Jamale's mind, there was no doubt; Tiffany could be the queen of acting a fool.

"Uh, huh. That's perfect. Now I don't have to wonder what I was going to eat. How was church?"

Ignoring her question, Jamale knew she really couldn't handle the truth about him meeting Cee-Cee. Besides, he wasn't trying to make small talk. "So, six o'clock. I'll see you then." He hung up without giving Tiffany time to respond.

Friday's was more busy than usual for a Sunday evening and that made it all the better for the occasion. When Tiffany arrived, she of course was trying to look extra cute for Jamale, but Jamale was totally out of his norm. He had on an old tee shirt with a pair of faded blue running pants and some awfully old dirty sneakers. Tiffany stood there for a moment just staring at Jamale and finally asked, "Damn, you think we're that comfortable with one another that you can meet me out in public looking like that?" Jamale tried to ignore all the people who were waiting to be seated who were also smirking at Tiffany with all of her attitude as she asked her question. He tried to be diplomatic by returning the smirks to the people while he ignored her by walking to the hostess desk to inquire on the wait time. But when Tiffany fronted Jamale a bit louder, and a bit bolder telling him not to walk away from her when she was talking, Jamale snapped and went left on her ass.

Jamale got so close to Tiffany that the sprinkling of saliva that escaped as he talked landed on her forehead. "Bi..." Pausing before he called her the name he vowed never to call a female. "....Girl, don't you ever think you all that and can talk shit to me. I wanted your ass to meet me here so I could tell your silly butt that you wouldn't be spending any more time with me. And I wore this jacked up outfit because it matched the jacked up person I was meeting. I was gonna try to be friendly with this ending, but your silly ass thought you could front a brotha in public. Oh, hell no. I messed up once by giving you some of my time, but now I realize you are one messed up in the head female. I'm gonna get in my car and forget I even belittled myself by spending any of my valuable time with your silly ass." Jamale was pissed. His behavior and his language were uncharacteristic. He didn't stop to watch the expressions of the people who once wore smirks. He didn't care what they thought. And he certainly could care less what Tiffany's reaction would be. He turned around brushing past the couple entering the restaurant and hurried to his car.

It took an hour drive around the city for Jamale to calm down. Meanwhile, Tiffany was back at the restaurant trying to convince the people that her man was having some legal things going on in his life, and he wasn't himself. Tiffany wasn't accepting that bull Jamale had just delivered as being the end to anything. If there were going to be an ending, it was going to be her doing it.

Tiffany wasn't letting go. The calls continued. The gifts and flowers were being delivered to his office, and occasionally she would make an appearance at Jamale's job. One morning she had caused such a scene in the lobby that security had to be called. Security escorted Tiffany from the building, and that's when she finally disappeared. Drama. Drama. Drama.

And then there was Jeannette, his long-time supplier of funds. She was bearable when he first met her. And truthfully, she had been good for Jamale in his younger years. She taught him so much about the pleasures of being with a mature woman. She schooled him on the needs and desires of a woman and how to meet those desires. She taught him that banging a woman and damn near bruising her guts was a far cry from getting a woman to have an explosive orgasm. Jeannette taught Jamale that a dick was just a dick if a man didn't know how to use it. And she also taught him that a woman was the best friend he could ever have if he needed his ego stroked. Give her an hour of immature sex and she was going to return the favor and fake an orgasm. Have your ass thinking you're the shit. That is until the next sista, who ain't so nice tells your worthless ass to get the hell up off her.

But with every good, there's a bad and what goes up must come down. The flip side of having Jeannette in his life was that ten years and gravity had affected her.

Jamale had had enough of the drama from Jeannette the last few months. She was in full bloom of menopause and was going to be the spark that set off his fuse. She had become possessive, one minute up and the next down. She wasn't sensual any longer; she was controlling and basically a pain in the ass. Jamale had learned his lessons and didn't need her for anything. He tried to sever their ties several times, but she would somehow find her way back into his life. He recalled using desperate measures that should have humiliated her. He took brochures on cosmetic surgery to try and make her understand her body had gone from firm to flab. He also pointed out some people walking the mall who were in total denial of the way they looked in the clothes they were wearing, but she wasn't getting it. He eventually had to break it down real raw for her and tell her all the money she was trying to buy him with, she needed to invest in herself because she was looking jacked up. Jamale could really be a jackass when he needed to. But it wasn't enough. Jeannette may have been insulted and hurt, but mostly she became challenged to win him back.

The gifts became more elaborate each time she sent them. Jamale had in his possession a wine collection that included a vintage bottle of Pinot Blanc, great white Burgundies, Germany's finest Rieslings, and Sauternes dated twenty years. She was spending her husband's money on Jamale like a crazed woman. But Jamale could no longer pretend to be bought. He didn't care what she did and how much she spent. There wasn't enough money on this earth for Jamale to continue with the relationship. It was over, and that was that.

As the sun beamed down on Jamale, he shook himself back into reality and joined in with the fella's role play of Scarface. Time had passed quickly, and they were drunk and needing to get back to the hotel before it got dark.

Days two and three were a lot like day one. They ate good food, drank plenty, partied with the beautiful people, enjoyed watching the women on the beach and smoked the cigars that made them look like the big ballers they knew they were.

Their vacation in Cuba was great. They returned to Dallas resuming their lives and by the first of the year Tiffany had stopped calling and Jeannette had stopped trying. Jamale and Cee-Cee's relationship grew stronger, and Marquis, Adrian, Peter and Austin had accepted that their boy was in love.

Seasonably Correct

There were hard times growing up in the James household. Mr. James drove the Metro train for the DC transit company and Mrs. James did housekeeping for several families in the Dupont area of Virginia. Family vacations in their household were rare mainly because of the extras Mr. and Mrs. James had committed to for their twin sons. Although times were challenging and there wasn't a lot of extra money, it wasn't about the money with this family. Peter and Austin were always aware of how hard their parents worked, and they always let their parents know the love they offered was more than enough.

Growing up, Peter and Austin had everything in common but their complexion. Peter had taken his mother's fair and creamy color, and Austin was a paper bag brown. Other than that, they looked identical and they shared everything to include their dreams. Dreams of going to college, making big lute immediately afterwards, and living a lifestyle most young bachelors only dreamed of. Peter and Austin realized at that moment they were dreaming their future. But they also knew these were dreams not far from becoming a reality.

The brothers never lost focus, even when times were hard in the home. Hard times none of their classmates at the private school they attended could imagine. If you get right down to it, the James family was struggling to make ends meet and in the eyes of most of their classmates, they were basically poor. When most families were either dining out or enjoying two vegetables, a starch and a meat, Peter and Austin were enjoying a hearty plate of smoked neck bones over rice. It was neither here or there for Peter and Austin, what mattered was their parents never let them go to bed hungry. It was real love in their home. And although they knew some of their friends looked down on them, the James brothers rested comfortably knowing they didn't have the alcoholic mom and the cheating father that most of them had. Their family foundation was strong, and nothing could divide them, not even the highway miles ahead of them when they left for college. And, although they had agreed to go their separate ways for college, they also agreed they would return to their family home after graduating to share the responsibilities of taking care of their parents. Peter and Austin recognized how hard their parents worked to send them to a private school and then college, and taking care of their parents was a minor comparison.

When they entered their freshman year of high school, both boys were promised a car in their senior year if they could maintain highest honors their first three years. It was a given for Peter and him meeting the requirements would come naturally. But for Austin, it was a different story. It wouldn't be easy for him. As the promise was being made, in the back of Austin's mind, he felt his parents made the agreement knowing he wouldn't be able to meet the requirements, and he was right with his assumption. Basically, one car was really all their parents could afford, if that. But their parents knew Peter would be responsible and share with his brother.

Just what they assumed would occur when the deal was made, happened. Austin messed up with the chance for a car in his first year. He maintained marginal grades in math, which kept him off the honors list. Austin wasn't discouraged, however. It was no secret that he didn't possess the smarts that Peter had. But he had other talents. When Peter was studying, Austin was making extra money to help his parents. He worked at his weekend job as a disc jockey at the roller skating rink, and he also earned the opportunity to intern at the local radio station. Radio was his passion. If taking advantage of the great transit system the District had to offer was how he was going to get there, then no problem. And, as far as the car went, it was eight years old with a dent on the rear passenger door. But how the car looked wasn't an issue to either of the boys. That Cutlass Supreme took them to every young girl's house they needed to get to.

Attending separate colleges was the first time Peter and Austin had ever been apart. Distance, however, couldn't stop them from being best friends and spending most of their free time together.

Peter graced Hampton University and Austin charmed Howard University. These men had it going on and they took full advantage of it later in life.

On Peter's most recent visit to Howard, Austin could see the car named Ol' Bessie was on its last wheel. Austin also realized how important it was that Peter had the car with him down at Hampton. So, being the caring brother that he was Austin took his saved money and got the car in good running condition. Without Ol' Bessie, he wouldn't be able to see his brother on the weekends. So getting it fixed was a must.

Having pledged a year earlier than Austin, Peter experienced the hidden thunders of pledging alone. Although he had his Line Brothers, many nights Peter wished he had his biological brother to share the experience with. As distressing as pledging had become, he made it through. However, it was undoubtedly an experience no one could prepare you for....literally. There were many long nights of coming to know his Line Brothers and the honored code of the fraternity organization. Those twelve weeks while pledging were the longest time Peter and Austin had been apart with little, if not any communication. As much as Peter wanted to prepare Austin while he was pledging, the oath was taken, and Peter knew something great for Austin was in the making. Peter and Austin would be brother's trifold; biological brothers, Christian brothers and fraternity brothers.

Peter, a computer science graduate and with a master's degree in computer engineering and Austin with a degree in mass communications, their parents were so proud. It wasn't long after Peter finished Grad school that both parents passed away.

Soon after graduation, Austin landed a job at WFLG TV as a production director and floor director. Although television was not his preference, he wasn't going to turn down an opportunity. Austin decided to give it a go until a position at one of the local radio stations opened.

Every day had been a challenge. His immediate supervisor was an "Uncle Tom" who felt Austin had something additional to prove to him. Austin struggled daily watching how his supervisor had his nappy black head up the asses of his superiors and kissed the asses of all his equals.

The White females at the station thought Austin was gorgeous, and he was the solution and their opportunity to put the old myth about Black men to rest. But Austin wasn't thinking about any women, but one; Khadijah. She was the love of Austin's life throughout high school, and when she left for college, Austin harbored a place in his heart for her. Often times he wished she could have been there to comfort him when he was missing his parents.

Austin and his father had an immeasurable bond and Peter admired it. Their mom was the most nurturing mother any child could have wished for, and she always encouraged them to get their education because she never finished high school herself. Mrs. James got pregnant with the twins in her junior year of high school. Mr. James was in his second year of college when he met her. She was stunningly beautiful, so he did what any red blooded American male would do when he saw the woman of his dreams; he pursued her. He fell in love with her and unfortunately, got her pregnant.

William James was incredibly mature and intelligent so when the woman he loved got pregnant, he married her. He tried to continue with school, but the twins were too much without help from her family. His family being down in Selma, Alabama wasn't any help, so he owned up to his responsibility and did what any man in that era did.

Although he loved and missed his mother, it was his father's death that Austin was suffering most with. Family time was very important in the James household, and Mr. James gave his sons the gift of knowledge like no traditional school had ever. He instilled in his sons the importance of knowing the history of their culture so they would be sure of who they were and why. He also taught them to strive for higher goals than what society would set for them. It was because of Austin's inability to grasp the book smarts and his father's ability to make him understand that book knowledge wasn't everything, which made their bond so tight. It was important to know he couldn't give up on learning regardless of where the lesson was being taught and that every day he would learn something from someone. Austin loved his father for being the strong Black man that he was.

As the weeks passed, Peter watched as his brother's life was being disrupted. No job was important enough that he would allow his brother to suffer. Peter needed his brother to be assured that nothing, to include money, was more important than their bond and happiness, so Peter suggested to Austin that he quit his job and relax until the job he wanted became available.

For a while, Peter and Austin lived in the two bedroom family home they were raised in. But living there without mom and dad became emotionally exhausting for the boys, so eventually the house was sold, and they moved into a two bedroom townhouse in Alexandria, Virginia.

Although the brothers developed some differences in their personalities, they shared so many commonalities that living together was something they knew they would do until the time came when one decided to get married.

Six months later, Austin was offered his position at the radio station in Dallas. The timing couldn't be any better considering Peter was between contracts at the time, so Peter agreed to follow Austin to the Big D. Peter was aware of the growth rate for Dallas' corporate headquarters and assumed there would be plenty demands for computer engineers.

Prior to the job offer, leaving the DC area was something the guys talked about often. They wanted to experience time away from the East coast, and the job offer in Dallas was the icing on the cake. The home of their favorite football team....the Dallas Cowboys. As you can imagine, being a Cowboy fan, life hadn't been easy living in Redskin territory.

One of the perks of being in a fraternity was the potential to link to one of their Kappa brothers in the world. After a few calls and faxes to their brother Marcus, who seemed to be on top of the real estate game in Dallas, the work was done. Peter and Austin purchased and moved into a three bedroom house in a small town north of Dallas where the average homes valued in the $250K range. Peter and Austin were surprised with the amount of house they were getting for their money. Up, all across the eastern border, a $250K house would be a starter home that needed an additional fifty thousand dollars worth of work to make it livable.

When they first moved into the neighborhood, Peter and Austin were bothered by the fact that they didn't see many Black people in the area. But in a short period of time they realized that Dallas, specifically north of Dallas only had small pockets of progressive Blacks. Dallas was very different from the chocolate cities in Maryland and Northern Virginia and unquestionably, the capital of chocolate people, Washington DC.

Peter and Austin adjusted to Dallas quickly, however. Peter landed a contract that lasted several years at the prominent company owned by Ross Perot, EDS and Austin became the voice that enticed his listeners with his poetic verses and romantic tunes on the Nice and Easy Show on 105.7. Life was good. They were very pleased with the move to the large metropolis in Texas and Dallas became their home.

In the years passed since graduation, Peter had not been out of work for more than a week at a time. The technology industry was slowing down causing Peter to be without a contract for three weeks. But he didn't mind. He enjoyed every minute of the break. It gave him time to visit with some of his female friends outside of Texas and while in Dallas to enjoy the comforts of home.

Peter had some time on his hands after the contract with EDS ended. He wasn't complaining because it gave him time to enjoy life. Life meant women. Each morning Peter would zero in on the women who exercised in the yard outside of his bedroom window. The four women were beautiful; a Hispanic, an Asian, a White, and a sexy, full figured Black. Granted, they were each fine as hell, but there wasn't anything more beautiful to Peter than a Black woman, especially one with a lit'l something on her bones. The others were just nice to the eyes.

In his mesmerized state, the incoming phone call was a relief for Peter because had it not rang he would have been wasting most of his morning looking at unreachable ass. His relief and savior for the moment was Marcus.

"Dawg, you won't believe what I'm looking at in my neighbors back yard. Man, ass for days. Females bent over showing their goods and not even knowing it. Dayum women know they can flex that ass."

Marcus laughed a minute and asked, "So should I be on my way over? I don't want you to hurt yourself tryin' to make 'em all scream."

"Nah Bruh. Ain't no way I could handle it all. But ain't nothin' wrong with a brother dyin' tryin'."

"You crazy, but I feel ya. Say man, now that I know you ain't got shit to do, why don't you meet me over at Grits and Eggs. I'm hungry as hell."

46

Peter was relieved to be rescued from the window that held him hostage. The decision to agree to meet with his frat brother for breakfast was a good one. He was a freed man. Peter said his good-byes as he waved to the women through the blinds. He didn't care that they were unaware of him being a fan. Peter just felt obligated considering he'd been given such a private and eventful show. Thank God, I have errands to run crossed Peter's mind a couple of times as he shook his head while closing the blinds.

4

"*Y*eah, hello. Hold on, I'm in a bad spot...I'm losing my signal," Driving up the tollway, headed to the stadium, Marquis noticed the passenger window going down on the black Lexus to his left. He glanced over and saw a beautiful female signaling him to get off at the next available exit. Marquis told whoever was on the other end of his cell phone to hold on. Marquis watched through his rearview mirror while the woman followed him to the parking lot and parked behind him. When he grabbed his cell phone and saw Adrian's number on the display, Marquis told him to hold on because he had some business to handle.

Marquis confidently stepped out of his car wearing a silk knit sweater that fit his developed chest and black jeans that showed off everything left for the imagination. He wore a leather Polo belt and matching Polo boots with a hint of cologne that made him tempting and inviting. He knew he had it going on, and he also knew he was a whole lot of man in a small package. Marquis was a classic case of an old saying with a lot of truth behind it... "big things come in small packages."

He removed his shades before the lady stepped out of her car. He wanted to be clear with what he was about to witness. He watched the door open as her left foot slowly was revealed. Marquis thought to himself, dayum she has a big foot for a woman, but that wasn't all he thought when she stood from out of the car. Dayuuuum! She's an amazon!

The woman stood about 6'2" and was wearing a short skirt that revealed her muscular legs. Her shoulders were as broad as Marquis', and her neck was as thick. When the woman approached Marquis and said hello, he could have hit the ground when her voice was as heavy, if not heavier than his. Granted, she was beautiful, but she was no she. She was a he and Marquis wasn't playing that game.

"Hello", she seductively whispered.

Marquis was a little agitated by his admirer, but he didn't expose it when he responded. "Hey. Listen, I don't wanna hurt your feelings, but, ummmm, I don't go that way."

"No problem, baby. You just looked so good in your car and hey, you gotta try, or you'll never know." Ol' girl smiled, waved good bye and turned away walking a sexier walk than most women.

As much as men want to deny it, there was a lot of "in the closet" men and the ones who had found their way out of the closet, would admit the diva was fine. Before reaching the car, Mrs. Doubtfire turned back to look at Marquis as if asking, are you sure? Marquis wasn't taking another look back. He got into his car and pulled off quickly.

"Adrian, you there? Man, you aren't gonna believe what just happened. Man, this chick asked me to pull over and damn, she was a dude. A sexy dude." They started cracking up laughing. Adrian made a few remarks causing Marquis to pull over to check himself. "Nupe, I know I look good, but I ain't that fine I got the brotha's wantin' me too." When Marquis got into his car, they laughed a few more minutes.

"Alright, enough of that, what's on your mind? What you want?"

"Hey, I was just calling to see if you were headed to the stadium and what you were bringing to the game tomorrow night?"

"What you mean, what am I bringing? I'm bringing what I always bring, top of the line beef. Tomorrow will be filet mignon."

"Well, you can believe, if you got the filet mignon, I got the Dom Perignon."

"Uh huh, we'll see."

"Listen, I'm on my way to the office for a few. I got this new female project that was handed to me. If I don't talk with you, I'll see you at the game."

"Cool. Talk with ya."

Marquis grew up in Decatur, Georgia off Memorial Drive. He and his crew used to frequent the strip just west of I-285 and would hang outside of the retail establishments. From time to time trouble would erupt, but mostly the trouble came from the local small time drug dealers.

One particular time, in his senior year of high school, Marquis got into confrontations that lead to fighting, and he found himself in and out of court for six months. Marquis had knocked out one of his opponent's teeth, and when the law appeared, Marquis had an outlawed weapon called a Black Jack on his possession. A first degree assault charge with a weapon was handed to him and almost caused him to lose his scholarship to college.

This wasn't the first time Marquis had had a brush with the law and the judge reminded him of it each time he entered into his courtroom. It was made very clear to Marquis the only reason the judge wasn't going to sentence him to juvenile detention was because of the academic scholarship Marquis had earned and his potential to become someone great. Judge Davis was the only Black judge in Decatur County, and he wasn't going to allow young Black people to think because he was Black he would be more lenient with them. Marquis knew he was standing on his last leg so Marquis promised the judge he would never see his face in his courtroom, and he lived up to that promise. Marquis learned that day that his temper could be his worst enemy.

As Marquis sat at the red light, his phone rang again, but this time Marquis checked the caller ID and noticed a Chicago area code.

"Hello." He answered unsure of who was calling.

"Hi Marquis, this is Candace. I'm calling from the airport in

Chicago. I hope this isn't a bad time."

"No, not at all. How are you?"

"I'm fine. My usual flight was changed to Dallas and, well, I thought I should let you know I would be in your neck of the woods."

"Really? So when will you be here and for how long?" Marquis was happy Candace was visiting, but he wasn't expecting an out of town guest. He had to juggle a few things on his calendar so he could enjoy her while she was in town.

"I fly in tonight and should be leaving on Tuesday morning. Will you be available for me?"

"Baby, you know I'm always available for you. I may have some things to do tomorrow night, but other than that, my time is yours. Should I assume you're gonna stay with me tonight?"

"I guess so. I probably need to get a room though since you have plans tomorrow night."

"Okay, Bay, I wish I would have known that you were coming sooner. I wouldn't have scheduled anything. Maybe next time."

Obviously lying, Marquis knew his traditional game with the fellas was not something that required planning, it was a tradition and no woman was going to make the difference. "Well Bay, I gotta get ready to handle some business, give me your flight information, and I'll pick you up at the airport, and we'll go from there."

His evening was unexpectedly occupied, but who better to occupy it than Candace. Candace was 5'8, two inches taller than Marquis and more gorgeous than any woman at the airlines.

Cautious as the wind, Marquis' mind calculated a mile a minute. Marquis had to make certain all his t's were crossed, and all the i's were dotted making sure Charita knew she wouldn't be spending the night tomorrow night. He needed to be free so he could spend time with Candace after the game. Marquis came to the conclusion a long time ago that females were unique creatures. Very nurturing by nature and extremely territorial. You give them an inch, and they automatically expect a mile and the craziest fact is they don't always realize they do it. For instance, if a woman is allowed to spend time with him and his boys, that woman assumes they have a place in that man's bed that night. Yes, most men would expect that woman to know they'd have a place in their bed that night; however, for the most part women would include a few more nights that could lead to a lifetime.

Marquis recalled one woman a few years ago who spent two nights with him, and the next day she had returned with a larger bag containing the personal items she felt belonged in his bathroom. When Marquis saw the toothbrush in his holder, he had to put her in check. The woman went into a frenzy that freaked Marquis out. He learned that day that two nights in a row were one night too many. As he was recalling the incident, he laughed out loud striking the attention of the man in the car waiting for the traffic light to change.

"Hey man, I'm not crazy. I'm just thinking about some of the things our beautiful Black women do."

"No problem man. I laugh too. I gotta woman right now who's trippin'"

They both laughed as they drove off. Only a few miles from the stadium, Marquis turned up the volume on his favorite funky ballads CD and started singing along with the artists. "...somebody rockin', knockin' the boots." Grooving to the song, Marquis couldn't help himself as he started thinking about the many woman who had the need to have their boots knocked. He slipped his car into fifth gear, and speed dialed number three on his cell to set the record straight one final time. "Hey Adrian, man, I had to call back. I'm in my car jammin' and started thinking about Rupal back there. Damn man, I know I look good, but damn, a dude? Not this brotha. That was a trip."

"Yeah dawg, that shit was crazy." In between his laughter, Adrian sat in front of his office building gathering a few things off of his front seat. "Listen man, I'm here at the building. Let me hit you back later after I listen to the tape of this female they got waiting for me in my office. The chick must be all that for them to want me to check it out on a Sunday."

"Yeah, alright. Talk with ya. Peace."

Exiting the 22nd floor of the skyscraper, Adrian stopped at the receptionist desk to grab a Jolly Rancher from her candy jar. Apple was his favorite, and he could always count on Kenya having one readily available for him. Sucking on the candy, Adrian turned the key to unlock the door to his executive suite. His office was remarkable. Gold and platinum framed record albums and CD's covered the walls and photographs of him and some very well known R&B celebrities. Across the room was a baby grand piano and to the left of his office was an enclosed listening area that had a stereo system developed into the wall that had a sound incredibly crisp and clear.

Walking over to his desk the realization of another dud package was positioned neatly on his chair. Adrian had experienced it all too often. He couldn't help his thoughts. There it is. Another package of the supposedly next mega female R&B artist; I don't even wanna check ol' girls picture out. I just wanna hear what she's got. Reaching into the FedEx package, Adrian removed the thin plastic case. "Well at least she had it pressed onto a CD", he grumbled. "She has more sense than some of the wanna-be's who submits their make-me-a-star dreams to me." Before entering the listening room, Adrian removed a bottle of sparkling water from the refrigerator and poured it into one of the crystal glasses from the small bar. He placed the CD into the player, sat back in his leather chair, his feet resting on the ottoman, with remote in hand and hit the play button.

The intro was a piano solo which faded into a piano and tenor saxophone duet. There was a brief pause when a three part female A Cappella harmony came in. "I want a man, who understands that

I'm a woman. Wanna be the one, who cooks and cleans and sets the temp in his bubble bath...gotta make him laugh...rub his body down. Don't wanna fuss...gotta make him smile when he's down..."

The solo voice that followed was unique and raw. It was a sound Adrian had yet to hear since he landed his elaborate position. It was the sound he'd hoped for and knew he would watch develop into a huge star. He sat there in awe as he listened. He had to hit replay for the third time.

"Oh shit! This female is raw!" Adrian stood up with his glass in the air in one hand and kissed the CD jacket in the other. Adrian was so excited with his new project that he pimped over towards his desk, and exploded, "let me see what ol' girl looks like. Damn, with a voice like that she can't be no scaly-wag." Adrian removed the remaining contents from the package and saw a folder with a bio, a photo and a DVD too! "Ahhhh!" Adrian started cracking up with excitement. After opening the folder, he sat behind his desk when his mouth dropped open. It was a head shot photo, and she was stunning. In script and in bold, the bio read: Ms. Chanel Rayson, Vocalist.

"Whoa! Get the hell out of here. Dayyummmm!" Spinning around in his executive chair, smiling at Ms. Chanel's picture, Adrian reached for the DVD that sat on his desk. He placed the video onto his lap; put his hands together as if praying and begged God to please let the rest of her be fine.

As he walked over and placed the DVD into the player, he let out a sigh, and that's when he realized he was really tripping. "Damn, I am off the hook over this female. Let me chill for a minute." Adrian relaxed in the chair across from the television and sipped on the remainder of his sparkling water. Thinking he'd better create an ambiance, he hit the remote that controlled the lights and dimmed the room. With all of his apprehension, it appeared he was preparing himself for the unexpected. Much to his surprise, Adrian was blown away with the quality and content of her demo tape.

It began with a sound of thunder and then a quiet rainfall and in the background you could hear the very sensuous sound of a woman breathing with a slight moan. While the breathing continued, bright red letters began to fade in and out, one letter at a time. C.H.A.N.E.L. Coupled with the pulsating sound of a heartbeat, the name Chanel quickly faded in and out twice. Suddenly the silhouette of a woman appeared, and a chilling sensation went down Adrian's spine. Her body was swaying slowly when she motioned as if caressing herself seductively. Before she was visible, she froze into one position when the music started, and there she was Ms. Chanel Rayson; Gorgeous, sexy and talented. Adrian knew what his next move would be, and he didn't hesitate to make it.

In Adrian's junior year at Fisk, he was given a marketing assignment that would change his life. He had already learned in his first two years of school that there weren't any local clubs or piano bars showing off any local talents, so he knew what the project would be. But being in a small southern town 50 miles east of Memphis, there just wasn't anything going on like what he'd planned. Adrian figured there had to be some unexposed talent somewhere, so he put on a talent show, and like the saying, "the freaks come out at night" goes, it was live right before his eyes. Every ghettofied, Jerri curl, gold tooth bamma and big country that could be there was there. What tripped Adrian out the most about the situation was the competitors were each complimenting the other on how good they looked. It was crazy. Adrian was in a twilight zone. But in that zone he found exactly what he was looking for. In between all the no talent, need not ever open their mouths and try to sing contestants on the stage, Adrian saw what he needed to see. He had a gift for spotting talent and knew he could make it work for him. He pieced a band together and marketed them in the hotels on the weekend. From that band grew several bands and Adrian became the top, actually the only booking agent within a two hundred mile radius.

Their Season

Driving into the two car garage a couple of hours later, Peter was surprised to see Austin's car parked that time of day. While shouting through the house, he placed the brown paper bags onto the kitchen table. "Hey man, what you doin' home!?" Austin, you in here!?"

While waiting in the den for Austin, Peter could hear the garage door closing. He hurried to the kitchen when he startled Austin. "Man, don't be jumpin' out on a nigga like that. You'll get your ass kicked up in here."

Peter looked at Austin, threw his head back and quipped, "Yeah right. Negro, please."

Austin's clothes were drenched and funky. When he walked past, Peter had to ask, "Damn man, how far did you run? Your shit startin' to look as tight as mine and damn man, you funky as hell."

Austin looked at Peter through the corner of his eye while drinking some ice water. "Ahhh. Man that's good. Whatever. You know as well as I know, my shit is ti-ight."

They laughed and started talking noise to one another asking what the other had as they put up their hands pretending to box. A few missed jabs were thrown when Peter asked Austin what he had planned for the rest of the day.

"Why? What you got planned for me?"

"Just go upstairs and wash your funky ass. We're going over to the Cafe."

"The Cafe? What's happen'n over there?"

"Don't worry about that lil' bro. Have I ever misled you?"

"Don't start with that "lil' bro" mess. You're all of four minutes older than me." As Austin relieved his tired feet by taking his running shoes off, he continued. "The Cafe? Hmm, yeah, aiight. I'll get ready." Looking backwards at his brother and smiling, Austin put on his back in the hood attitude and pimped towards his bedroom.

Forty-five minutes later, two gorgeous brothers walked out of their bedrooms and were ready to blow the minds of anyone who could stand to be near them. Jeans and a calfskin jacket never looked better on Austin. Then Peter stepped out with his powder blue turtleneck sweater and dark navy jeans. They checked one another, gave the look of approval and got into the Mercedes of choice.

The weather was unusually warm, so they decided to give Dallas a taste of the James brothers. They put on their east coast attitudes and wore it well. They put on their shades and dropped the top and pumped up some Reggae. Reggae hadn't made its impact on Dallas as it had on the east coast.

At first Austin and Peter thought the drivers to their left and right were staring at them because they were Black in a 500, but that wasn't unusual to see in Dallas, so they settled that it had to be the Reggae. Dallas wasn't ready for the James brothers and all that came with them.

Peter and Austin drove into the lot of the Cafe. Back in the day, the Cowboy Cafe used to be owned by a couple of Cowboy football players and a guaranteed spot to meet one of the current players. Down the street from the headquarters and practice field made it convenient for the players to stop for a cocktail or a game of pool. It was also a place where "The Boys" were guaranteed to get themselves into trouble. The color challenged women were all over the players, and before you knew it their asses would be in court for one reason or another. The owner of The Boys got fed up with his boys always appearing on the news for one thing or another. It always seemed to be related to someone they'd met at the Cafe. Jerry, being the hardnosed owner that he was banned all of his players from going into the place. Needless to say, business slowed down.

The establishment wasn't anything more than a sports bar with a couple of big screen TV's, a few pool tables and Cowboy memorabilia. If it wasn't for the periodic drop-ins from the old players, there really wasn't anything special about the establishment anymore.

The owners weren't happy with Jerry's decision, so they reacted quickly by selling the place. The nightly events changed in what soon became known as "The Cafe."

Anyone with sense knows, if a new venue is introduced, the young and lively are going to be there ready to party. The new owners were on top of their marketing game, so they invited K104 to host one evening a weekend and featured karaoke twice a week. Naturally, it became a hit. Give a sista or a brotha who could sing a microphone and they're going to go platinum plus, live in concert on your ass. And that's exactly what happened. Both nights were standing room only. It was ridiculous. Folk drove all the way across town to Irving to be in a sports bar with a DJ and an open mic. That was the scenario at night. During the day, the bar had a relaxed atmosphere where you could sit back, enjoy a beer and watch a game.

Peter and Austin wanted to park the Benzo at the front door, but all the spots had already been taken. They drove around the already packed lot hoping to find something close when they noticed a car with a Washington Redskin's decal in the rear window. "Peter, check it out. There's a Redskin fan around. But they aint' no Washingtonian, they're from Michigan."

"How you know they're from Michigan?"

"The license plate."

"Yeah but maybe they moved to Michigan later. Being from Michigan, you would think they'd be a Lion's fan." Thinking for a moment, he added, "Maybe not. Hell we grew up in VA, and we're

Cowboy fans. I guess it's possible."

"Well, let's check it out when we get inside."

Taking a quick peep at himself in the mirror on the visor, Peter ran his finger over his mustache and winked. Austin laughed and jokingly added, "Man, get your punk ass out the car and let's go in."

Walking into the dimly lit cafe, Peter walked ahead of Austin searching for the best available table. As they walked in the room, they passed several tables with some gorgeous women making remarks about how good the James brothers looked. On a couple accounts, Austin could hear the remarks clearly and smiled thinking, "Women are no different from men." Austin nudged Peter to get his attention a couple of times, but Peter ignored him.

"Peter, man, what's wrong with the tables we've passed? Better than that, man, what's wrong with you? Did you not see some of the females you walked past?"

"Man, I'm just looking for a table where we can see the TV. You know The Boys play today."

Austin heard what was coming from his brother's mouth, but he couldn't believe what he was hearing. A beautiful woman not taking precedence over, hell, anything. Austin examined the room for a moment when he stopped Peter to ask, "Well, do you recognize anyone from back home?"

"Nope, I sure don't. Come on, let's sit here."

"Man, stop complaining like a girl."

"I got your girl." The words between them were in fun. They seldom disagreed and allowed it to escalate beyond rational communication.

Austin sat with his back facing the door across from Peter. After a ten minute wait, their laminated menus where brought over to their table by a slim woman wearing very short cut-off denim shorts. Neither of the men thanked her. She had wasted ten minutes strutting around trying to be seen.

As Peter began scanning the menu Austin reached over and pulled it from his hand and asked, "So, what was the big deal with getting me to come to the Cafe?"

"Man, you ask a lot of questions. Can't a man just want to take his brother to lunch?"

Austin looked at him as to say, "yeah, right" and continued scanning the menu.

Peter decided on an entree that was named after a famous football player. As Austin was flipping his menu over, he noticed the legs of a woman walking towards him. He raised his head slowly as his eyes captured every inch of her walnut brown legs and was speechless. The woman he saw standing before him shocked him. For a moment, he thought his eyes were playing tricks on him. But they weren't. Austin stood in awe, wrapped his arms around her and whispered, "Oh my God."

Austin pulled away, and through all of his excitement, he bumped the table spilling his glass of water. He didn't care. He wasn't at all satisfied with the service he was getting from the need-a-little-junk-in-her-trunk waitress who strutted around in her shorts. She needed some work to keep her busy.

The woman he loved back in high school was back in his arms, and he knew he had to hug her once more. The hug lasted for a moment when she responded with a girlish giggle. They paused and stared into each other's eyes while Khadijah's eyes filled with tears of happiness as she began to whisper, "Hi baby."

"Awe, come here." He cradled her in his arms as if she were a young girl who had lost her favorite toy. "Girl, look at you. Wipe those tears. Oh my God, how long has it been?" He couldn't help his sweeping smile. Standing within arms reach was the woman he had dreamed about in high school hoping one day she would be his wife. In his presence was the very woman who'd broken his heart after vanishing after high school. The woman he wanted to make love to when making love was merely getting it in. When they fell in love, they were immature high school kids who had planned their future together; a plan that never evolved.

Khadijah left for UCLA after high school graduation and lived in California with her aunt. After the summer semester, Khadijah enrolled for the fall term and attended some classes, but soon realized school wasn't something she really wanted to do at the moment. She figured she'd give modeling and acting a try and later return to school to complete her degree. But her aunt wasn't following the same program. The plan was to have Khadijah for the summer and then she would live on campus beginning in the fall. Khadijahs plans were different, and she didn't care what upset her aunt; she'd gotten a touch of the limelight with some local commercial spots and speaking parts in a few low budget films. Khadijah thought she was on her way to stardom.

She was like most people who moved to LA with "that dream." She got caught up in the plastic lives of the wanna-be's and found themselves struggling to survive. With the little bit of money she'd made, Khadijah moved into her own efficiency apartment in East LA. It was a far cry from Beverly Hills, but it was a start and all she really could afford.

The strains of making ends meet became second nature and acting gigs became far and few between. She was starving for another gig. After trying the modeling thing she found out quickly the best way to start in that business was to model nude. Struggling had grown old, so Khadijah tried it and realized the money wasn't worth her dignity.

From LA Khadijah moved to Vegas and worked in the casinos making money, but better than that, meeting some very influential men. Khadijah had a classy charisma, so meeting the right man wasn't a problem. Once she decided which man she would settle with, she lived the glamorous lifestyle of a kept woman. She did the kept woman thing for a few years and finally decided she'd go back to school to get her degree.

Still very excited about seeing her, Austin asked, "So, what are you doing in D-Town?"

She couldn't help her smile. After running into Peter at the market and setting up the surprise meeting, Khadijah imagined her and Austin's reunion the entire morning. Before she answered his question, Khadijah reached for Austin's hand and spun him around slowly to check him out from top to bottom, front to back. Austin was still as fine as he was back in high school. "Umm, umm, umm."

Peter sat checking them out when he started laughing. Peter had never seen his brother blush. Austin James, the man who mesmerized women every night on the radio airwaves was blushing. Peter couldn't believe it. He chuckled and excused himself from the table before he embarrassed his brother.

Austin knew Peter had to be tripping on him and thought he'd humor his brother further. "Hey big pimpin', I know you not hatin' on a brotha." Austin smiled at Peter's nigga please look before he walked away.

Peter left, and Austin invited Khadijah to sit next to him. He had a million questions running through his mind, but the only thing that mattered at the moment was how long she would be in Dallas.

"So beautiful, you never told me what you're doing in Dallas. I'm not even gonna think you've been here and hadn't gotten in touch with me. There's no way you could be here and not hear me on the air. So, what's up with you in Dallas?"

"So you're living your dream. You've made it to radio."

Smiling and being very proud of his accomplishments, Austin explained how he wooed the women on his Nice and Easy show at night. Khadijah put on her girlish jealous look and added, "Oh, the ladies are being wooed by my man?" She couldn't help her smile and knew she was flirting with temptation. Before he could respond, Khadijah continued. "Truthfully, I just got to Dallas yesterday, so I haven't had the opportunity to listen to the radio and get wooed by Austin James."

Reaching for her hands, he told her she didn't need to get wooed over the airwaves; she could have the real deal. Hearing Austin speak his words made her happy. It was like old times. They began laughing and teasing one another about who was more in love with the other back in the day. While they were teasing, Peter returned to the table.

"So Bro'. What do you think about Khadijah living here now?"

"Man, we hadn't gotten that far into the conversation." Looking over at Khadijah, he asked, "So, is it true? You're going to be living here permanently? Is that what I'm hearing?" Austin was elated. If him loving this lady, was to be a secret, then let the secret be told. The three women across the room who had been staring at Peter and Austin the moment they walked in were whispering and then turned up their lips at Austin and Khadijah. And the lady at the bar who had just ordered a cocktail for Austin was stopping the waitress before she delivered the drink. Even the females who had followed Peter and Austin to the cafe were paying their tab so they could be on their way. Sista's know when a man is considered out of reach. Yeah, they may try their luck from time to time, but this was not the time to test their luck. Only divine interference could break up this "Hallmark Moment."

Khadijah was smiling equally as big and as excited as Austin. Nothing else seemed to matter. "Yes, I'm here permanently." She gave a few giggles and asked him to hold her once more. Austin had no problems standing and extending his arms to feel the pulse of her beating heart. With her in his arms, Austin stroked her back gently and kissed the top of her head. Khadijah rested her head on his chest and held on tighter. Their eyes were closed as they stood their savoring their moment and not caring that they were in the cafe. It took Peter to clear his throat unusually loud to bring them back to reality.

"Hey man, why don't you two go to the house and talk? I'll find something else to get into. In fact, there's this fine honey on the other side of the room I've been talking to that I may need to share some more time with. So go ahead on without me. I'm cool." Peter was wearing his devious expression that Austin understood clearly. Austin gave Khadijah a what do you think look, and when she okayed them leaving, Khadijah grabbed Austin's arm as they started towards the door.

"Hey baby girl, slow your roll. I need your car keys so I can get home."

"Oops, my bad." Khadijah tossed the keys to Peter and smiled as she and Austin walked away.

5

$\mathcal{P}$reoccupied with what was being aired on the news, Marquis answered his telephone after the third ring. "Hello."

"Hey man, the Boys got their butts kicked!" Being as animated as Peter could, he put as much emphasis on each word as he possibly could. Hoping to mask his disappointment that the season was over for his team, but more importantly how upset he was about the substantial bet he'd lost.

"Yeah, yeah, yeah. Hey, I'm not trippin'. Now I can do the conference and then have a few weeks off." Pausing as Marquis flipped through the disc player until he reached the song he wanted to hear, he then asked, "So, were you at the stadium?"

"Nah, I checked it out at the cafe with this sexy female. Dawg, these young females seem like they gettin' thicker earlier and earlier. This female was bad as hell. I was thinking about taking her up to the box, but then she told me her age, and I knew that mess was potential bullshit in my life, so I kept it right where it was. Besides, I don't give a female that much progress that fast. She's gotta pass the test, and ya know what I mean."

"Boy, you're crazy, but I hear ya. Say, what you got planned for the night?"

"I don't know yet, gotta check the calendar."

They both started laughing when Peter's phone beeped in another call. "Marquis, hold on for a minute, let me get this call."

Changing into his for the ladies voice, he answered, "Hello."
Her voice was deliberate when she spoke and she had no problem

with getting to her point. "Hi Peter, this is Tiffany, Jamale's woman. I just need to know if you've seen Jamale, and if you can tell me where to find him."

Peter was thrown off by the call. He thought for a minute and tried to place the name with a face, when it finally hit him. It's been months, he thought. What is she calling for, he wondered. Not giving a damn about the answers, he responded. "Tiffany? Jamale's woman?"

As matter-a-fact as she could be she shrieked, "Yeah. Jamale's woman. Damn, I met you at the football games a couple of times."

Knowing exactly who she was, he faked a little just to see where her head was. "Oh yeah, Tiffany. You're the one with the really long weave." Pausing for a moment, he changed his attitude. "Hold up. Before we go any further, how did you get this number?"

Catching on quickly to the change in Peter's tone, she tried to mellow out her attitude so she could get the answers she needed. "One night when I was with Jamale I saw it on his caller ID. I didn't mean to interrupt you; I just wanted to know if you've seen Jamale? I've been calling him, but he hasn't answered his phone."

Not giving a damn about her politeness, Peter went straight for the jugular. "First things first. Honey, you calling me isn't cool. I ain't your nigga and secondly, checkin' for my boy is definitely fowl. But I can guarantee you this, when I do speak with him, I will tell him you're lookin' for him. But in the mean time, don't you ever feel comfortable dialing my number looking. I don't keep tabs on Jamale."

Tiffany was so angry she didn't wait to give a response before exiting, she just hung up. With Marquis on the other end of the phone waiting, Peter clicked over and explained the call to him. They laughed for a while at Jamale's fatal attraction and how Peter handled the call. After their laugh, Marquis surprised Peter with his next question. "Say man, how much money you put on the game? You better chill on all that betting. That mess gonna get your ass in some deep shit one day. You know them crazy ass White boys don't give a damn 'bout nothin' but their money."

"Yeah Dawg, I took a hit for three G's on the Boys. But I'm gonna make up for it on the last game before the play-offs."

"Aiight, keep fucking' with them nigga's. They ain't got no love for your ass when you come up short."

"I got this."

Marquis left the subject alone. He presumed his boy had control over his life. He wasn't going to start doubting him now. Besides, Austin would step in if the gambling got out of control.

Changing the subject, Marquis told Peter how one of his friends was flying into town and thought it would be nice to double date with him and one of his selected few ladies in North Dallas. Peter laughed at Marquis when he put emphasis on the words "selected few ladies." Peter told him to give him a minute, and he would call him back. He also made it clear that all of his selected few ladies were polished to perfection.

Before Peter would call Marquis back, he had to check his calendar and voice mail. Scheduling was the key to Peter's successful system, and the system was cut and dry. He called it "the rotation." Either you're in, or you're out. He didn't include many women in the rotation, but those who were Peter treated as if they were the only special woman in his world. The way he explained it, the women understood their position and had no problem with being involved. And, if there were one who didn't understand, he simply dismissed them. Peter made it very clear his intent was not to fall in love and the details of his desires were outlined and concise to include his specific needs and wants the very moment an interest was sparked. The way he figured, if the woman listened, understood and respected him and his position on relationships, then the choice was entirely hers to remain a part of the rotation. If she tripped later and fell in love, which is a no-no from the beginning, then shame on her. With Peter, it's very simple: love simply is not an option and if that particular emotion somehow sneaks up on him, creeps into his heart and takes harbor, then there would be no need for other women or a rotation. She would unconditionally be the rotation.

Peter randomly set a night aside for himself, but occasionally a twist here and there added a little zing to his own expert planning. He believed a twist is what made him such the expert. Marquis' request was easy. Peter humored himself as he pondered his decision. Peter was confident the perfect plan would soon be in the makings. After all, he had dominion over his calendar and never allowed a woman to control or dictate the way he spent his time.

Hmmm, he thought. He spoke at a devilish whisper to himself, "this may take a minute. How am I going to finagle the days, so none of the ladies feel slighted? Crystal? Hmmm, she needs to be put in check a bit. I've never thrown her off guard; maybe it's time for me to see how she handles it. She expects to be with me tomorrow night. I'll throw a wrench in her plans and invite her over tonight."

Always one step ahead of things, Peter applauded himself at his well-timed success at getting Crystal to agree to join him on a last-minute double date. But, as usual, making her feel special was the key and with an accomplished grin on his face, Peter hung up and called Marquis.

"Hey man, it's a go. What you wanna do with the ladies?"

"I was thinking we could go over to Arthur's in Addison and have a candlelight dinner; then you can do what you say you do best." Clearing his throat, he threw both hands up in the air. "You're on your own."

Laughing at Marquis, Peter agreed he did do his thing best. "Yeah. I do have the shit under control. Man, the only time I can think when I could have been sprung was with the female out in LA. Remember China? Ol' girl was off the chain. Fine as hell! But I knew she was full of game and at that time I couldn't try to make her work into my "master plan". But, I sure do wish I could catch up with her ass now. If I had to put my money on it, I'd bet she had some nigga just eatin' out the palm of her hand." After a few minutes of reminiscing and saying the past is the past, Peter finally asked the details of the evening.

"So what time does the lady arrive and what time do you want to meet?"

"In about thirty minutes. After she gets settled in, I figure she should be ready about eight or nineish. In fact, I need for you to make the reservation for nine."

"Bet. Let me give Jamale a call and let him know he has an if'n on his hands."

"Man, what you call her? An if'n? What the hell is that?"

"Yeah.I.F.N. An ignorant fatal nut case."

"Man you are crazy."

"I may be crazy, but I can guarantee I don't have a woman like that fool. In fact, let me go so I can give Jamale a call."

Jamale was resting on his bed when the phone rang; he was hoping it would be Cee-Cee. After the second ring, his baritone voice was whispering hello.

"Jay, dig this, fool. I hope you're sittin' down. Man, a blast from your past just called me looking for you."

"Who?"

"Ol' girl. Tiffany. Man she just called a few minutes ago. She said she got my number off your caller ID."

"What!?! Tell me you're bullshitting'. This chick is out of her mind! I kept seeing these anonymous calls on the box, so I never

69

answered them."

"Yeah well, I'll bet it's her crazy ass. I wouldn't kid about some crazy shit like that. You better put her in check before she does something stupid...have your ass hemmed up somewhere. Damn, how long has it been since you went off on her?"

"Man, please. It's been months. Right after I met Cee-Cee. In fact, it was the day I met Cee. Man, I'm not worried about what she may do. I know how to handle silly females like her. Trust me." Wearing his exceptionally broad smile he continued, "right now I have bigger and better things to handle. Don't trip on her crazy ass. Man, I gotta go handle some business. I'll holla at you later."

Peter shook his head and went along with Jamale's decision. He had no reason to question Jamale's judgment. Peter knew his friend would handle it appropriately. Besides, he also knew, females like her came a dime a dozen. The manipulative games were only as strong as the man was weak.

Jamale sat in his chair thinking about the woman who kept his heart and mind in sync. He reminisced on the months gone by, and the very moment Cee-Cee entered his life. Every detail was vivid and as gratifying as the day they met. This relationship was different from any Jamale had been in. Firstly, she was a single parent. Secondly, he never thought he would meet another man's child and love him like his own. And thirdly, he never thought he would be able to love so unconditionally and experience true love so unexpectedly and so quickly and he never thought he was ready to date a woman exclusively so early in life. Jamale had to learn, as much control that he had over his life, he actually had none. When God is ready, He'll show you what you think you know about your life. Or, when you think you're in total control of what you will and won't allow to happen, He reminds you just who's really in control and will introduce to you what He already had planned for you. Reclining in his chair, Jamale closed his eyes and recalled their precious beginning.

It was four months ago when Cee-Cee gave him her phone

number. He was rushing to his car, and he tucked the small piece of paper away before he misplaced it. The next night as he went to call her he began to panic. Looking through his day timer, he couldn't find the torn piece of paper. He had been cautious with the number so the thought of how he could have lost her number pounded on his mind. He searched and fumbled through his papers when it dawned on him, "I placed it in the most sacred place; my bible." Flipping through the pages, the small torn yellow piece of paper was neatly placed inside. He smiled after he realized it was in the Book of 1st Corinthians, at the 13th chapter. For those who don't know, that's the chapter on love.

For a while, Jamale stood there staring at the book when he was inspired to read the chapter before making his call. After reading it, he meditated on the verses and began dialing Cee-Cee's number.

It was so vivid. Jamale smiled as he thought back to their first telephone conversation. She cleared her throat and excused herself before saying hello. When she heard his voice, she became quite excited. The beginning of their conversation was slow, but eventually they progressed into a more intimate conversation which lasted for hours. It was unusual for Jamale to hold such a conversation with someone he'd just met, but he knew he didn't want to hang up. Thinking with his heart was something he needed to do, and although it was something very unfamiliar to him, it was refreshing and new. It made him realize the man he'd become was actually very lonely and hoped for the kind of love he'd discovered with Cee-Cee. Jamale was excited and willing to put his guard down and allow himself to love this woman.

The conversation was natural. Not a lot of fluff as he called it. They were talking as if they'd know each other forever. They shared some things they had in common when Cee-Cee became shy and hesitantly shared with Jamale what she experienced in church the first day their hands touched.

It was uncanny how similar their stories were. They admitted it was electrifying and rejuvenating. Their hands held and their hearts connected. They were both in shock when they listened to each other's story. They began laughing and thought it was weird as they continued their conversation.

He recalled having to be honest about his urge to kiss Cee-Cee that afternoon in the kitchen and he was honest with how he still wanted to kiss her. He knew his last comment was pushing the envelope, but he had to tell her.

It had been a long time since Cee-Cee felt butterflies in her stomach. She held her pillow tight and sighed as he defined his unexplainable feelings. She wanted his kiss the very way he wanted hers, but she didn't let him know. But it was obvious she wanted to see him after he had asked her out for ice cream.

Preparing for a date was something of her past. It had been nine years since she left Jeff. The man she thought she would spend the rest of her life with. Jeff was her first love. They were a family. Something she'd hoped would be very different from the dysfunctional relationship she watched with her mom and dad. Cee-Cee could recognize an unhealthy relationship instantly, and she vowed she would never be with a man because she was lonely, scared or wanted a father for her son. She had almost given up on the idea of loving anyone or even starting the process of loving someone.

After hanging up the phone, Cee-Cee went into a complete frenzy. She jumped to her feet, walked in circles for a moment and realized she needed a sitter for her son, Jaylen. She hurried over to her neighbors and asked Yolanda to keep him for a few hours. Cee-Cee went into details about having a date and after a few minutes of you go girls and high fives, Cee-Cee rushed back to her apartment to get ready. In her bedroom, she ran directly to her closet, pulling shirts and jeans from its hangers. After trying on outfit number twenty-five, she had exhausted herself. Cee-Cee plopped down onto her bed and came to the conclusion that she was going to be very comfortable with what she put on, and he would have to accept her as casual as she came. With that thought in mind, she decided on a black, white and blue Polo sweatshirt and a pair of navy Polo jeans with black boots. Cee-Cee pulled her hair in a ponytail, added a light touch-up of makeup and a splash of Jivago perfume. She was ready to see Mr. Jamale.

After taking Jaylen to Yolanda's, Cee-Cee waited patiently for Jamale. When he phoned her from his cell phone indicating he was parked in front of her apartment property, Cee-Cee began to panic once more. He asked if he could meet her at her apartment door, but Cee insisted it wasn't necessary. She stopped in front of her bathroom mirror, said a few words to herself, took a deep breath and headed towards the front of the property. There he was finer than she remembered double parked in his glistening Mercedes.

They were both smiling like school kids on their first unescorted date. As Cee-Cee approached the car, Jamale had stepped around the passenger side and opened the door for her. He smiled at her for a moment and then began to chuckle. When they both were strapped in and ready to take off, he looked at her and began to gleam. His smile relaxed Cee-Cee and stirred up the opening conversation that opened the gates of love.

"So brother, what're you smiling so hard for?"

"Brother, huh? Let's leave that at the church. I'm Jamale, or any other sweet name you can think of." Again, that broad smile took over. "Now, to answer your question. I'm smiling because I'm happy you agreed to have ice cream with me on such short notice and you are more beautiful than I remembered."

Cee-Cee tried not to blush as she thanked him. She could feel herself losing her self-control. The fact that this man was causing her biological percolator to brew some juices that had not brewed within a long, long, time, had her stunned.

They sat at the traffic light for a moment not saying a word. When a love ballad started playing on the radio, she closed her eyes and bobbed her head to a slow groove. Periodically a grin would come across her face, and she'd shake her head thinking, umm, umm, umm. Cee-Cee was envisioning that kiss he'd talked about earlier and was hoping he'd follow through with his desires.

Jamale didn't say a word. He enjoyed watching her with her eyes closed and her rhythmic groove. He could feel her passion, and he imagined her motions coupled with his. He, too, wanted the kiss. His body was beginning to react to his thoughts, and with the jeans he had on, Jamale knew he'd better maintain some control. They were only half of a block away from the ice cream parlor, so what an ideal time to interrupt the mind wandering that was going on at that particular moment.

Pretending to be paying close attention to the road, Jamale stretched his head a little to look at the driver ahead of him while breaking their silence. "Cee-Cee, we're almost there. So what's your favorite ice cream?"

Cee-cee opened her eyes suddenly, turned her head towards his direction and smiled. "I like pistachio. What about you?"

He smiled at her and scanned her body slowly while answering her question. "Without a doubt, I like butter pecan." Again, Cee-Cee found herself blushing, and Jamale loved every minute of it.

Considering Jamale's directness in his question at the church and the way he had just scanned her body, Jamale was still very much a gentleman. He opened the door and reached his hand out to Cee-Cee to help her from the car. When their hands touched, both of their bodies reacted which caused them to pull away quickly from one another.

Darkness was starting to take over, and because it was getting late, they agreed to eat their ice cream in the car while driving to the lake. The temperature had dropped a little, and it was brisk out, but that didn't matter, they were together and why not the lake to share a first kiss.

They stood side by side looking out at the water. The moment was right, and before Cee-Cee could finish her sentence, Jamale reached for Cee-Cee pulling her close to him. He carefully placed his lips on hers. She responded by placing her arms around his waist, entering her tongue into his mouth. His arms rested around her waist, and his hands caressed her back as they stroked tongues.

The kiss was forever, so it seemed and their emotions were running rapid. They held hands as they walked closer towards the water while admitting to one another their desires to make love. Cee-Cee knew they were moving too fast and had to take a stance to put an end to admitting to their needs. So Cee-Cee asked the question, "So, how do you feel about children?"

Stunned by her question, Jamale stepped back and gave a bewildered look. Changing the subject, he asked if she were getting cold and suggested they get into the car. Cee-Cee agreed it was cold and wasn't sure if Jamale had intentionally ignored her question or if he was preparing himself to give what she may have thought to be the correct answer. Whatever the case, Cee-Cee had already come to the conclusion that not too many professional and successful men sincerely welcomed single parents into their world. Besides that fact, she had two other strikes against her. She wasn't a professional or a college graduate. Therefore, Cee-Cee knew she would not allow it to devastate her the way it once had in the past.

Jamale turned the warmer on the passenger seat for Cee-Cee. He set the dial to the local jazz station and turned the volume moderately low before turning to her with such concern. "Your question. Why such a serious and unexpected question?" Trying to relax the mood a bit, he followed with a little humor. "I thought we would date a little, perhaps fall in love, get married and then talk about children." He smiled at her and reached for her hand when he noticed her smile wasn't as genuine as it had been.

"You're serious. I apologize. Children? How do I feel about children? Well, I like children and hope to have a child or two someday. I haven't given the subject much thought, but, thinking about it right at this moment, I'd have to say, children would definitely fit into my lifestyle. I've had a lot of fun being single, and professionally I'm stable. I have a home that was designed for a family, and I've done a lot of traveling. I guess a trip to Disney could be a nice vacation to plan." Again, a little humor to relax the mood, and this time she joined him.

Jamale's thoughts of their beginning have become the anchor in his life and nothing could stir him away from his hearts compass that kept him in love with Cee-Cee.

6

Their timing was impeccable. Both Mercedes' pulled up in front of Arthur's with two of the finest brothas, and should I say, maybe two of the only brothas in the place. The valet attendant didn't do his ordinary rush to the car, smile, help the driver out, and get the keys and hurry around to help the lady out. Instead, he opened the door for the lady and helped her to the curb. He admired her ass out of the corner of his eye and then went towards Marquis who was already standing in front of the car checking out the young Black attendant admiring his date. Peter and Marquis both smiled at the young man as they tipped him before he parked their cars. Peter winked at the young attendant and placed a twenty in his hand. Peter let the attendant know if he would take good care of their cars he'd take better care of him when they came out of the restaurant.

The ladies were beautiful and proud to be on the arms of their men as they continued their arrogant strut. While waiting for the hostess to return to the front of the restaurant, Candace made conversation about the imported black and white Italian marble floor. She spoke of the time she had been to Italy and how the restaurant reminded her of a place she had dined at while there. Marquis interrupted her story by telling her how beautiful she was and how happy he was to have her with him in Dallas. He knew if he hadn't stopped her, she would go on the entire night talking about her experiences around the world.

Marquis had come to the conclusion that there was something about Candace that he didn't like, and that was it. She talked too damn much about what she owned, where she'd visited and what she'd done. But he wasn't going to burn any bridges. Marquis also realized her stay was temporary, and if it was going to be a successful one, he'd better get with the program. So naturally he had to give her what every woman wanted and expected; full attention and the highest form of praise. So he did what he knew would work; he kissed Candace's hand and told her how beautiful she was. After all, he didn't need an invitation to be the man of the hour. Regardless, he was going to be that to any woman he was spending time with.

While Peter was finessing Crystal with his debonair ways, a woman passed and quickly glanced at him with a seal of approval. He was surprised by her coy flirtation because that was his area of expertise, but he had no problem sharing the wealth. There was no unwritten rule that a woman couldn't have "game" of her own. Unfortunately, it was not the appropriate time for him to react and put his game plan into action. You can call Peter many things, but you can't call him disrespectful. He would never make a woman feel as if she were second to anyone.

With a peacocks strut, the refined gentlemen and their ladies passed through the dimly lit room. The ambiance in the room was very romantic, and if you played your cards right, you were guaranteed to get your groove on later in the night.

The room wasn't very large; maybe twenty tables filled with smug people who thought they were in a class of their own and intentionally gave looks of disbelief and disgust. To the right of the room was a well stocked bar and a couple of men talking with a gentleman who appeared to be of some influence. Along the wall, in the rear of the dining room were five private rooms that separated them from the open dining room. Each private room had a red velvet curtain and a private wait staff which provided the guests complete intimacy. Of the five private rooms, three of those rooms were being occupied. You'd have to wonder who was behind those red velvet curtains that were drawn as their private waiter stood patiently outside waiting to be summoned.

Arthur's had an impeccable reputation that had earned the respect for its culinary greatness. But also, the restaurant was known for its famous and very wealthy clientele. When Marquis, Peter and their ladies entered, they looked as well suited to be there as any of the other guests. While Marquis, Candace and Crystal were being seated at the table near the bar, Peter waited behind to ask the requirements for being seated in one of the private rooms.

As Marquis and the two women passed the couple dining at the first table, Peter overheard a petite older White woman with the overly teased hair that covered up her balding spots whisper in a quiet, yet intentional murmur. "They must have won dinner for four coupons off the local radio station. Surely they couldn't afford to eat here. Look at them; they must have spent every nickel of their welfare checks to buy clothes to wear out."

Peter couldn't believe what he'd just heard and was pissed by her remarks. It took every fiber of Peter's soul not to unleash the "Nigger" that some White folks believe dwelled in all Blacks.

Needless to say, Peter was poised when he joined his other guests for a few minutes, still fuming inside. Unable to contain himself he gently excused himself from the table and headed towards the foyer to ask for the manager.

The older gentleman at the bar was interrupted by the hostess and immediately joined Peter at the foyer. As Peter explained the racism he was just subjected to, an offer for complimentary dining was extended along with a sincere apology. Peter made it very clear he wasn't there for free food and was quite capable of paying for his meal. However, he did appreciate the gesture. As he was walking back to his table, the older gentleman called Peter back and explained that he was the owner and truly didn't appreciate how Peter and his guests had been treated. The owner then asked if he could seat Peter and his guests in one of the restaurants private dining areas. Pleased by the suggestion, Peter thought it would be a great way to separate him and his guests from any other patrons unable to accept the success of beautiful Black people.

Because Peter was the only one of the four to hear the comments from the old bigot, the ladies and Marquis didn't know what was happening, and why they were moving to the private room, nor did any of them question it. For all they knew, Peter was definitely the man and was working the people at Arthur's.

An appetizer wine was brought out with a serving of Porta Bella mushrooms that were deliciously stuffed with blue crab meat. Marquis sniffed and tasted the wine and accepted it; something obviously not new to these gentlemen, and the ladies were very impressed. Satisfied with the night, Peter raised his glass and toasted to the two most beautiful women in the city.

Loves Season

After minutes of thought, Jamale interrupted his deep and loving memories to call the woman he'd grown to love. Meanwhile, Cee-Cee sat curled up on her recliner wearing her favorite flannel night gown enjoying a good movie. She could always count on a good movie on the Lifetime Channel.

On the weekends, Cee-Cee planned most of one day around nibbling on her movie snacks, watching a good movie or enjoying her time to bond with her son, although her bonding time with Jaylen was beginning to dwindle right before her eyes. Cee-Cee had become accustomed to not having a man in her life, and like so many other single mothers with sons, companionship was directed towards the sons who replaced a man in their lives.

Jamale's timing was impeccable. He entered into Cee-Cee and Jaylen's life at the perfect time. A time when she feared her son was drifting away from her maternal clutch and her becoming too comfortable with not having a man in her life.

After her divorce from Jeff, the man she should never have married in the first place, she became a happily divorced, and I mean a thank you Jesus, happily divorced woman. Whereas things may have been difficult from time to time and accepting her situation as a single mom, she and Jaylen were doing fine with their particulars. They traveled together, went to the movies, dined out, spent quiet time reading books, did amusing things outside of the home, and shared endless conversations on any subject a young child with an inquiring mind could conjure up. She did everything with her son that she could do with a man, except the obvious. Granted, this was all good for Cee-Cee most of the time, but she, just as any other woman wanted to have a male companion she could call her own and hope to build on a relationship that would last forever.

The relationship Cee-Cee shared with Jeff was explosive. Reflecting on her past wasn't something she did very often, but it seemed her time in front of the television helped her to recall some sad moments. She recalled the day after she brought Jaylen home from the hospital, she was so exhausted from not feeling well throughout the day that when Jaylen woke up to be fed in the middle of the night, Jeff being the insensitive jerk that he'd become pushed her off the bed and onto the floor. There had been so many repeated instances throughout the years that constituted domestic abuse that Cee-Cee unhesitatingly ran away from the relationship before she became a domestic violence statistic.

Cee-Cee was five years younger than Jeff and deeply in love when she married him. He joined the Marines directly after graduating high school and wanted his wife to join him at his permanent duty station. Cee-Cee really didn't want to leave her family in Arkansas, but she had no other choice. She was a young mother, and he was her husband, and they were her new family.

Moving away from her mom and her few family members allowed Jeff to be in total control of what she did, where she did it, when she did it and whom she did it with. Keep in mind "it" could be any and everything. No matter what she did, it became good reason for Jeff to hit her and make her feel as if she were less than anything of value. Jeff had everyone who knew him fooled. They thought he was great, and their marriage was perfect, but Cee-Cee wasn't fooled. She lived with the mental and physical abuse for the three years they were together, and she learned very well never to judge a book by its cover.

It was one cold morning in upstate New York when Cee-Cee found herself running with her three year old son through the snow away from the man she thought would beat her to death. Jeff promised her that day she would never be with any other man for as long as she lived and if she tried, he would kill her. That day became the end of her hell and the start to a new life away from Jeff. Cee-Cee got on the first Greyhound headed to New York City and connected onto a bus that would lead her back to Little Rock, Arkansas. He harassed her for a while over the years, but for the most part, he really stayed away. Until last month, Jeff started calling for Jaylen and trying to find his way back into their lives.

Despite the years passed, her life with Jeff always brought tears to her eyes. And watching the Lifetime channel didn't help much. Watching movies that mirrored her life with Jeff only added fuel to the fire.

Deep into her thoughts, the ringing telephone startled Cee-Cee. She sat staring at the handset for a few rings and thought not to answer it. She wasn't expecting any phone calls, and besides, she was engulfed in her movie and consumed by her thoughts. And she knew the one person she wanted to hear from was out doing his own thing.

Jamale and Cee-Cee had agreed months ago that one weekend day was to be spent as "we time" and yesterday was that day together, so there were no required phone calls. After the fourth ring, she answered the phone, and much to her surprise, the voice was charming, inviting and pleasant and started with an innocent "Hello." Whenever she heard his voice, the sensitive woman kicked in. It was her sweetheart, and she was always elated to hear his comforting voice. They were both very much in love with each other.

The conversation started with small talk and general questions when suddenly Jamale asked a surprising question. "Baby, I was thinking about how we met and our first date and wondered do you ever think about it?"

Cee-Cee started laughing. "Silly, you know I do. I told you how I reacted during our first telephone conversation. What's goin' on with you?"

In an unusual tone, he answered. "Nothing really. I was just thinking about us. Where we've been and where we're headed."
Cee-Cee was caught by surprise, so she had paused for a moment before she asked her question. Her eyes paralyzed to the floor, and in a discouraged tone, she asked, "are you thinking about the children thing?"

"Yes and no. I was just thinking about us. Don't start reading more into this than there really is. Baby, I love you, and that's what matters for now. Everything will work out."

Not feeling as confident as Jamale, Cee-Cee knew the topic had the potential of getting too deep, so before allowing it to go any further, she agreed with Jamale. It was her cue to leave well enough alone. Cee-Cee gave the excuse she had a few errands to run as she hurried off the phone.

Their relationship was that of a love story. But as every love story goes, there always seems to be some kind of sadness that goes along with it. This was theirs: Cee-Cee was six years older than Jamale and with a son who was twelve-and-a-half. Jamale had no children and wanted at least one child together with the woman he planned on marrying. Cee-Cee had a tubal ligation ten years ago after experiencing a miscarriage with her ex-husband, plus she knew her childbearing days were over. She was approaching forty and was close to finally having her life to explore without a child. The option of having children just wasn't something Cee-Cee wanted to consider.

Open Season

Dallas, Texas was everything Khadijah had hoped for and more. The sexy sounds of New Birth played on the radio, and the climate was far from the cold winter days of Detroit. Plus she had the man next to her that helped her to rekindle long lost and forgotten desires.

Austin's hand gently cupped the top of Khadijah's hand as his fingers interlocked comfortably with hers. Each time Austin glanced over at Khadijah, he gave her a beguiling smile. She was mesmerized. The unspoken words that came from his alluring eyes made her quiver by the thoughts that took over. Although their words were few, their desires were loud and clear. Khadijah was on her way to an unforgettable journey with the captain who could possibly rock her boat.

Driving in the middle lane of the busy interstate, with no exit near, Austin began slowing his car. He turned his right signal light on as Khadijah watched for a moment unsure why he was pulling off onto the median. She asked if there were a problem, but he didn't answer. When the car came to a stop, Austin put the car in park and turned towards her. He raised Khadijah's hand to his lips and lightly kissed it a couple of times. Austin smiled and in a compassionate influence he spoke, "I've missed you more than you could ever know. I wish I could make you understand how very happy I am being with you at this very moment." Again he kissed her hand and smiled. Khadijah made every attempt to relax, but deep in her heart she didn't know how to react. It had been so long since she felt the kind of love Austin was displaying. "I needed to tell you that before we got to my place. I wanted you to know how special you are to me." Khadijah stared at Austin while he found his way back onto the interstate. She was speechless. All she could do was smile as she looked away.

Khadijah's heart began fluttering when Austin turned the corner into the President's Circle Subdivision. There was no doubt that Mr. Austin James had it going on. When he pulled in front of the red brick house at 2312 Lincoln Square, Khadijah's face lit up. She was proud of her two high school buddies and their accomplishments.

Before getting out of the car, Austin turned to Khadijah and asked if she were okay. Girlfriend wasn't crazy; hell yeah she was okay. She was with the sexiest man, and the only man she every truly loved. If he could feel the pulse of her libido and read the thoughts in her mind, he would think he'd just walked onto the land of erotica. But because of the woman she'd become and her experiences and decisions, Khadijah had other thoughts beginning to occupy her mind. Fortunately, over the years she'd become very good at camouflaging it all. She had put on one of her charming smiles before Austin realized something was beginning to trouble her.

Ordinarily Austin would pull into the garage if he had a female companion visiting. This time was different. He wanted the world to witness his joy and the woman who brought such joy into his life. He opened the door and reached for Khadijah's hand to help her from the car. Austin held her hand up the walkway until it was time to unlock the door. When the door opened, he stepped away so she could enter first then followed her in and locked the door behind them. Before they went any further into the house, Austin began their evening of amorous passion by delicately reaching for Khadijah's face, and stroking her skin as he kissed her.

Although his fabulous bedroom was near and available, where the scents would burn from candles and the romantic sounds of some Brazilian jazz would flow from his stereo, instead it was at the marble entranceway that Austin tenderly kissed her lips. And as each button from her blouse was unlatched, his tongue stroked every inch of her revealed flesh. She stood there savoring every stroke of passion when she found herself removing his shirt from his sculptured body and massaging his neck and shoulders with her lips. Khadijah unzipped and began removing his pants. While he was stepping out of his clothes, he was unzipping her skirt. Their breathing became heavier as her sexy black thong fell to the floor. They held hands and kissed until they were kneeling in front of each other. Their kiss stopped as they stared at one another waiting for approval. Austin's lips were wet, and his mouth was warm when he devoured her succulent juices. Khadijah's approving moan helped Austin to take her to a place beyond recollection.

The tears streamed down Khadijah's face as the thoughts consumed her. She thought about the man she had promised to always love. How she had forgotten his touch. How she'd forgotten about their love. How her body was reminded how a woman felt when a man truly loved and appreciated her when he made love to her. How she was being loved by a man whom she hadn't seen in years. And most importantly, how she hadn't been loved by a man she vowed to love forever after being married five years ago.

Austin gently kissed up Khadijah's stomach, onto her breast and finally her lips again. When his eyes opened, he saw the tears streaming down her cheeks. He stopped, held her and whispered, "Baby, why are you crying?" Khadijah clutched him closer towards her and cried quietly. Stroking her hair and trying to comfort her, Khadijah pulled away from Austin with a look of despair. Needing to surrender to the words that pained her had Khadijah trembling when she spoke. "Baby, this is wrong. I have to be honest with you." With tears flowing down her face, she paused for a moment wrestling with the words to come. "Baby, I'm married."

Austin's surprised look made her tears fall faster. He put his head down and was speechless while they both sat paralyzed by her confession. Words that time could not change. His heart and soul was heavy as he raised his head slowly. Austin looked into Khadijah's eyes and with tears in the wells of his eyes, he quietly told her, "we'll get through this." Austin reached for her hand to help her off of the floor.

Khadijah stood there not knowing what to say or do when he walked away towards another room. Her dreams were becoming her nightmare. Losing him again couldn't be happening. It wasn't until Austin returned that Khadijah knew he loved her. He covered her with his treasured crimson and cream bathrobe. Austin felt it in his soul that Khadijah was the only woman for him, and he confirmed it as he uttered the words, "I love you and if I lose you again, I'd lose my whole world."

7

(A)lthough Adrian had been introduced to many potential superstars, he was not behaving like his usual composed self. He was tripping on a "project" without any negotiations or hell, without even talking to the artist, but Adrian was sure he'd come across a shining star. Adrian had an ability to recognize a star, and he knew exactly what his next power move should be. This female would be on top of the charts for a long time and without question would be one of the century's top divas. And let's not leave out what it would do for his career. Adrian would be known in the industry for being the most diverse multi-platinum A&R's in the industry. This would confirm him to be the commodity he'd always known he was.

Adrian was certain that there wasn't any more need for his procrastination. He sat his butt down and began pressing the numbers listed on the bio below her name. Adrian exhaled a loud sigh of anxiety as he pushed the last number; he leaned back onto his chair and swiveled around looking outside of the window that overlooked downtown Dallas when the phone began to ring.

The phone rang a couple of times when an older woman answered the call. The sound of a crying baby shadowed all of what should have been a comprehensible greeting, and it was almost impossible to understand what the woman said after Adrian asked for Chanel. Adrian repeated himself twice when he finally apologized for calling the wrong number and hung up. He stared at the number on the bio for a moment, when he spoke above a whisper. "I know I called the right number. What was all that drama goin' on over there? Let me try this again."

The aching sound of the crying baby amplified over the old woman when she muttered, "My Lawd, what ya cryin' 'bout? Hush up all dat dere noise." While stumbling to put the handset to her mouth, the woman finally got around to saying hello.

"Uh, yes, may I speak with Chanel please?"

"Who you askin' fo'?"

"Chanel Rayson."

"Baby there ain't nobody by dat name livin' here. Wait, who you askin' fo' again?"

Undeniably, Adrian was becoming a little frustrated. He rolled his eyes as he raised his voice a pitch to answer, "Chanel Rayson." Feeling the need to clarify himself, he added, "She's a singer."

Between trying to hush a crying child and decipher what the man on the phone wanted, the woman finally blurted out, "Well, there's a Nannie Olivia Rayson livin' here and she sings."

If anyone could have witnessed the buck-eyed and stone faced expression Adrian was wearing, they would have known he'd just been slapped with some dreadful bit of reality.

In a very well hidden and condescending tone, he dreadfully repeated the name Nannie Olivia and asked if she were available.

"Well, no, no she ain't. She's at church. Her and her sister should be comin' home in a minute…ugh, ugh, here they go now. You wanna hold dah phone a minute?"

Almost relieved Adrian responded, "Yes ma'am. Thank you." He looked at his watch trying to imagine why anyone would go to church twice on Sunday, both in the morning and at night and shook his head. It was when he heard the beautiful sound of her voice that Adrian stopped wondering and concentrated on her voice and nothing else.
It was beautiful. The voice of an angel singing, "Great Is Thy Faithfulness." It was undeniable that he'd reached the right

number. The old woman tried to shout over her singing, but Nannie Olivia, Chanel or whoever she wanted to be called intended on finishing the verse and stopping to hear her grandmother wasn't an option. Chanel was doing what she loved most, and it was echoing across the phone line.

"Nannie Olivia, you hear me! Girl, some man is on dah phone asking for a Cha-something Rayson who sings. I guess he talkin' 'bout you. If you hush for a minute, you can get yo'self ova here to see who it is."

Chanel was paralyzed. Her mouth hung open, and not a sound came from it. When she finally could speak, it was at a whisper. "He's asking for Chanel Rayson? Oh my God, grandma, please, gimme, gimme, gimme....clearing her throat....please give me the phone."

Chanel sat down exhaling for a moment. Her sister who had come in the house with Chanel stopped in front of her when she noticed how big and bright Chanel's eyes were. Chanel's sister knew something exciting was going on, and she wanted to be in on it.

Part countrified and part urban, Chanel's sister Doris let out a squeal that could have shaken all of Houston. "Ooooooh gerl, whatz up wit' you? Why you look like you trippin'? Who dat on the phone?"

Cuffing the phone receiver, Chanel whispered to be quiet and tried shooing her off, but that didn't work. Doris plopped down on the sofa beside Chanel, with her arms crossed and her mouth twisted with attitude, and positioned herself to listen to every word.

Not really caring if Doris heard or not, Chanel knew this was the phone call she had been hoping, wishing and praying for ever since the packet had been mailed. Chanel looked at Doris with a facial expression that told her true feelings... if you would relax and sit your hot butt down maybe you would realize who was on the phone. Then maybe, and I do mean maybe Doris would go into a moment of total shock, and her mouth would follow shut. But before Doris could get deep into the conversation the baby started crying, so she had no choice but to leave the area to take care of his nasty diaper. So, I guess shit isn't always a bad thing because it was exactly what Chanel needed so she would have some privacy.

Clearing her throat and with a long exhale, Chanel managed to speak. "Hello."

"Hi. I'm trying to reach Chanel Rayson."

"Yes, this is Chanel. Who am I speaking with?"

"My name is Adrian McGowan, I'm with Milestone Records. I hope this is not a bad time to be calling. I reviewed your packet earlier and must tell you, I was very impressed. I'd like to schedule a time for us to get together and talk."

Chanel jumped to her feet and did some kind of fancy footwork that looked remarkably close to an Indian rain dance, and she did everything possible not to let her excitement slip out when she spoke. "Are you serious? Oh my God, yes, I would love to. When?"

"Well, I'd like to meet sometime this week if that's possible. I can fly into Houston or Milestone will fly you to Dallas. Whichever..." Thinking strongly about his next words, Adrian cringed at the thought of having to try to conduct business with a crying baby in the background. Not that Adrian thought he was above being around her people, but certainly not to conduct business with a potentially lucrative client.

"Why don't you plan on coming to Dallas? Take down my telephone number at the office, and give me a call early tomorrow morning and we'll discuss the best time for you to fly out."

Without thought or hesitation, Chanel jumped at the opportunity facing her, "Uh, Mr. McGowan, I don't need any time to think about when I can leave. Uh, I'll be ready first thing in the morning if you'd like."

Finding the humor in Chanel's excitement, Adrian chuckled before interrupting her. "Okay. Let me have my secretary make the necessary arrangements, and we'll go from there. You should be hearing from either me or my secretary Jasmine with the details to fly out tomorrow some time. And you're sure you can leave right away?"

"Yes! I am more than sure."

"Okay then, it's a plan. You'll be getting a call in the morning."

Before Adrian could say good bye, Chanel blurted out his name with such sincerity, "Mr. McGowan, thank you so much."

"Thank you Chanel for sending the packet. Get a good nights rest and I'll see you tomorrow."

Adrian and Chanel took in a breath of relief after hanging up. Chanel whispered her thanks to God and turned to run into the kitchen to share the news with Doris, but Doris was already standing in the doorway with her hands on her hips and her lips turned up waiting to hear what the phone call was about.
Although Doris and Chanel were born identical twins, there was truly something God also did. He made them two totally opposite people in character. Talking about opposite ends of the spectrum, well, Doris and Chanel had earned their prominent places.

As a young girl, Doris was considered the more ambitious of the two sisters. From early as she could remember, Doris had big dreams of becoming a famous dancer. She danced from the age of three and loved it more than anything, but it was at the age of sixteen and after the tragic death of their parents when Doris changed. Actually, everything changed. She and Chanel had to leave their home in Ft. Lauderdale, Florida and move to Houston, Texas with their elderly grandmother in an environment they were not familiar with. And the move meant having to give up on the dance lessons she had enjoyed for thirteen years.

Although Chanel and Doris' parents had a will with their

grandmother as beneficiary and custodian of the minor children, their grandmother was old and set in her ways and not prepared to raise two teenagers in the lifestyle they were accustomed to.

In Ft. Lauderdale, Doris and Chanel lived in a middle class neighborhood, and their parents enjoyed giving their children almost everything they wanted. Doris was in dance class, and Chanel took private voice lessons. But it was Doris who proved their parent's hard earned wages weren't a waste of money.

In high school Doris was on the drill team and in the local dance theater. Having to move to Houston to a high school that did not offer any dance program and wouldn't allow her to join the drill team, she was devastated. As far as Doris was concerned, life itself was over when her dream was abruptly taken away from her. One would think the sisters would draw to one another for support, but just the opposite occurred. Doris didn't want much to do with Chanel. Chanel was disappointed with the way Doris was handling their situation, but Chanel was growing up and becoming quite a young lady, identifying with her own talent.

With as much attitude as Doris could deliver, she asked, "So, what was that call about?"

Initially Chanel hesitated, but she realized there was nothing Doris could do to mess up her music career. Telling her the good news wasn't any big deal.

"Girl, you are not going to believe this. Shulandra, my producer sent my packet to a record company, and they want to meet with me. Girl, that was the man who makes all the decisions on who will and who won't be signed to a deal."
"What kinda deal you talkin' 'bout?"

"Girl, I'm talking about a major recording deal. This could be it!"

"Yeah well, what is that gonna mean for grandma, me and Demetrius?"

"What you think?" Trying to get Doris to join in with her, Chanel started singing the theme song of the well-known '70's sitcom, The Jefferson's. "...moving on up, to the east side..."

"Gerl, you are trippin'." Doris changed her tone and hit Chanel with a flurry of questions. "Do you really think this is it? Where is this record company? Did they really like you? Was he Black who called? Did he sound fine?"

Chanel couldn't believe how man hungry her sister had become. She shook her head at Doris and giggled. Chanel sat on the worn sofa and began telling Doris the details of Adrian's conversation. As Chanel reached the end of the story she started to walk away, but before she reached the dining room, Chanel turned to add, "And yes, he sounds fine."

"Un, un, hol' up. I wanna go." It was rare, but Doris knew how to sound sweet and look innocent. Doris was very familiar with what's known as the full of shit mode, and this was her time to perform. "Can I go to Dallas with you? Tell them you want your sister to come with you. Pleeeeeease, NO." Doris only called her sister NO when she wanted something. It was a name their mom used to call Chanel when she was a little girl. It was short for Nannie Olivia. "NO, I promise, I'll behave. Pleeease."

"Girl, that's not up to me. But I promise I'll ask when he calls."

The devil in disguise. A sheep in wolves clothing. Master of deception. Full of shit mode was in full affect. When Chanel left the room, Doris flipped Chanel the middle finger, lipped the words, fuck you and twisted her ass into the bedroom.

8

$\mathcal{N}$ot quite four o'clock on a Monday and his telephone was ringing for the fourth time in the last ten minutes, and Jamale's deep sleep and sensual dreams were being interrupted. And although getting angry had become something rare for him, at the moment he was on the borderline of becoming pissed.

"Yeah. Hello." Adding some force to his voice, he tried again, "HELLO."

The dial tone had Jamale curious, but he quickly dismissed the thought of it being someone of importance. He thought how he wished the number showed up on the caller ID. It being zero dark thirty in the morning, his thoughts were cloudy as he tried to remember the code to block all private, unknown or unavailable numbers, but nothing was clear. "Damn, who the hell is calling me like that? They can't be too damned important 'cause they would have texted me. And only the most significant people in my life know to do that." Looking at the clock on the night stand, he said aloud, "Damn, it's only four o'clock in the morning."

Sitting up in his bed after the first ring, Jamale grabbed the phone and shouted, "HELLO!" There was obviously someone on the other end, but his greeting was being ignored. He tried saying hello again and asked if there were anyone on the other end needing to speak with him, but still no response. At that point, Jamale had had enough of the games. He knew that if he'd planned on getting a little more sleep, the only sensible option was to hang up and turn off the ringer.

Unable to rest, Jamale wiped the crust that had formed in the corners of his eyes while thinking, damn that's some silly immature shit. Who the... Almost stunned by his thoughts, Jamale sat up suddenly in his bed. Jamale's voice was raspy when he questioned who could be acting such an ass so early in the morning. "I know damned well that crazy ass Tiffany ain't playing games after all these months. Nah, that's not her style. If she had something to say, she would have no problems voicing her opinions." His mind was racing as he thought about the threat Jeannette had made just two weeks prior. She threatened to destroy his house and his car if he didn't pay back all the money she had given him over the years. Jamale had to laugh out loud when he remembered the last time he saw Jeannette and told her he had fallen in love with Cee-Cee. She was pissed. She swung at Jamale and promised she would make his life a living hell. Jamale laughed while he was telling her to get past herself and to enjoy the time they had together over the years. Jamale thought about the time that passed and was certain it couldn't be Jeannette. It had been almost eight months since the last time he'd spent any time with her and decided to dismiss Jeannette as his crank caller.

"Let me get my Black butt some more sleep. I got a serious day ahead of me."

It seemed as if minutes had passed when the annoying beep woke Jamale from his sleep; but, however annoying, it was his text message which earned Jamale's full attention.

The message read: Baby, are you okay? I called, but your voicemail came on twice. Call me.

"Damn, the ringer." He reached for the phone, hit Cee's number on speed dial and walked toward the bathroom smiling when he heard the sultry sound of the woman he loved. Needless to say, just as most men wake up, so was the rise of Jamale's masculinity.

"Hey baby. I'm okay. I turned the ringer off 'cause someone kept calling and hanging up on me around 4 o'clock. What you doing up so early?"

"I got a couple of hang up calls myself, but I thought it was Jeff being the king of all assholes. Then I started thinking about my sexy, sexy, sexy Black man."

Jamale's attempt to use the bathroom would have to wait. Hmmm makes you wonder if it's possible for something hard as a rock to get any harder. Jamale gave up on standing in front of the commode and leaned back onto his bed with his eyes closed and his manhood in hand. Cee-Cee was familiar with the moans that he allowed to escape. Those sensuous moans were playing along perfectly with her plans. Cee-Cee asked if she could come over to cook him breakfast and take care of him. Jamale didn't hesitate to answer. "Baby you know you don't need permission to come over to let me feel that sexy body of yours next to mine." Jamale had no time for second guessing when it came down to enjoying the pleasures presented to him by his woman.

With a hint of sarcasm Cee-Cee asked, "Unn-unn, remember the part about me cooking for you? Did you miss that part of the conversation? I didn't say one thing about our bodies being next to one another. I said cook for you, baby."

Jamale laughed before he responded, "Oh, my bad. I meant have you cook for me."

The appointment Jamale had scheduled on his calendar was removed from his list of things to do. At the moment, making Cee-Cee happy was far more important than the appointment, and Jamale's plan was to be Cee-Cee's genie in the bottle and make all of her wishes come true.

Before they disconnected their call, Cee-Cee added a few instructions to set her plan in action. "Oh, and by the way, I'd like you to stay in the room until I call you down to the kitchen. Can you do that for me?"

"Anything for you, my lit'l lady."

Jamale liked the idea of his lady wanting to cook breakfast for him. He didn't understand what else Cee-Cee had planned, but if staying in bed until she told him to come downstairs was what she wanted him to do, again, her wish was his command.

Thirty minutes later, Cee-Cee was downstairs in Jamale's living room wishing her man good morning from the bottom of the stairway. She was almost singing the words as she told him breakfast would be ready in about twenty minutes. But Cee-Cee was surprised to see him coming out of the bedroom and reacted quickly hiding the large carry bag behind her.

"Get back in the bedroom. I told you on the phone I'd tell you when I wanted you to come down." She was being secretive and sexy at the same time and turning Jamale on even more if that's possible. He gave her a tantalizing smile, and as if surrendering, he put his hands up before returning to the bedroom.

Cee-Cee was so excited and with good reason. Her intentions included a morning filled with pleasure and indulgence. First things first...start breakfast. Fresh strawberries and thin wedges of mango and pineapple, Belgian waffles with a light sprinkling of confectionery sugar, maple brown sugar sausage links and a glass of freshly squeezed orange juice. Secondly, the ambiance had to be right. Cee-Cee put the large carry bag with all of the makings of the second part of her plan in the downstairs bathroom. Thirteen small votive candles and a bag of red and white rose petals, her favorite George Howard CD, massaging oil and her white chiffon robe that revealed every inch of her curvaceous body.

Of course, Jamale had a few surprises of his own going on upstairs. Candles were burning at each corner of the king sized bed and the emperor who had positioned his naked body across the cream-colored, satin down filled comforter was waiting for his queen.

Cee-Cee tapped on the bedroom door and was surprised when she peaked in to ask if she could come in. Jamale's alluring tone made Cee-Cee giggle after he responded, "Oh baby, the question is, can I come in?"

Taking very slow steps towards her man, Cee-Cee answered one word per step. "I...want...you...to..." She stopped two feet in front of him, smiled and finished her sentence, "...get up and go downstairs with me to eat the breakfast that's getting cold."

"Why I gotta go downstairs to eat breakfast when I got breakfast right in front of me?" The site of Jamale licking his lips made the invitation extremely inviting.

"Baby, you're real sexy right now, and oh yeah I want you, but ugh, right now we are goin' downstairs to eat the breakfast I worked so hard preparing for you. Now come on." She turned around slowly, took a couple of steps, intentionally stopped to bend down to pick a small piece of lint off the carpet. Jamale thought she was cute and laughed out loud. Cee-Cee knew exactly what she was doing and what bending down in front of Jamale would do to him. Jamale always felt Cee-Cee's rear end was the sexiest part of her body and her bending over was a definite tease.

When Jamale entered the kitchen, he was truly impressed. Cee-Cee had prepared all of his favorites and was sitting at the table looking beautiful. Everything she had done was reminding him why he loved her so much.

As they sat across from one another, Cee-Cee was timing his every bite. If she wanted her plan to run smoothly, she needed to excuse herself from the room at the right moment. Jamale was being very cooperative. He never once asked what she had up her sleeve. Instead, they kept the conversation minimal throughout breakfast. However, both of them were making statements with their seductive stares and sexy gestures with the fork as it entered and exited their mouths.

Before Jamale finished his meal, Cee-Cee asked him to please stay in the kitchen until she called for him. Jamale was willing to be as cooperative as she wanted because based on the reaction his manhood was experiencing he had no intentions on interfering with the moment. Besides, he had no plans on suffering with what people refer to as the blue balls all day.

While Jamale patiently waited to be called on, Cee-Cee was

arranging the room with candles and rose petals. Setting the mood was the key that would authenticate her well thought out game plan. She began by placing a lit candle on each step leading upstairs. Beginning at the entranceway of the kitchen, up the stairs and into the bedroom was a path of red and white rose petals which ended at the bed, which, too, was covered with petals. Before calling for Jamale, Cee-Cee changed into the chiffon robe and stood at the top of the stairs. She touched the play button on the remote control of the stereo as soon as she saw the kitchen door opening. When Jamale stepped out of the kitchen, he stood there as noble and gentle as ever. Jamale knew there was no need for words, so he did what any man in their right mind should do; he allowed his bath robe to fall to the floor as he seductively followed the petals up to the woman he knew he would be affirming his love to.

Jamale stood in the entrance of the bedroom for a moment admiring the beautiful creature of delicate and refined femininity. When he looked at her, he saw something very different about Cee-Cee today. She fit into his life and for the first time, Jamale admitted it.

Cee-Cee delighted in the man she loved and smiled with happiness. She was positive she was achieving the results she'd hope.

The enticing woman stood in the doorway of the bathroom soliciting him over with her index finger, and she spoke in hushed tones as she invited him to the warm bubble bath she had prepared. Jamale's body was declaring something other than a bath, however, but if putting him in a bubble bath was part of her plan, he was in no way going to interrupt. Jamale stopped to admire the petals and then slowly turned towards her. Acutely satisfied, he dropped his head and shook it in disbelief. Jamale turned his head slightly, looked at Cee-Cee and began to smile. She was beautiful to him. She was everything he knew he could love forever.

Jamale walked slowly towards her and stood face to face as he whispered the words I love you. Her heart digested his every word as he removed her robe. Their bodies brushed as he stepped past her towards the large garden tub, and for a second, Cee-Cee had to ignore her body as it quivered from his touch.

Jamale stepped into the warm water and rested his head on the silk bath pillow Cee-Cee had waiting for him. When she turned the lights off, the flicker from the candles glowed around the large bathroom. The crisp sound of the saxophonist played in the background while Cee-Cee's body swayed influencing Jamale to sink lower into the water as he sighed in satisfaction.

Although there were several white bath rugs, Cee-Cee placed one of the large floor pillows from the bedroom near the tub so she could kneel onto it. She gently bathed her man as if he were a young child and neither of them spoke any words for the duration of the bath. When she helped him out of the tub, she began to dry his virile anatomy. She reached for his hand guiding him to the bed when she began to delicately massage him. But, before she could finish, Jamale turned over, brought her close to him and passionately began to kiss her. It was his turn to show her how appreciated she was.

Seasoned Love

Assuming there's always a first for everything; with sex, that is, or perhaps I should say, without sex. Imagine sleeping beside the one person you once desperately loved and not knowing if sharing fervent lovemaking would be a good decision. Khadijah knew her moisture was running down his leg and she felt his strong penis pressed against her buttocks throughout the night. Her burning desire was consuming her, and the eruptive thoughts overcame any thoughts of sleep as she desperately tried to ignore her pulsating clitoris. Dayum!

Eyes may have been closed shut, but I can assure you, wasn't much sleep going on in that bed last night. It was more of a cross between cravings and suffering, which made it damn near impossible to keep their eyes closed. There wasn't anything easy for Khadijah about being in the bed next to Austin, wanting him so frantically and not being able to touch him passionately.

The situation wasn't a cake walk for Austin either. He was struggling with their dilemma and his desires. His only thought at the moment was shit, shit, shit. Austin had a solid erection, and when his leg wrapped between and around Khadijah's, he could feel the heat and wetness between her legs. He was handling the situation the best he could until temptation got the best of him as he surrendered and began caressing Khadijah's erect nipples.

She was married and it made the situation extremely awkward. But there was no turning back once they got started. The sounds of her sigh relaxed his trepidation and his imagination took off like a horse running wild.

Khadijah and Austin thought they had successfully made it through the night without cause for guilt as they slept in each other's arms. Frustrated, Austin's next thought was, to hell with this shit. He turned her over and slowly removed her black panties. Austin stared into her eyes for approval, and when he didn't see any resistance, he inserted his pleasure into her delicacy, and they finally made music unlike any musician could have ever composed.

Their bodies were drenched, and their breathing was intense. Khadijah rested on Austin's chest with a satisfied smile. When she looked up at him, all Austin could think to utter was, "Yes. Yes. Yes." He'd reached the conclusion, Khadijah was no joke. She'd done something to Austin most women had tried to do with no prevail. Khadijah made Austin reach his height of ecstasy while she was pumping and grinding her body while on top of him. The only person Austin could fool would be himself if someone asked, but the truth of the matter was, his mind was blown. The man was damn near speechless. Austin had reached some point where one word sentences were all he could speak. "Damn." "Wow." "Baby."

When he tried to speak, he stuttered. "Ba-ba-baby, I love you." Khadijah didn't want to make Austin uneasy, so she closed her eyes and held him tightly.

She was relieved to hear those words from Austin, but the words "I love you" weren't the stimulus of her excitement. Khadijah's body had gone through some transformational journey that had her in la, la land. Her face was flushed; her body quivered as if she were standing outside with her flesh exposed to cool air and her head was as light as a feather in the wind. She laid there for a bit unsure if she should move, actually, she couldn't move, when without warning she began to giggle. When she turned to look at Austin, she noticed him staring at her trying to figure out why she was giggling. She took his hand, kissed it softly and tried to explain. "No, no, no. I'm not laughing at you, babe." Khadijah was dealing with her own realization. It just hit her like a ton of bricks that she had just done something she had never done with any man. She experienced her first orgasm. Dayummmmmmmm!

Austin started tickling Khadijah as he questioned what she was laughing at. In between laughter, she tried to assure him she wasn't laughing at him, but her body was still too limp, almost paralyzed when she balled up into a fetal position. "Bay...bay....bay..." Austin interrupted her pleading by pressing his thin, but very moist lips against her full and supple mouth. "Ummmmm." They both moaned. It was one of those long and deep kisses that made the juices start to flow again.

Austin's manhood was speaking to Khadijah and she was hearing him loud and clear. Khadijah wasn't a fool. She knew exactly what she had to do to put out her burning desire. She reached for his solid manhood and put it just where it was supposed to be at the moment. And like the old saying goes, "That's all she wrote."

Half the morning was gone. Any other day, staying in the bed making love to his woman would be great. But Austin knew he had a 10:30 meeting with the Program Director at the radio station and he couldn't afford to be late. And Austin knew he wasn't going to ignore Khadijah's needs by rushing their session. He had already decided a morning shower together would be the icing on the cake. Nothing was going to short change their first time together after all the years apart. Austin subconsciously knew, however, what business needed to be taken care of, and he also knew with Khadijah being married and them not discussing the details of the marriage that he wasn't sure what the consequences would be regarding her being out all night. He trusted she had it under control, and when the time was appropriate, they would discuss the details in full. As for last night being the appropriate time, well, neither one of them were going to disturb their happiness.

9

$\mathscr{I}$t was later than normal for Peter to have his juice maker grinding and pureeing, carrots, apples and celery. His famous juice that he said ignited his energy reserve. Austin came down looking exhausted and aggravated by the loud machine, but Peter leaned against the refrigerator sipping on a glass of his juice, ignoring Austin's painful expression and smiled at his brother as he offered Austin a glass of juice. "Hey man, I know you don't really like my juice, but you look as if you could use the vitamins and a massive boost of energy." When Khadijah followed Austin into the kitchen seconds later, naturally Peter had to make some remarks on the way she looked.

"Well dayum. Maybe I need to make another batch of juice. Y'all look whooped. What's goin' on here? Oh, oh, let me guess…two love birds who don't ever plan on being apart from one another ever again. So when's the wedding?"

Neither Khadijah nor Austin responded. And based on the expressions they both wore, Peter assumed something was up, and it wasn't anything good.

"Hey, is everything okay? What's up with those expressions on your faces?"

"Man, I'll talk with you later. Right now Khadijah needs to get home, and I need to get ready for my appointment. I don't mean to leave you hangin' or anything, but you know how it is."

"Oh, it's like that. After I got you two together? No problem, we'll talk later. I need to get out of here anyway. On the serious tip… I hope everything's all right."
Peter gave Khadijah a hug and a kiss on the forehead and knocked

knuckles with his brother before exiting into the garage. One thing Peter could be assured of was Austin wouldn't put himself in any position that he couldn't handle.

Before starting the powerful 302 horsepower, V8 engine, Peter pulled out his black book that had his bookie's number in it. In his three quarters, full black book, his bookie's number was the only number that didn't belong to a woman.

Peter James sat in his car thinking about the bet he wanted to put down before making the call. He knew he had to make up for the loss he'd taken on the Cowboy game and couldn't afford to fall short on the playoffs.

Peter called his bookie Franco, an overweight Italian from Brooklyn, New York. Peter didn't really know much about Franco other than he was the man who had the underground betting locked up.

Peter wanted to place a bet for five G's on the upcoming Baltimore Ravens, Pittsburgh Steelers game. He'd heard the line was Pittsburgh by a seven point spread. As usual, Franco answered with his raspy voice. He listened to the bet Peter attempted to place and started laughing almost choking when he heard Peter's request. "Are you outta your damn mind? Man, I ain't frontin' you that kinda bet. The word is you haven't made good on your bet in Vegas on the 'Boys game yesterday. You know the word gets out fast."

"Hey man, I'm good for any bet I lay. When I get off this call, I'll be on my way to the bank to get Phil's money. In fact, let me get off the phone and give him a call now."

"Yeah. I would suggest you do that. Oh Peter, when I hear you handled up on your bet, I'll talk with you about the bet you wanna place. But I'm tellin' you, you mess with my money, you gonna wish you never did."

"Yeah, whatever. Just put me down when you hear that I'm good for it."

Phil was a hot tempered Trinidadian asshole from Philadelphia. Peter had been threatened by Phil once before when he was late paying his debt and Peter wasn't up to hearing the same kind of threatening message from Phil that he'd just gotten from Franco, so Peter figured he'd better wait until he got Phil's money in hand before making the call.

Rushing into the parking lot of the bank, Peter frowned at the Caucasian man who winked at him as he hurried into the bank. There were several people waiting for the next available teller and Peter really didn't want to wait for what could have been ten minutes at the rate the old lady to his left was moving. Peter was smart; he knew he had his ace in the hole if he needed to have his business handled quickly.

He stood in front of Margaret and flashed her one of his gentle smiles. She had given Peter every indication that she was interested in him, but it was against the policy of Dallas Mutual for bank representatives to date their customers.

"Good morning, Margaret. How is the morning starting for you?" Really not interested, he continued smiling.

"It's going super now that you came in and gave me such a wonderful smile. How can I help you this morning?" She gazed at Peter through her bifocal glasses that sat on her short and unusually wide nose.

"I need to do a bank wire for three thousand. Here are the bank details to wire to."

"No problem, Mr. James. It's going to be a couple of minutes, but you've done this before. You already know. Are we pulling from your savings?"

Flashing his charming smile, he answered, "Margaret, you know more about my finances than any woman ever. Yes, from my savings."

Turning away blushing she added, "I'll be right back." Peter hadn't even noticed the extra twist in her backside as she walked off.

Peter sat in his car for a moment studying the transfer details and his balance receipt and was stunned when to see that his savings account balance was just over three thousand. He looked almost surprised, but in his mind he knew he had been making more bets than usual and losing more times than winning. Peter wasn't concerned though. He had a good feeling he would win the spread in the Steelers/Ravens game.

After minutes of "Don't mess with my money and I'll fuck you ups" from his conversations with Franco and Phil, Peter decided he'd better do something to relax the headache he felt coming on. An image of a beautiful and cooperative woman always seemed to work wonders.

Peter thought about his evening with Charita last night and felt good about not allowing her to spend the night with him. He'd concluded a long time ago that if he allowed a woman to spend two nights in a row with him, it could lead her to believe more than she needed to about his intentions. He'd done his job at making her feel good by allowing her to spend one night.

As Peter drove down I-35 into traffic, he called Charita to confirm their date for the night. She was excited about finally going to one of the Monday night football gatherings she'd heard about from one of her coworkers who had been one of Marquis' dates. Peter was humored by her excitement, but he was more interested in the car he saw in his rearview mirror. As he approached the parking garage, he could see the very familiar car behind him. The windows had a dark tint so he couldn't see who was driving, but he knew he'd seen the 300M before. Peter tried to dismiss the car, but he was certain he'd seen it before, so he watched it pass as he turned into the garage.

Not being familiar with the garage, Peter followed the young men in suits towards the elevator. As he exited the elevator, he was facing a beautiful atrium with huge trees and a small fountain that had tables and chairs around it for people to sit. The Thanksgiving Tower was the tallest and perhaps the most attractive building in the Dallas downtown skyline.

Although the building was unfamiliar, the series of events to follow was not anything new for Peter. Being a contractual computer engineer had its advantages. He could work in any city or any fortune 500 company and meet people from all over. And because he was one of the best in his industry, getting a contract at top dollar wasn't anything difficult for him. It also allowed him flexibility.

Peter entered the atrium from the underground garage, and everyone seemed to be still. Women's heads were turning, and the few women seated eating their bagels had already started their inquisition. "Girl, who the hell is that?" "Damn, where the hell did he come from? Negro is fine." He was the most polished and attractive man in the area. There were professionals and non professionals that looked good around him, but Peter had a sense of confidence that most men lacked.

Peter stood for a minute admiring the view, or perhaps I should say, all of the fine sista's trying to get to their destinations. He was astounded by how many professional Black women worked in The Towers and he never even considered checking out a happy hour somewhere in the near area.

As Peter strolled throughout the atrium, he studied the many women who were obviously checking him out. This was nothing unusual for Peter. He smiled at most of them, and before a few of them could even consider a minutes time with him, he'd come to the conclusion to dismiss them. The first and the only reason the few women had been dismissed without thought was because they were White. Not that he had anything against White women. They just weren't his cup of tea. Although, he had to admit, one of the women was very attractive. But his rule was his rule; Peter did not and would not date any women other than Black women. But that was not to exclude his Caribbean sisters. Hell, they're one of us. He was convinced White women were too weak in the mind, and he admired the strength of his Nubian sisters.

Peter got a few flirtatious gestures and sexy hello's along with a couple of business cards passed his way, but Peter's objective was to be on the 23rd floor ten minutes before his scheduled arrival time. There wasn't enough time for Peter to sort through the women he'd scoped out, but he was certain there had to be, at most, two, who would be perfect candidates for his system of rotations.

Before he could reach the elevator, he recognized a familiar face and refused to miss the opportunity to say hello. Wearing his gleaming smile, Peter walked a slow stride towards the woman. She wore her 5'10 statuette physique like any supermodel on any glamour magazine. And when she glided across the floor, even she was impressed with her stride. The lady knew she had it going on and had no shame with putting that little extra umph to her step to make her onlookers do a double take.

The rhythmic tap of her Italian leather pumps as they struck the tiled floor gave her a sense that her steps had her hips swaying and enticing all of her onlookers. However, Peter was the only person that mattered at the moment. While heading in his direction, the sexy diva's freaky thoughts began to stimulate her genitalia as she began to undress him slowly. When she finally imagined his fine sculptured body, she concluded that his fine mocha male organ could give her what the double A batteries wasn't…nothing but absolute, fleshly pleasure.

Although getting a man to thicken her pudding wasn't a problem, Karyn didn't lend out her coochie like it was sugar for the neighbor to borrow. When a man had possession of what she felt was her million dollar stock, he was sure he had carefully managed the investment and was pleased with the dividends. Admittedly, from time to time Karyn had to let her fingers do the walking. That was okay with the sex starved woman so long as when the pudding had thickened, there was someone she knew she could rely on to lick the bowl clean.

Assuming Peter could very well be that candidate, her mouth salivated, and her pulsating erotic desire ached as she approached him. But, before she reached him, she quickly diverted towards the elevators that would go to the even numbered floors. Karyn was working her business and was very good at doing it. She made her presence known and made it very obvious to him that she had recognized him by the smile and nod of her head. There was no question, Peter was intrigued and thought it may be time to try to work his rotation in another way. He thought to himself, why not make her day? Even if it is just for one day, a woman with game sometimes had to be reminded that a man wrote the rules to the game. She was just a player. Peter rushed to the elevators where she stood so he could begin his mission.

When Peter approached her, Karyn was pleased, but not as pleased as Peter appeared. She had her own thing going on when it came down to who and how she would acquaint herself with a man.

Peter positioned himself directly in front of her. He stood close enough so she could smell his scent and see the moisture on his lips as he slowly tucked them into his mouth and swept them with his tongue. Peter's slow and deliberate words had Karyn burning like a ball of fire. She had already made a mental note to stop in the ladies room to insert her vibrating, remote controlled operated sex toy into her ignored genitalia.

Ready. Camera. Action. Peter began his role. "Hello. I saw you at the restaurant last night. How are you?"

Casually controlling her desires Karyn answered, "I'm fine. How are you?"

Peter was intrigued with her calmness. He was certain that working his plan and getting to first base with this woman was far more important than arriving ten minutes early to his new job. With a woman like her, he had to follow the steps as if he were on the firing range taking aim to his target. First step... breathe. Second...

relax. Third... aim. Fourth, squeeze. BULLSEYE! Peter was feeling pretty darn confident. His prey was within arms reach and with his aim she was surely to be caught in a matter of minutes. Peter could feel his blood warm as his anxiety climbed. But like the saying goes, Never let'm see you sweat. Instead, he began some small talk. The next move was to put on his debonair smile.

"I'm also doing well. But I must tell you, you are far more than just fine, you're exquisite. In fact, you're more beautiful than you were last night." Peter was feeling good. "So, do you work in this building or do you have business to conduct here?"

Impressed with his compliments, Karyn smiled, but don't be fooled, that wasn't enough to win him any brownie points. "Well, let me interrupt you for a minute. Firstly, I don't even know your name or anything about you...." shifting her body with more confidence. "....other than you like to dine at Arthur's." Karyn could imagine the chill that must have run down Peter's spine. Hoping to avoid his reaction, Karyn looked down at her gold Presidents style Rolex and added, "And secondly, I am pressed for time, so I need to get on the next elevator going up."

Karyn was spreading her funkiness a little thick, but she wasn't being rude. There's a fine line between the two, and if you're not careful reading and distinguishing between the two, you could easily lose out on a wonderful opportunity. Peter being the astute man that he was had mastered the two, so he smiling and accepting her brash attitude came without fault.

No doubt, Peter was surprised by her response. But he, in no way allowed her to think or believe she had accomplished some great feat, although she had. In one breath, this female had politely squashed Peter's intro to his ironclad plan. But being Peter, the rotation super hero that he was thought quickly, smiled and pardoned himself to add, "Well if an introduction is what you're needing, allow me. My name is Peter James. I'm in IT, and I like a good New York style pepperoni pizza. Is that enough or do I need to say more before I can at least invite you out to dinner?" Shifting his body, it was his turn to be more confident, borderline arrogant when he spoke. Looking down at his gold TAG Heuer watch and adding a quiet smack of his lips, he added, "Oh, but the time. You're pressed. I'm sorry to keep you."

As she listened to Peter, it took every bit of strength not to bite down on her lip and tell the man how fine she thought he was. But instead, when she noticed the Greek letters on his key chain she responded with, "JAPAN" and turned to press the call button for the elevator. Peter began to chuckle before asking what she knew about J.A.P.A.N. when suddenly the elevator door opened. Karyn got onto the elevator, seductively turned her body, smiled and said, "Just Another Pretty Ass Nupe" as the door shut.

This was a first; a female with some strong game. Not that it came as a surprise to Peter, he knew she had game when he saw her at the restaurant, but he had no idea she would have it going on like that. He couldn't help but laugh as he walked towards the other elevators.

10

$\mathcal{A}$lthough two twin sized beds occupied the small room, it routinely only had one of the sisters sleeping in it at night. Doris worked the night shift while her grandmother watched Demetrius. Chanel didn't agree with the arrangement and often expressed her objections to Doris, but Doris didn't give a damn what Chanel thought. Doris figured if her grandmother wasn't complaining then Chanel should consider minding her damned self-righteous-always-knows-what's-best-for-some-fuckin'-body-else-business. Doris certainly wasn't going to quit her well paying job. That easy money was what kept her looking good, smelling good and rolling around in her small convertible looking flyy.

After graduating from high school, Doris and several of her female friends used to spend most of their afternoons sitting at Bookers Lake watching the variety of cars going in and out of the parking lot of the gentlemen's playground. Based on the valet attendants greeting, Doris and her friends would speculate on which of the men would be classified as regulars or high dollar droppers. Each day the girls tried to imagine how much money the men dropped on the stage until one day Doris couldn't take the suspense any longer. She drove onto the lot and asked the attendant what the age requirement was to work in the club. His response was music to her ears. She was old enough to waitress, and one year shy of being old enough to dance so Doris stepped into the world of exotic temptation.

One year later, Doris was ready to become a dancer and learn the hard knocks of making fast and plentiful money. She was the only Black dancer that worked the evening shift and the men loved her. White men who fantasized about the beauty of a Black woman's erotic charm was being fulfilled, and the brotha's, well, they knew fine when they saw it.

All the years of her parents' hard earned money became well spent money. Doris was not only an incredible dancer, she was skillful at the art of removing her clothes and making the men relinquish their pay checks.

A veteran dancer gave Doris advice that stuck with her since her debut on the erotic and electrifying money-making stage. The trick to being seductive was keeping in mind that most of the men were in the club to see women remove their clothes because most of their wives were either too stupid, shallow or narrow minded to be the freaks in the bedroom that men wanted. Doris used to wonder why other women hadn't learned what most sista's were taught. It was as if a traditional secret had been passed down from generation to generation in the homes of most Black families' that a woman should be a lady during the day and her mans whore at night. Not that there was any disrespect intended. Most Black women simply learned what to do to keep their men happy at home and out of the strip clubs.

Doris' last set on stage ended at midnight. When she turned onto Hannah Road, she could see the corner room of the small brick house lit. Doris wondered with frustration why Chanel wasn't in her usual deep sleep.

Chanel had every intention on getting as much rest before her big day, but anxiety wasn't allowing it. She sat up with her back against her pillows imagining the days on the road to perform from city to city. She imagined her acceptance speeches at the music awards. She envisioned the entire lifestyle of being a multi-platinum star. Chanel was excited until Doris walked into the room asking why she was wearing the stupid grin on her face.

Chanel shot Doris a look that clearly expressed kiss my ass, but it was her words that followed that told the story. "Doris, I am so sick and tired of you thinking you can say what you want, and I'm supposed to roll over like some dog and take it. I've been waitin' for the day to tell you what I think, but you know what, it ain't worth it. You ought to be glad I recognize the saying about blood being thicker than water, 'cause if I didn't, you would be one miserable sister. If you don't like me, that's fine. If you wanna take your anger out on me because mommy and daddy died, that's fine. If you're so pissed, you aren't pursuing your career as a Broadway dancer because you gave up on yourself and started stripping instead of being the great dancer you could have been, then fine. But don't you hate me because I refuse to hate you. I have a big day ahead of me tomorrow, and you can't rob that joy from me. So you can say whatever you want, but if you know like I know, you'd better make sure whatever you say isn't directed towards me. Goodnight."

Doris stood there stunned with a blank expression until Chanel was finished. Chanel had never put her in check before. Doris may act a fool, but she was in no way a fool. She knew every dog had their day. She walked over to her side of the bedroom, put her bag down, undressed and got into the shower. She wasn't going to let Chanel know how deep her words had plunged into her heart.

While in the shower, Doris thought about the major deal Chanel may be landing soon with Milestone Records. She thought about the perks she would gain by being the superstar's sister and didn't want to ruin her chances at enjoying them. Doris had it all mapped out. Chanel's success would be the gateway to her fame and fortune. Doris figured she would be Chanel's dancer in every video and at all of her concerts. Knowing this was the break, the opportunity that would get her off of the booty stage and onto the celebrity stage.

As she finished her shower, she thought about what she would say to Chanel to bring her back into the light, but it was too late, Chanel had drifted off to sleep.

Getting a lot of sleep last night was out of the question. Chanel's adrenaline was higher than any time she could remember, to include the first time in the studio singing and making her own music. Her confrontation with Doris and the thoughts of fame and fortune made it almost impossible.

When Doris woke up she was prepared to deliver her rehearsed kiss my ass speech to Chanel, but it wasn't necessary. Chanel was in a happy mood and behaved as if nothing had occurred between her and her sister, so Doris went along with Chanel's self-righteous attitude because she really wasn't in the mood to put on an award winning performance. Instead, Doris decided she would be her old bitchy self. The way she figured it was if Chanel had been putting up with her shit all the past years and still could not curse her out and hold a grudge for at least twenty-four hours, why should she change now.

Chanel was anxious and the phone constantly ringing that morning didn't help. But so far there was no call from Dallas. They didn't have call waiting, so when Doris tried to hold a go nowhere conversation with someone who probably didn't matter, Chanel stood in front of Doris with her hands on her hips making it very clear she needed the phone line to be free. Doris tried to ignore Chanel by raising her voice and laughing unusually loud into the handset, but Chanel wasn't having it. With as much attitude as Chanel could muster, she postured herself in front of Doris and simply told her to do what she felt she must, but not to expect to ever go with her to Dallas on one of her many trips. Chanel cut through Doris' layer of attitude and caught her by surprise. Doris let her mouth get her ass into trouble. "Nannie Olivia, don't ever think you can get away with threats 'cause baby I ain't no punk."

"Oh, is that right? I'll keep that in mind."

Chanel sat on the couch with her legs crossed and her thumb in her mouth. Thumb sucking was a habit Chanel hadn't broken since a young child and Doris made jokes about it as often as she could.

Chanel waited most of the morning for Milestone Records to call. Finally, she decided to get into the shower. She thought a shower would help her to relax and not wait anxiously by the telephone. Just as Chanel was going into the bathroom, she turned to ask Doris a favor. Chanel caught Doris standing in the doorway of their bedroom mimicking her with her thumb in her mouth. With squinting eyes, Chanel reluctantly asked Doris to please stay near the phone. Doris agreed, but because Chanel had pissed her off earlier, she really didn't give a damn about her or her phone call. When Chanel closed the bathroom door, Doris made going to the Quick Mart for a bag a chips and a drink a priority.

The phone rang six times. As Chanel turned the shower water off, she heard the last ring and rushed to answer it. While rushing around her bed, she hit her toe on the corner of the bed and came close to cussing. Although she was suffering through the ache, Chanel was mostly pissed because she missed the call. But more so because she had to rush out of the bathroom to answer the call she'd asked her sister to be on the lookout for and then hitting her toe. The fact that really sent Chanel over the edge was because her hard headed, don't give a damn about nobody but herself sister couldn't do the one small favor she'd asked. She yelled across the house for Doris, but realized she was nowhere around. Chanel stood in the middle of the living room floor with her towel wrapped around her, and her gut feeling telling her she'd missed the call she'd been waiting on. As she walked back towards her bedroom, the tears were beginning to fill in her eyes when suddenly the phone began to ring again. Chanel leaped onto her bed and answered it on the first ring.

Slightly winded, she answered. "Hello."

"Hello. May I speak with Nannie Olivia."

Unfamiliar with the voice on the other end, Chanel hoped it was the call she'd been waiting most of the morning for. In a very faint and resistance voice, Chanel spoke. "This is Nannie Olivia, but please call me Chanel." Hesitantly Chanel asked, "Is this Jasmine?"

"Yes it is." Jasmine spoke with a French dialect. Her words were very pronounced and sounded very eloquent. "Hello Chanel. I'm following up on Mr. McGowan's call yesterday. He said you would be okay with any flight arrangements I made for you today, so I went ahead and guaranteed your flight. I have you scheduled on the 3:15 flight out of Hobby Airport into Dallas Love Field. You'll be flying out of gate 15, and you will arrive…" Frantically,

Chanel stumbled through the things on the kitchen table looking for a pen. Chanel was soon relieved when she noticed the black pen sitting on the countertop. She tried to catch up with Jasmine's instructions, but the pen didn't write. She was in a desperate panic looking for another pen. She scanned the room like a sniper looking for its target when suddenly a glimmer of hope was hidden underneath the table.

Moving quickly, but missing what Jasmine was saying, discouraged, she sat in a slump on the floor. Did she miss the most important information of her life? She thought to pardon herself, but she felt embarrassed. Nonetheless, she asked Jasmine to repeat the information.

She carefully repeated the information and continued, "Mr. McGowan will be there to pick you up. We left your return trip open. They suspect you'll be in Dallas for a week or so. There will be several people meeting with you, and, well you'll see when you get here. Mr. McGowan doesn't expect he'll have any difficulties identifying you. Welcome to the Milestone Family, Chanel." Jasmine's salutation was considerably warm and very professional. Chanel felt welcomed and was ready for her *invitation into the frightening, and all that glitters is not gold,* world of entertainment.

Just as Jasmine was ending her call, Adrian walked up to her desk. He signaled to Jasmine to put Chanel on hold, he wanted to talk with her briefly before she left Houston. Before placing her on hold, Jasmine said good-bye and was surprised when Chanel responded with, Au voir.

While Chanel was on hold, Doris walked into the bedroom shooting a, what the fuck you gonna do about it look. She ignored Doris and turned as the call was reconnected. Chanel was surprised and very pleased when she heard the next voice.

"Good morning Ms. Chanel Rayson. This is Adrian McGowan. Did you get any rest last night?"

Chanel giggled a little before she answered realizing this was no joke. "Good morning." Immediately Chanel reverted to the mature woman she was. "No sir. I did not. You had me thinking all night. You have me so excited." Okay, perhaps she was mature in life, but very immature in business. Saying he had her real excited wasn't the brightest thing to say, and it made her feel like a real idiot.

"Is that right? Well, I'll have to make up for my being the cause of you losing sleep."

"That's okay. You can make me lose sleep any time you want. You've made me the happiest woman in the world. Thank you." However immature in business, Chanel was excited, and her comments were intended to be very innocent. She had no intentions on doing anything degrading or foolish. She was confident with her talent and knew she didn't have to make foolish mistakes to be successful in the doggy-dog music industry. It was Adrian's responsibility to see through her innocence.

"Thank you, Chanel. We have a big day planned for you. Try to get some rest on the plane and I'll see you this afternoon. I have your picture, so I shouldn't have any problem identifying you when you exit the plane. You do still look like the woman in the picture?" Adrian started laughing when Chanel attempted to convince him that she hadn't changed. Adrian continued with his antics about how women send fake pictures to strangers all the time. He went on telling her about how they're actually crossed eyed, with gold teeth and too fat or too skinny. Chanel continued trying to convince him and Adrian enjoyed listening. Before hanging up, he apologized and admitted he was joking. Adrian's humor helped Chanel to relax knowing he could be fun too.

Jasmine was a few years older than Adrian, and she had tried on numerous occasions to capture his attention, but he made it clear that he didn't mix business with pleasure. When Adrian opened his office door, Jasmine was giving him a perplexed look as if she were looking at a stranger. Jasmine saw something in Adrian's eyes she hadn't seen in the five years she'd been working for him.

He looked mesmerized.

Before Adrian could speak, Jasmine found an opportunity to question him. "So boss, what's all the buzz about this Chanel person?" Adrian smiled when he responded, "You will see. You will see." Jasmine didn't appreciate Adrian's response, but she was smart enough to know to let it go.

Adrian asked Jasmine for a copy of the arrangements she made for Chanel's visit. Scanning over the schedule, Adrian looked at the small clock on Jasmine's desk and realized he had enough time for some last minute preparations. Adrian made a few business calls and finally the one very important call that took priority over all calls.

It was Monday night, and the Steelers and the Ravens were fighting for their place in the playoffs. This was definitely a game he didn't want to miss with his boys, but he knew Ms. Rayson was someone worth missing his traditional game for.

The phone rang twice when Marquis answered. "Marquis, what's up? Check this out, I'm gonna have to cancel tonight. I got a client flying in this afternoon."

"No problem man. I was gonna cancel too. I gotta fly to Houston for the convention. Man, I can't even catch up with Austin and Jamale. Let me give Peter a call, and I'll let him know the deal."

"Kewl. Hey, while you're in Houston, check out that spot I told you ol' boy owned. I'll give him a call to have you put on the guest list."

"Man, that ain't my thing. No. Hold up. Yeah, do that. If I gotta entertain some White boys, that's where I'll take them. Tell your man it may be four."

"No problem. I'll check with you later." Adrian and Marquis both stated, Black Power before ending their call.

Saying Black Power at the end of their conversations used to prompt jokes, but then they realized the truest meaning behind the saying and they had to question exactly what was wrong with reinforcing the hope of Black power. The term was something the men picked up from Austin, the revolutionist of the group. Austin had even gone as far as attending a few meetings with the New Black Panther Party (NBPP), not that he had any intentions on committing to the organization. But Austin knew it was a definite source for keeping abreast on what was happening in the local Black community.

11

$\mathcal{S}$he front entrance into the Westin Hotel was very busy for a Monday. When Adrian pulled up towards the red carpeted entranceway, several luxury vehicles were ahead of him. But it wasn't the cars that had the people's attention; it was the beautiful woman with her entourage of seven men who had them in a frenzy. Standing at the revolving door was Oprah Winfrey. She nestled comfortably in Stedman, the love of her life's embrace. It was her birthday, and as a gift from him, he selected several cities that she could enjoy a shopping spree; Dallas being the first.

When Adrian reached the front of the line of cars to be parked, he handed his car keys to the valet attendant and rushed past the crowd of fans. He was pressed for time and based on Adrian's attitude towards the clerk he didn't give a damn who was in the lobby. "Pardon me. Hel-lo. I have a reservation and would like some assistance."

"Hello sir. How may I help you?" The middle aged woman smiled with clenched teeth as she acknowledged Adrian.

"Yes, I have a reservation under the name of Milestone records. I am a representative of theirs."

"Well, I see your reservation, but sir we need to have a first and last name for our records." The clerk wasn't being as polite to him as she had been towards other guests, and Adrian identified it immediately. Fortunately for her, he didn't have time to submit to her petty attitude.

"Well, guess what? I have both." Pausing and giving the woman a dumbfounded expression. "A first and a last name." Tilting his head to the side and smirking he continued, "Adrian McGowan.

That's M.c. capital G. o.w.a.n."

Raising her eyes without moving her head, the clerk looked up at Adrian as she typed his information. She offered him his keys and sarcastically extended a good day as he picked up the keys to suite 716.

The Galleria Mall entrance was connected to the lobby of the hotel. As he walked into the mall, considering how he found his way to the third level to the Godiva Chocolate Shop, it was clear he was very familiar with the mall.

After making his purchase, Adrian returned to the hotel and exited the elevator on the seventh floor. He was very pleased with the two room suite that was waiting for the next R&B "Artist of the year".

The large box of chocolates Adrian purchased were placed centered on the pillow on the king sized bed. Across the room on the table nearest the patio door, Adrian set the twelve long stemmed roses that were arranged beautifully in a stunning vase. He knew this woman had all the qualities of several first year Grammy nominations, and the suite she was staying in was just the beginning to the elaborate lifestyle she would soon become accustomed to.

Adrian had timed his afternoon perfectly. Rushing wasn't necessary. It was 2:35 and he was only a few exits away from Mockingbird Lane. He assumed he would have time to find a parking spot, get through the security check point and be at the gate waiting for Ms. Chanel Rayson. He was wrong. Mockingbird Lane was shut down to one lane due to construction, and more obstruction was contributed by the old Buick parked on the side of the road with its hood up and steam shooting from the radiator. The scrawny and balding man in blue was doing all he could to divert the traffic and keep it moving, but it was a very slow process.

When Adrian finally reached the airport parking garage and found a parking spot, it was three levels up and at the back of the garage.

When the elevator eventually arrived, it had a family of four to include a stroller and large luggage occupying it. Adrian was frustrated and wasn't chancing the squeeze, so he waited for the next available car down. As he tried to get to the walkway of Love Field, the departure traffic and cabs were moving quickly. Adrian was not as relaxed as he had been. He actually was becoming more frustrated as he waited another few minutes before being able to cross the walkway.

"Damn. This shit is unbelievable." Speaking loud enough to catch the attention of the couple standing in front of him.

Before going through the security checkpoint Adrian looked at the monitor with the arrival information and began to panic. Flight 220 was on time and on the ground. He hurried through security and ran down to the gate. Fortunately he had a short run to the gate. He saw the plane from the window just pulling in. Adrian hurried to the men's lavatory. He didn't want to look frazzled when she saw him for the first time.

Adrian stood in the back waiting for the passengers to deplane. When Chanel reached the doorway into the airport, she smiled when she noticed Adrian standing amidst the small crowd holding a sign that read her name. Adrian returned the smile when he got a glimpse of her. She was more stunning in person than on the picture and her video. Chanel was shocked with how fine Adrian was, but she masked her thoughts very well.

His smile could have told a story of love at first sight had he not made every effort not to let this woman know how fine he thought she was. He had never allowed pleasure to interfere with business, and this would be no exception.

Extending his hand to shake hers, he introduced himself. "Ms. Rayson, hello. Adrian McGowan." He couldn't help the erotic thoughts that crossed his mind.

"Hello Mr. McGowan." As she smiled trying to restrain herself from giggling too much.

Their conversation was minimal as they walked towards the baggage claim area. Adrian appreciated the way Chanel was dressed in a pair of no name blue jeans. His mind was made up that she was a very basic woman who was truly oblivious to her physical assets. She was genuine, and it enticed Adrian more knowing there wasn't anything pretentious about her. Adrian had more than enough opportunities to associate himself with the wanna-be's in America. In fact, one of the many wanna-be members was no more than ten feet from where he was standing. She was checking him out from the time he reached the gate to the time he and Chanel reached baggage claim.

This woman was dressed nicely and very attractive, but she was so transparent. The small lines around her eyes and the texture of her skin proved she was much older than she wanted to admit. And anyone with any know how about fashion could see she did a lot of bargain shopping by the knock-offs she was wearing. And if you looked down at her feet, the shoes told the real story....her ass was a pay less and get less try-to-be-a-diva who was clearly faking the funk.

Chanel leaned close to Adrian to whisper, "Gee, do you see that woman checking you out?"

Adrian laughed at her innocence and responded, "Yeah, she sees you with me, but I guess she made the determination you're not my significant other. Consider it a lack of self respect. Some women haven't learned if they let the man choose them, maybe they would have the man of their dreams."

Chanel didn't respond, but she was reflecting on his every word and Adrian admired her. He liked the fact she listened and absorbed. There was no question in his mind, Chanel was a winner.

"So, how was your flight?"

"Well, it was different for me. I mean, I'd never been on a plane before. If I ever thought I had a fear of flying, that fear went right up in the clouds. I was too excited about coming here to be afraid."

She pointed out her bags as they came around on the carousel. Adrian bent over reaching and talking at the same time, and Chanel couldn't make out what he was saying. She decided to lean closer to Adrian's ear to make a joke. "Get da cotton out ya mouth boy, dunt nobody know what ya tryin' t'say." Her deep southern draw was worth the laugh.

Adrian looked up at her, and they both laughed. He didn't expect the ice to be broken then and there. Never mind in that way, but he was certainly happy to learn early in the game that she had a sense of humor. It would make the time together much more relaxed.

As they approached the black sedan, the tail lights flickered as the alarm was turned off by the remote on Adrian's key ring. Chanel smiled. She couldn't resist telling him how beautiful his car was and how happy she was just being there. As he loaded her luggage into the company car, Adrian went into some of the details about what to expect during her visit. As they approached the tollway, Adrian suggested two choices, "We can either get something to eat now or we can go to the hotel, and you can settle in and I pick you up later. You're the boss."

"Hmmm, decisions, decisions. I'm hungry now, but first I need to know where we're going to eat and if I need to change."

"Well, it depends on what you want to eat."

"Wow, I'm really the boss. Okay, let's see. I would like some seafood, but I want to go somewhere we can maybe eat outside on a terrace. That way I can stay in my jeans and not worry about tryin' to eat cutesy."

"Is that right? Oh so in other words, you wanna throw down. Kewl, I know the perfect spot. Are you sure it's not too cool outside for you? I wouldn't want you to get in the studio tonight talkin' 'bout you got a cold."

"Nah, it ain't too cold. Besides, I could still flow even if I did have a cold. So now." Her matter of fact attitude was sexy, yet innocent, and he took it in like a breath of fresh air.

Adrian liked her spunk. Chanel was easy to have fun with. He knew from her packet that she was professional and took her singing seriously. They talked and laughed until they reached the area of town called Lower Greenville. After minutes of searching for a parking space, they lucked up on a spot in front of the restaurant named Awshucks. Chanel studied the building that looked like a fisherman's shack along side of a beach. She didn't have to say a word, her eyes spoke for her.

"Don't worry. The food is great. You'll see." Adrian remembered the first time he was introduced to Awshucks. He must have worn the same expression as Chanel because he recalled hearing the same "the food is great" speech he'd just given.

The damned if you do, damned if you don't atmosphere had been accepted by the repeated customers for years. On a Texas summer day, you would either suffer the heat along with your meal or during the winter months you'd stiffen your lip to sit outdoors. Either way, your choices to avoid the Texas climate was slim. There was limited seating inside the small restaurant. The majority of seating offered was on the outdoor terrace that during warm days would be exposed to the sun, and the colder days enclosed by durable plastic mock windows.

The floor was covered with broken clam shells that had been cemented together, and the wooden park bench tables were covered with rolls of paper towels. Like the birds migrate south when the cold weather came, the flies migrated to Awshucks.

There was a line of people waiting patiently to order what was known to be the best fresh seafood quick order joint in town. Repeating the four people ahead of them, Chanel and Adrian both ordered a summer platter with enough Cajun shrimp and crab claws for four. Just like Chanel's eyes had spoken for her earlier, they were telling a story of delight as she finished cracking the last crab claw.

Adrian enjoyed watching her devour what was once a feast for two. He studied her as she ignored the roll of paper towels and licked the Cajun seasoning from her fingers. Adrian couldn't help but appreciate her attempt to relax around him.

While she was making a large dent into her platter of food, Adrian had only knocked off a small corner of his. Before reaching for another shrimp, she unraveled a few towels from the roll, wiped her hands and mouth before surprising Adrian with her small talk.

"Adrian, I feel really comfortable around you. I feel as though I can say whatever is on my mind."

Cautiously interrupting her, "Is there something you need to say to me?"

"Yes." Adding a charming smile before she continued. "You eat like a girl on a first date." Surprised by the stab in the side, Adrian sat back on his chair with perplexity. Chanel started giggling. "No. Really, you do. Women act nervous about eating in front of a man for the first time. You know, women order a salad like they're not hungry or pretend to be watching their diet, but deep inside they be starving."

Adrian started laughing. "So you're trying to say I'm nervous about eating in front of you and deep inside I wanna dig into this shrimp and stuff my face?" Adrian thought he'd give her a small jab in her side when his expression made her know that the "stuff my face" comment was intended for her.

Embarrassed but humored she went along with the joke, "Oh, so it's like that. Makin' fun of how much I'm eating. Okay." Adrian smiled at her as she popped another shrimp into her mouth.

"Dang, keep that up, and we're going to have to roll you into the studio."

"Ha. Ha. Ha" She responded sarcastically not quitting on her shrimp. "Hey, I told you I was hungry. I didn't want to waste your money."

"Yeah aiight. Don't get to full 'cause you got a long night in the studio." Chanel assured him there wouldn't be anything that could keep her from staying alert.

Another Season

Towards the end of the season, the athletic trainers from across the country would have an annual conference. This year it was being hosted in Houston, Texas. The conference was designed to introduce the future trainers to the lifestyle of a trainer for the NFL. It also allowed the current trainers to speak on some of the obstacles and challenges to be expected by groupies and fans. It was designed to emulate the conference held for the NFL players and had been a success the last two years.

Like the trainers previous to Marquis, when he landed the job freshly out of college, he was excited about traveling and working for the NFL. The conference was definitely needed. He recalled how it took him a minute to adjust to the new lifestyle. In fact, he actually got caught up in it.

On Marquis' first road trip with the Cowboys, the females were like roaches on bread. Their by any means necessary attitude was to hook up with anyone associated with the NFL. Marquis being young and dumb thinking he could get the coochie and leave, felt the repercussions the following days.

Marquis had a few drinks too many that infamous evening, and while being captivated by the moment, he didn't think about using protection. It was the next city and two days later that he realized the mistake he'd made. Peeing wasn't anything easy for him. He let out a scream that could have shaken all of Philadelphia. He may have been a fool for not protecting himself, but he wasn't any dummy. He knew his ass had VD.

After his struggle in the bathroom, Marquis sat on the bed in disbelief as he fumbled through the yellow pages searching for family planning. That was a sure place to have a quick check up without having to use his insurance. Cash for services is what he needed, besides the hearty dose of penicillin. After that ordeal, women, he played get the coochie with were totally scrutinized and the jimmy was like a second skin.

Although the conference was beneficial, it wasn't something he looked forward to. Not because he was tired of traveling and being away from home, but because it meant hanging with the new trainers and getting them broken in for the road away from home. That usually meant partying and being preyed upon by a lot of women. The women part wasn't all that bad because he had control over that, but Marquis knew he had more than his share. One more would be more than needed.

There were more than ninety men standing in the lobby. Each wore the same blue trimmed paper name tag affixed to their clothing. Most of the men were laughing with some of their old colleagues. The few new hires seemed to have located one another...I suppose them wearing their newly distributed NFL sweat suits had something to do with it. They stood out like a sore thumb. Of the twelve new hires, there were only two minorities. It was hard to imagine there not being more than two minority kinesiology graduates in the world this year. It seemed a diversification quota was making its' mark. The new hires each migrated towards the corner near the wall and Marquis took immediate notice.

"Yo dawg, check it out. Out of all the men in this room check out how many brothas are here. What? Eight, maybe? Nuttin' but the good ol' boy system."

Marquis' East coast colleague spoke fast and with a lot of exuberance.

"Yeah man, I see it. But you know if we bring it up, then we'll be the ones trippin'. Fuck 'em. I'm gonna get mine and then some from the NFL." Jerry was intelligent but real ghettofied. Marquis nodded in agreement as he listened to his two colleagues discuss the NFL's diversification problems.

The registration process was long. The trainers moved from one table to the next getting all the literature from the league, and the pharmaceutical vendors who were promoting their products. Marquis was captivated by an attractive woman at the end of the table and zeroed in on her making eye contact. She was pecan brown with short hair with gold highlights. She had an unusually wide mouth and a beautiful smile. When she focused on Marquis smiling at her, she returned the gesture. But for anyone who knew better, they could see she had more of an interest in the woman walking across the lobby. Marquis told Jerry he was going to make some things happen in about five minutes, but Jerry helped to open his brothers' eyes.

"Yo dawg, female ain't thinking about your johnson, she's thinking about ol' girl's cat."

Jerry and the East coast brotha started laughing when Marquis frowned as he realized Jerry was right. "Damn. What's up with that shit? Oh well, whatever floats the boat." Marquis swatted at the air and walked away. "Man, I'm gonna go get a seat; they should be starting in a few."

Marquis and Jerry sat in the rear of the room paying attention to their watches. Three hours later and they were dismissed. Marquis figured he'd take Adrian's offer and take a few of the guys out to Club L & G and call it an early night. Marquis liked the name of the joint and hoped it was as nice.

Before leaving for the club, Marquis sat with three men in the hotel restaurant for dinner. Two of whom he had just met and agreed to show them the town. The new guys, Chad and Andrew were cool, but if the truth were told, they were honky-tonk White boys; Chad was from Kentucky and had never really been to a big city, so this was like an Earnest goes to Houston adventure.

"Hey dude, this is pretty awesome. Houston rocks." Chad's head was bobbing up and down like a bobble head doll. He went on and on about not knowing how to get around in a big city and how he wanted to go everywhere in one night. Marquis of course nipped that thought in the bud.

"Hold your jets, John Boy. You guys are hangin' out with me tonight. So first things first, you need to relax." They appreciated the idea of having someone who knew the city to hang out with, but a Black man? It was written across their faces, and Marquis didn't pretend that he couldn't read them.

"What's wrong, the Klan won't let you hang out with a Black man?" They were stunned and speechless until Marquis started laughing.

"You boys need to chill and relax your Wrangler jeans. Go to your rooms and meet me in the lobby in about an hour. I'm going to show you guys a night you will never forget. Relax. Relax." Marquis left them standing paralyzed as he turned away laughing and singing the song, "I met my ex in Texas…"

Chad and Andrew started laughing when they realized they weren't in their Wrangler jeans. They gave one another the look of approval and decided what the hell.

When it was time for the three men to meet in the lobby, Chad and Andrew were stunned when they saw Marquis. In their opinion, Marquis was a city slicker wearing clothes that made him look like he was a celebrity on his way to a high dollar function. That was a typical country-boys-can't-dress-for-shit perspective. Marquis did look good in his smoked gray Brioni suit with black crocodile shoes and matching belt. Escaping the dress for success look, instead of wearing a necktie, he wore a black silk mock turtle neck sweater to compliment the suit.

When Marquis got off the elevator and saw his two running dogs for the evening, he shook his head in amazement. Chad had on a plaid shirt with a pair of black jeans and cowboy boots that showed off a two inch heel. Andrew wasn't much better. He tried to spruce up a bit when he matched the three shades of black in his pants, shirt and tie. It was clear who his fashion idol was but everyone can't get away with doing the black tie on a black shirt thing like

Regis Philbin. But he tried so Marquis gave him a point for effort. But that point was retracted when Marquis got close enough to catch a whiff of Andrew. He had over splashed that inexpensive Chaps cologne that you can buy at any drug store.

"So, you guys ready to roll with a brotha?" Marquis asked as he rubbed his palms together as if he was getting ready to cut into a Thanksgiving sweet potato pie.

"Well, hell yeah..." Chad responded.

Chad offered to drive his rental car, and Marquis thought why not until he learned it was a Ford Taurus. It wasn't a family car kind of night so Marquis told Chad to put his keys away and get ready to hang with a Nupe. Chad and Andrew had no idea what a Nupe was, and they didn't question it when they heard the locks pop up on the black Lincoln Navigator.

"You have got to be kidding me. Is this what you're driving while you're here?"

Marquis laughed at Andrews southern draw, but he was more amused with Chad standing there scratching his head as if he'd never been in a luxury vehicle. It really was beginning to appear like an adventure. When Chad and Andrew got into the vehicle, they were blown away by the Navigator's features. These boys were hilarious, so to top the evening, Marquis figured he should entertain his colleagues by slipping in a CD of The Man, Mr Tupac Shakur.

Tupac was blaring in their ears hard as hard could get. As Marquis' head was bobbing to the beat, he watched in his rearview mirror at Chad trying to catch the groove. He was pathetic, but Marquis gave him credit for trying.

"So Chad, you diggin' on Pac? What's up with that?"

"I heard some of this guys stuff from one of the Black kids down the hall in my dorm. It's dope." Adding a bit more effort in hopes to impress Marquis, he tried to catch the groove even harder by throwing in an extra shoulder move, and by using the dated word "dope" to make him feel like he was current with his slang or ebonics. Marquis decided he wouldn't front the man and let him try to catch his groove.

Looking over at Andrew, Marquis noticed Andrew seemed disconnected and wasn't getting into the beat. "So, Drew, what's up with you? How you livin'?"

"How I'm livin'? I'm sorry, I don't get it." Not being rude, just ignorant to the whole slang/ebonics thing.

"You know. How ya livin'? How's it going? What you up to?" Rolling his hands forward in front of Andrew as if coaching him to roll with him.

"Ohhhh, how I'm livin'? I'm livin' huge." Smiling as if he had caught on and finished with the right answer.

Marquis looked at him with total disgust and dejection. "That's livin' large, not huge." Marquis was definitely ready to get out of the truck after driving around for 15 minutes with Ork and Dork.

Finally, the lit sign he'd been looking for...Club Ladies and Gentlemen, aka Club L & G. the finest titty bar in Houston. Luxury cars, professional athletes and high dollar men surrounded the entrance. Chad and Andrew gawked for a while. They had never seen anything like it in person, but they'd seen enough TV to know how to fit in. And what they didn't know, they knew they were in good hands. They had their coach, the Nupe to lead the way.

With Chad and Andrew in tow, Marquis walked to the doorman and told him his name. The over-flexed man wearing all black with an earphone and microphone stuck to the side of his face allowed them in with no cover and directed them to the VIP section of the club. Needless to say, the guys were impressed, but they almost shit their clothes when they walked in and saw the beautiful woman on stage.

"Oh my God would-ya-look-a-there." Chad said with excitement.

She was a beautiful Boriqua woman entertaining her onlookers. Her long black hair swept across her brown skin and her piercing dark eyes complimented her pearly white teeth.

Across the stage, her glistening body was moving in a groove to every beat of the song that she danced to and Chad was falling in love. Andrew, being the ebonics professional that he was, and in all of his excitement blurted out, "Wow, she's PHAT."

Chad didn't take that too kindly and asked, "What the hell do you mean she's fat? She's not fat."

As nerdy as he could be, Andrew began to explain himself. "No, Chad. Not fat as in f.a.t. I mean phat as in p.h.a.t. It's slang for pretty hot and tempting." Chad started smiling and then they did the good ol' boy punches to the shoulder when Marquis interrupted them.

"Boys, boys. If you're gonna use slang, you need to get it right. P.H.A.T stands for just what you see up in here. Punnany, hips, ass and tits. Now sit down and enjoy the show." Chad and Andrew were so taken by their lesson on slang that they hadn't noticed how they were just treated like small children at an adult club.

Andrew laughed at Chad as he embellished the stage with dollar bills. Marquis shook his head in disbelief and was happy he didn't have to fantasize over any woman. Giving his money to a total stranger for a moment of fantasy was completely and totally out of the question.

While Chad and Andrew was being entertained, Marquis excused himself to go to the restroom. When Marquis returned, Chad and Andrew were slouching in their chairs looking exhausted as if they'd just put in a full days work. Marquis laughed at them before he asked, "So, have you two had enough? Ya'll ready to go back to the hotel?"

Chad stood before speaking. "Oh hell no. Definitely not!"

"Okay." Before Marquis could say another word, the music started, and the next lady had walked out on stage. A sista. A beautiful caramel skinned, stunning woman. She was incredible, and Marquis wasn't willing to pretend she wasn't. He sat up in his chair and enjoyed every minute of her captivating performance. When she exited the stage, he exited his chair to give instructions to the waitress to have the dancer to join him. Being in the VIP section, he had that privilege.

Ten minutes later, the lady was seated with the gentlemen. The introductions were brief, and the champagne was delivered.

"Good evening. My name is Marquis, and these are my colleagues, Andrew and Chad."

"Well hello gentlemen. I'm Alyssa." She smiled at Andrew and Chad while she continued holding Marquis' hand from his introduction.

Alyssa was impressed with the invite to his table and the champagne and didn't mind sitting with Marquis during her break. Andrew and Chad tried to join in on their conversation, but the next girl was on stage and that was far more interesting.

"So, Alyssa, I must tell you, you are beautiful. This is not a usual night out for me, in fact, this is extremely rare for me, but since I had to entertain colleagues and was given an invitation to the club, I thought why not. And I must add that I'm glad I did."

Smiling and enjoying each word he spoke, Alyssa responded softly, "Thank you. I'm glad you could make it out. I hope you enjoyed the show enough to stay for the next set."

"Well, actually I have to call it an early night. But don't get me wrong, staying is definitely something I would have done had I not had such an early and long day scheduled tomorrow."

Alyssa was used to the disappointment. She didn't put much stock into the men who came to the club. She looked at titty joints as an easy fix for most men. Marquis was no different. He was just finer than most.

Before Alyssa could respond, Marquis made a suggestion. "I don't know how you'll feel about this, but I have to try. I'm going to be in Houston until Wednesday, I'll give you the number where I can be reached, and if you'd like to have dinner, you can meet me at the restaurant of your choice. No strings attached; just dinner and great company."

She pondered the suggestion for just a moment and agreed. Marquis wrote the information on the back of one of his business cards and appreciated how she smiled. It was getting late, and Marquis knew it was time for him to leave. He asked her to reassure him, and before she walked off, she did by blowing him a kiss and whispering, "See you soon."

"Okay fellas, let's get up out of here. Damn Chad, how much money you throw away tonight?"

"Man, I don't care. I'm ready to give her the keys to my house." Before they walked away, Andrew let out a yahoo that was out of this world. That was Marquis' cue to get the hell up out of Dodge.

12

ℭ hen the doorbell rang, Cee-Cee stopped to look at the clock. She assumed it wouldn't be Jamale because Monday nights were reserved for the fellas. She shouted for Jaylen to answer the door, but he was in his room watching a movie. Cee-Cee thought not to answer it, but after the third ring, she thought it may be important.

Her neighbor Yolanda was getting anxious, so she began knocking, along with ringing the bell. Cee-Cee was starting to get very angry with whoever was on the other side of the door.

"Who is it!?!"

"Girl, its Yolanda. Open up."

Rushing to open the door, Cee-Cee was almost frantic thinking something serious had happened. "What's wrong? You okay?"

"Everything is fine. I got something on the stove, but I wanted to know if Jaylen could come with me to my friend's party. There's supposed to be some music celebrity there or something and I thought Jaylen would like to be there. I won't keep him out. I promise."

"Girl, don't you scare me like that. I thought something happened the way you were kicking in my door." She started laughing as she turned to go to Jaylen's room. "Lock the door, girl."

Jaylen had already been standing in the living room trying to see what all the noise was. He was happy to see his "girlfriend" and smiled as he spoke. "Hi Miss Yolanda."

"Hey baby. You're gonna hang out with me tonight."

"Yaay. Can I spend the night over your house?"

"You sure can if it's okay with your mom. What you think mom? I can get him ready for school and take him too if you don't mind."

It didn't take too much thought. Cee-Cee knew she didn't have enough opportunities to have a night to herself. Just the thought of being able to prance around naked, burn a candle or two, sip on some wine and listen to her favorite oldies CD made Cee-Cee smile. Oh yeah, it was definitely okay for Jaylen to spend the night.

"Jaylen, pack your overnight bag and clothes for school tomorrow." Jaylen had already started towards his room when Yolanda asked permission.

"Okay, mom."

"Girl, don't keep my baby out too late. It's a school night."

"Don't worry about your lit'l man. I'll take good care of him."

With bag in hand, Jaylen hugged Cee-Cee good-night and followed Yolanda out the door.

Besides the call from Jeff, Cee-Cee's evening was going wonderfully. She sat in her bubble bath enjoying her glass of Lambrusco and relaxing. An hour into enjoying her night of self indulgence, again, there were unexpected knocks on the door. She couldn't believe it. She knew it had to be someone at the wrong door, so she didn't even bother to put her robe on to talk through the door.

"Cee, open up."

"Jamale, is that you?" Peeping through the peephole, she confirmed he was alone before hiding her naked body behind the door as she opened it.

"Hmmm, what's goin' on up in here? Damn girl, where's Jaylen?"

"He's spending the night with Yolanda." In between short kisses, she continued, "Remind me to give you a key."

Jamale wrapped his arms around Cee-Cee and began kissing her intensely. She guessed she was in for a night of some serious love making, but Jamale had other plans. Instead, he told her to get some clothes on so they could hang out for a minute.

"Hang out?" She gave him a confused look and thought he had lost his mind.

"Yeah, come on Cee, it's getting' late." Patting her lightly on her ass, she headed towards her bedroom to get dressed.

Hanging out with Jamale was something she enjoyed. Jamale was a spontaneous person which always made evenings exciting. Jamale was casually dressed in a pair of jeans, a sweater and his leather jacket which made her decision easy, unlike the first date. Cee-Cee reached for her Old Navy jeans, turtle neck sweater and her denim jacket from the closet and was ready for the night.

Driving down the parkway Jamale didn't say much. Cee-Cee started a few conversations, but he kept the conversation very short.

"Baby, is everything okay? You're awfully quiet. Is there something on your mind?"

"Nah. I'm kewl. I heard about this new karaoke spot. I thought we could check it out. Maybe I can get you on stage and sing me a song."

"Yeah right. I don't think so."

Jamale looked over at her and knew he was in love. As they drove down the interstate, Cee-Cee could see the beautiful archistructure that held so many memories. The last time she had been in the area was on their first formal affair. It was like a fairy tale. There it was, the Morton Meyerson Symphony Center.

Cee-Cee smiled as she reminisced on the date. It was a Friday evening in September. The air was warm with a light breeze. Jamale had asked her to get beautiful for him that night; he wanted to take her out to a formal event that a good friend of his was hosting. It had been so long since Cee-Cee had been on a date that required her to get "beautiful" that she really wasn't sure what it meant. But she wasn't going to make a fool of herself by asking, so instead she probed about the event until she learned it was a black tie affair.

It had taken Cee-Cee and Yolanda three days to find the perfect gown and matching accessories. Yolanda did her hair to make sure she looked as elegant as she felt that evening.

The day started at the spa. Cee-Cee had won a day at the spa in Addison last year at her company Christmas party and figured this would be the perfect time to use it before it expired.

When Cee-Cee pulled in front of the building, she recalled admiring the large gold letters on the cream stucco building. She watched the women as they entered and thought how women with money really did enjoy pampering themselves. She didn't care that her day of pampering came by way of a gift card, it was as good as the plastic cards those women would be placing on the counter.

When Cee-Cee entered into the foyer, she remembered being so impressed with how everything appeared sparkly. The walls were covered with mirrors, and the fixtures were made of simulated crystal and the beautiful diamond like chandelier set off its splendor.

Cee was greeted by this overly chipper young woman, no more than twenty three years old. She wore all black; come to think about it, all the employees wore black. It gave them a chic look.

"Good morning. Welcome to Je m'aime." French for, "I love myself". The woman's French sounded as if she had studied for years and had frequented the French Riviera.

Damn, I took French for three years in high school and I still couldn't make it sound that authentic, Cee-Cee thought. Not losing a beat to the flow of the young ladies welcome, Cee-Cee continued, "Yes, I have a nine a.m. appointment. Nikkia Peterson."

Placing her French manicured finger on the third line of the appointment book, the young woman looked up at Cee-Cee and smiled, "Yes, we have you scheduled for a total spa."

A woman waiting to be helped gave Cee-Cee a smug look wondering how she could afford such a treat. But when Cee-Cee pulled out her gift card, the ladies expression read, Oh, makes sense now.

Cee-Cee looked at the woman with the obvious face-lift and thought, whatever cow. I'm getting ready to get pampered, and it ain't costing me anything.

"Your matron, Jodi will be with you in a moment. Meanwhile if you'll follow through the second door, your changing room will be number three. Jodi will greet you from there." Smiling, the woman handed Cee-Cee a key that had a large pink rabbit's foot attached to it.

Cee-Cee couldn't believe it. Even the dressing room or powder room as it was noted on the door was the bomb. It wasn't very large, but it was certainly larger than her bathroom at home. It had a pedestal style commode and sink with brass fixtures, a vanity that had high dollar perfumes and lotions covering the glass top and a brass table that held the thickest and thirstiest pink towels on it. Hanging on the brass rack was an sensational plush terry cloth bath robe with the spas name embroidered onto the front of it. Cee-Cee sat at the vanity for a moment reading the gold embossed card that instructed the ladies to have the disposable swim suits under their robes when their matron arrived. She couldn't believe how awesome everything was as she sat with her legs crossed.

The two taps on the door let Cee-Cee know it was time for her to explore and enjoy the world of pampering. Jodi was about 5'7 and a very handsome man. She couldn't tell if he were gay or straight nor did she care. He was getting ready to spoil her. Jodi smiled at Cee-Cee but didn't say anything. He reached for her arm as they walked over to the steam sauna, but Cee-Cee asked if she could skip that treat. "I really don't enjoy being in a sauna, could we move to the next station?" Cee-Cee wasn't sure if station was the correct word, but it seemed appropriate.

"No problem. I really don't enjoy them either." Jodi confirmed he was definitely gay when he spoke. "The next area will be the dead sea. You will be in this room for about twenty minutes." Stopping at the CD player outside the door, Jodi asked, "Would you like Kenny G?"

"That would be fabulous. Thanks."

When they entered the room, there was a large black sunken tub filled with water and brass hand rails with two steps leading down into the tub. Cee-Cee didn't know why they called it the Dead Sea room until Jodi began to speak. "At the bottom of the tub are dead sea mineral bath salts. It's going to feel slippery or muddy so be careful stepping in. Relax and I'll be back to get you."

Cee-Cee did just that. She didn't know what felt better; the tub or the body massage she got afterwards. After the tub and massage came a facial, a manicure and a pedicure. It was the most relaxed and pampered day she had ever experienced. For $350.00, Cee-Cee knew it would probably be her last.

After forty-five minutes of preparation, Yolanda, Jaylen and Cee-Cee were stunned by her beauty. She had on the most elegant black evening gown accented by silver and rhinestones. She was magnificent, and when Jamale laid his eyes on her, he was blown away. "Whoa. Look at you. I don't know if the Meyerson can handle all your beauty." Standing in the middle of the floor, Jamale slowly walked around her admiring every inch of her magnificence, and Yolanda and Jaylen enjoyed watching Cee-Cee get appreciated from head to toe.

The Meyerson was spectacular. The evening started with limousines filled with celebrities and city officials. The reception table had four women more beautiful than most of the females they greeted. The dinner tables were filled with the Who's Who of Dallas and leaders from around the nation. The show afterwards was as spectacular as any awards night in California; all for one man who made his millions and shared with the less fortunate.

Cee-Cee couldn't believe she was enjoying herself with the man she was falling for at an event that cost a minimum of five thousand dollars per table. She had arrived. She was mingling in a circle she only imagined existed. It wasn't until she went to the ladies room and listened to the gossip that went on that she realized, you can take the bamma out of the projects, but you can't take the projects out of the bamma.

Dressed in her multi-colored sequin gown the first woman began, "Gerl, did you see that mutha fucca with that hoe? I can't believe he had the audacity to bring her up in here knowing I would be here."

The next woman stood in her winter white chiffon gown and began, "Yeah gerl, that nigga ain't no good. But did you see how Councilman Carvins was checkin' out Patrice? I knew they were sexin' one another."

The third lady in the red sequin fitted gown joined in, "Hol' up. Did you see that fine ass Randy with his raunchy, old ass wife? I'm 'bout to get with that shit and have his ass all caught up in my cat. Give me about a week." The three ladies started laughing and giving high fives not caring that Cee-Cee was in the bathroom to hear the community low down.

This is crazy kept replaying in Cee-Cee's mind. These women are dressed to the hilt and they're acting as ghettofied as ghettofied could get. Unbelievable. Cee-Cee walked out of the restroom trying not to be noticed.

The entire day was like a fairy tale from start to finish. Jamale walked Cee-Cee to her front door and kissed her. She unlocked the door and invited Jamale in. They stood inside the doorway kissing when finally she invited him to the couch where they would continue their kiss. The kiss lead to caressing and the caressing lead to passionate love making. Cee-Cee had found her prince charming.

Reclined in Jamales car, Cee-Cee was enthralled by her memories and Jamale knew it.

Jamale didn't interrupt Cee-Cee's deep thoughts. He knew she reflected on their date each time she saw the Meyerson and he enjoyed watching her reminisce. It only confirmed for Jamale that she loved him.

The Adams Mark Hotel featured a night of karaoke each week. A few of Jamale's coworkers told him that some decent vocalist came out to sing, so he thought Cee-Cee would enjoy herself. Usually Jamale would valet park, but tonight he didn't mind self parking because he wanted time to walk hand in hand with Cee.

When they entered the lobby, the concierge directed them down the hall to the Fahrenheit Lounge. The room was smoke filled and the people were standing with their cocktails in hand singing along with the man on stage. When they walked in, Jamale noticed the open table directly in front of the stage. Jamale hurried Cee-Cee towards the front tables as if there were in a line of people rushing for the seat. Cee-Cee wasn't very impressed with the stubby man singing the country western song, but she figured he had to be doing something right because the crowd loved it.

As usual, every karaoke host thinks they can sing like any artists on their song list. The next song Lady, was a classic hit from Lionel Richie.

It was bad enough the people had to witness a 6'3, 300 pounds red headed man attempting to feel the groove of a Black man, but to have to listen to the first couple of notes that were off-key was asking for much. The man obviously had a cold and bellowed out notes that were ruining Mr. Richie's song. He cleared his throat a couple of times and tried to continue, when finally he stopped the song and asked if there were anyone in the audience who could finish what he'd started. Everyone looked around when suddenly this drunken guy stood and said he would be honored.

Some of the people laughed, others booed while some cheered him on. As he headed towards the stage, he tripped over a chair and fell to the floor. The crowd was in hysterics.

"I guess we got a real rock and roller here with us tonight", the MC said jokingly.

Again the invitation was extended. When no one stood, Jamale decided he would show the crowd how the song should be sung. The crowd roared when Jamale took the mic as if Mr. Richie himself was taking the stage. He was so handsome, and Cee-Cee knew it.

Naturally he began his efforts by staring into the eyes of the woman he loved and she loved every minute of it. Jamale's sexy baritone voice had the room's attention. But most importantly, he had his woman's undivided attention.

That boy could sing. He was crooning like he had just sold out at Madison Square Garden or something. The men in the room were taking advantage of his baritone voice as if it were them with the microphone sounding good. It was their opportunity to try to mack on the woman next to them, and the women were returning a starry eyed look at the men. Jamale had created an ambiance of romance in the Fahrenheit Lounge.

Three quarters through the song, Jamale turned his back towards the crowd, and when he turned around he switched the mic to his left hand. The spotlight was shining on him, and the sparkle off his finger was beautiful. The host turned the sound down a couple of notches as Jamale walked over to Cee-Cee. He held her hand and whispered into the mic, "I love you." She was in awe. Tears were forming in her eyes as everyone in the room remained still to watch. He removed the ring from his finger and whispered into the microphone, "Lady, I'm your knight in shining armor, and I love you. Will you marry me?"

The people in the audience were quiet until they heard her whisper into the microphone, "Yes." The crowd went crazy cheering, but Cee-Cee and Jamale were engrossed in a passionate kiss that temporarily muted the sounds of the entire world.

Jamale and Cee-Cee walked over to the MC and thanked him for a perfect night. When they got outside the lounge, she stopped Jamale and asked, "Did you have this entire night planned? Before he could answer, Cee-Cee startled Jamale. "Oh my God, what about Jaylen? I haven't even talked with him about this."

"Don't worry about Jaylen. I stopped over to Yolanda's house before going to your place and he and I had a little talk about me being his dad. He accepted."

"What? Are you telling me, the MC, Yolanda and Jaylen were in on this?" Cee-Cee wrapped her arms around Jamale and straddled his waist with her legs and gave him quick kisses between each word. "I. Love. You. So. Much." Cee-Cee stared into Jamale's eyes with tears falling and whispered, "You have made me the happiest woman on this earth."

As they walked hand in hand through the lobby, Jamale stopped to break their grip. "Hold on a minute. Let me ask the front desk agent something real quick."

"Okay." Gazing at him as he walked away.

Jamale had a brilliant smile on his face when he told Cee that the night had just begun. "I hope you're up to a few more surprises. I thought maybe we would spend the night here."

"Baby, I love you more than you can ever know." She couldn't control her joy. Cee-Cee was so totally in love with this man and knew she would have a life of happiness with Jamale.

The ride in the elevator was very slow. They kissed missing their floor, and when they realized it, they laughed. Finally reaching the room, Jamale carried Cee-Cee in and laid her across the bed to continue kissing her. The chilled bottle of Moet was finished, and the night was filled with passionate love making.

The next morning Jamale had a lot to share about their wedding. It was he who made the decision they would be married in the next couple of days. Cee-Cee was surprised that they would get married so soon, but she was more surprised by his wedding requests.

He wanted her to have all the bells and whistles of a well planned wedding in a couple of days. It was obvious Jamale had been planning this for some time because everything seemed to be in order. He pledged to make the flight arrangements for her mother to be there, and arranged for Cee-Cee to select whatever she needed at Sherrie's Bridal shop, the flowers and cake were on order and all the other necessary arrangements were made. All she had to do was be there with a matron of honor and bridesmaids.

Cee-Cee was in shock. It was really happening. She was going to be Mrs. Jamale LeTreau.

13

$\mathcal{A}$ustin held the number one position in most radio shows for the Southwest demographics. He broke arbitron records and one out of every three people in the DFW metroplex was tuning into his show.

As he waited outside of Kenneth's office for about ten minutes, he thought about Khadijah and how happy he was now that she had returned into his life. But he also wondered how they were going to get around the fact she was married.

When the door finally opened, the owner of the station came out and greeted him. It wasn't very often the owner of the station would be in town visiting. Something was up, and Austin didn't have a very good feeling about it.

Kenneth was sitting behind his desk with a blank expression as he greeted Austin. "Austin, how's it going? Come on in."

Austin was trying to communicate with his eyes to Kenneth, but Kenneth wasn't budging. Austin was on-his-own, and he knew it.

Mrs. Tyson was a slender woman in her late fifties. I suppose she would be considered attractive. Perhaps it was all of her money that helped her to clean up.

She inherited the station from her father and had done a tremendous job with improving the shows format and the ratings. She didn't interfere much with her director's and producer's decisions unless it was something she felt wouldn't be beneficial to the growth of the station. Austin couldn't imagine why he was included in the meeting with the station director and owner.

Mrs. Tyson was cordial but very to the point when she began. "Have a seat. Austin, I flew into town because I am faced with a decision that requires your input."

My input? He wondered.

"Over the years I have watched our competitors grow due to syndication. What I'm thinking is adding a twist to what they've done. Each of our competitors has used their morning shows for syndication and not their evening mellow format. So, here's my question. What do you think would happen with the growth of this station if we decided to syndicate your show?"

Austin was flabbergasted by what he'd just been asked. Mrs. Tyson was asking if he wanted to be heard nationwide. Austin understood his accomplishments were good, but he had no idea she thought his ratings were so good that she would consider syndication. Austin was ecstatic.

"Wow. I think"…clearing his throat… "Excuse me; I think it's a hell of an idea." Being modest, he continued. "But allow me to ask, what makes you know my show has what it takes?"

"Several things. You know how to romance women; you also know how to instruct men on how to romance their women without insulting them. And, another factor is that you're impressing folks in the southwest with your northeastern charm and selection of music. Music is very different on the ast coast. Because so many northerners and easterners have migrated to the southwest, they appreciate your choice of music and your flare. It's my opinion, there are people all over this nation having to suffer with the many radio personalities who have never been abroad or outside of their region and are stuck believing their show is the best thing since hot water cornbread." She surprised the men in the meeting with her well rehearsed analogy. Mrs. Tyson was tickled pink, literally.

"Think about what's happening right here in your own backyard. Your competitor does a whole lot of talking throughout his show. He plays a lot of music people on the east coast have never heard of and he usually gets caught up playing one artist too often." Before she continued, she closed her book with what appeared to be filled with statistics.

"I'm going to be quite frank with you. Austin, the best thing you have going for you is the fact you know when to shut up and give the people what they want to hear....hit ballads from the old school, good advice and your charm."

Austin started laughing when he added, "Hey, you don't have to convince me Mrs. Tyson. I know the people who tune into my show are satisfied."

Bobbing her head up and down in agreement, her eyes lit up when she asked, "So, are you willing to give this a go? Are you ready to be heard across the nation?"

"No doubt. I am more than ready." Enthused, Austin walked towards Mrs. Tyson to shake her hand.

"Great. I'll have new contracts drawn up for you to review and we'll go from there."

Kenneth, Austin and Mrs. Tyson were shaking hands when Nicole buzzed the intercom to tell Mrs. Tyson her guest had arrived.

"Thanks Nicole."

The agreement was made, and everyone in the room was pleased. Each one shook hands and Austin was beaming with enthusiasm. Mrs. Tyson and her guest, who turned out to be her brother were sharing the typical "good to see you's" and the three others aboard the elevator nodded and gave awkward smiles.

No question, Austin was truly hyped. At the moment, there was only one person he wanted to share the news with and he didn't have a number to reach her.

As he drove around town, a thought seized him. Since he'd

volunteered with Big Brothers of America, he hadn't been living up to his obligation. Austin drove around thinking about what special thing he could do over the weekend with his "little brother". He was having one of those moments when you just had to share the wealth. Austin realized something big had just happened to him and if he didn't do something for someone less fortunate, especially an underprivileged young Black male, his success wouldn't be worth having in the long run.

Austin was startled by the vibration of his cellular phone as a call came in. The caller ID said, Unknown Caller, which came close to not being answered, but the thought of it being Khadijah changed his entire body posture. Ordinarily Austin's body would be erect while driving, but when he heard her delicate voice, he rested his head back and started to lean a little.

Khadijah blurted out, "Hey baby. I had to tell you something really important. I was just thinking about you and, ummm, I had to tell you that I love you and miss you so much." Starting to giggle.

Austin drifted into this sexy transition that only he and his body could relate to. He reached between his legs and stroked his manhood. He didn't feel it necessary to let Khadijah know how he was feeling that very moment, so he listened and enjoyed every word she spoke.

Khadijah continued, "And I was just thinking how I would love to be somewhere kissing you from head to toe."

"All right now. Don't bite off more than you can chew. So, what's up? We can make all that kissing from head to toe happen, you know. If you don't have anything planned for the day, why don't you meet me at the café in about an hour?"

"I can do that and better. My husband has plans this evening, so if it's okay, I can hang out with you."

"That's kewl. Maybe we'll just chill and do some talking before you turn into a pumpkin."

"Ha. Ha. Ha. Well, I don't know how much I like the thought of just talking, but if that's all I can get, I'll take it."

"Watch yourself. I already warned you. Don't get yourself in any trouble. You know when we get to the house a lot more than talking can happen. I was just thinking about you, but, seriously, I gotta make a quick stop and I'll see you soon."

"Okay Bay, I'll see you in about thirty minutes. Love ya. Bye-Bye."

Austin felt really good. He decided to get ringside tickets to the live broadcast of upcoming wrestling at the arena. Wrestling wasn't something Austin particularly liked, but he knew Victor was a huge fan and it would make his day.

Austin thought he could probably get press passes and Victor would be the envy of his class or perhaps the entire school. But instead of chancing it, he stood in line for thirty minutes for the tickets. While in line Austin called Victor's mother to make sure the night of the show would be a good night for them to get together. Austin was very excited telling Victor's mother about the tickets and confirming her secrecy about their plans. That moment, Austin realized he'd made a good decision becoming a volunteer.

Driving into the parking lot, Austin spotted Khadijah's car immediately. She smiled when she saw him, and it seemed she couldn't get out of her car and into his car fast enough. Khadijah wasn't holding back, and Austin loved every minute of it. Thank God she wasn't bigger than a minute because another pound or two and she would not have been able to squeeze herself into the slim space between him and the steering wheel and onto his lap. Khadijah didn't waste any time kissing him before saying hello.

Jokingly, Austin began, "Oh my God. Get this heavy girl off of me. She's killing me." Straining while he spoke and smiling at the same time.

"What-ever." Play punching him on his shoulder and kissing him again.

Squirming over to the passenger side of the car, Khadijah rested her head back, licked her lips slowly and added, "Okay, now that I got that out of the way, what would you like to do?"

Clearing his throat he answered, "First I need to regain my composer. And then I thought we could drive across town, and you and I talk about what's been going on over the years. But now I don't know if that's the best plan." Austin looked over at Khadijah and smiled. "No, really, is that kewl?"

"That's fine. I wanna learn everything that makes you tick."

"I'm gonna take you to the Southside where we can get some real food. There's this joint called Elaines where you can buy the authentic Jamaican food. You down for some curry or some ox tails?"

"Baby, please. Jamaicans everywhere in the northeast and you know it."

They laughed and talked about the many delicacies they could get from the Jamaican bakery and restaurant on East L Street in DC. Rice and peas, jerk chicken, curry goat, ox tails, fish soup, cocoa bread and cornbread and cheese.

The ride was pleasant. They started reminiscing about their high school years and what they knew about their old classmates.

"I remember when Purple Rain came out, and you came to school with your new paisley shirt and Guess jeans. You thought you were the shit." Khadijah was humored by Austin's recollection.

"What do you mean? I was the shit. It was you who thought you had it goin' on when you put glitter all over your thick white socks and rolled up your black jeans to show off your socks. You really thought you had the Michael Jackson thing goin' on."

Laughing the entire ride to the Southside of Dallas, time escaped them. For a moment, they didn't notice the devastation of the community. Suddenly Austin got silent, and although Khadijah was as affected, she didn't say much. While living in Detroit, Khadijah was faced with much devastation and condemnation in the Black communities so this wasn't anything new for her to see. And although what Austin witnessed in Dallas was sad, it wasn't anything close to what he'd seen growing up. It didn't matter where Austin saw it though, urban desolation really impacted him.

"Baby, are you okay?" Khadijah whispered.

Austin's eyes began to mist when he saw the little boy no more than six years old sitting on the ground in his front yard drinking from an old beer bottle he'd found.

"This is the kinda shit that pisses me off about our people. Where the hell is his mother?" Becoming more agitated, he continued. "Why don't someone step up and stop them from putting all this destruction in our communities? Everywhere you look there's a malt liquor or Hennessy billboard. And then they make sure the people on them are Black and lookin' like they're having the best time of their lives. The shit ain't right."

Cutting from one street to the next Austin hissed at every form of desolation he passed. "I wanna show you a place where I hang out from time to time." He sped up and drove another eight blocks when he was in front of a store front that had black painted windows. Austin didn't say much for a few minutes when he finally apologized for getting so emotional.

Khadijah didn't know what to think, and she really didn't know what to say when he pointed out his hideaway as being the Dallas Headquarters of the New Black Panther Party (NBPP). Khadijah was silent. She knew she had to tell Austin what was going on with her and when would be a better time than now.

"Austin, I have to tell you something very important." He saw Khadijah was very sincere with whatever she was about to share, so he pulled into the parking lot of the local convenience store and gave her his undivided attention.

Khadijah felt her heart as if it fell into the pits of her stomach. Swallowing a couple of times before she spoke, she began. "My husband is White." Khadijah sat up straight in her chair and stared him in the eye as if she had just confessed to the most heinous act.

All Austin could do was put his head down and cover his face with his hands before speaking. He turned to her and asked only one question. "Does he love you the way you deserve?"

Based on what she'd determined about Austin's principals and philosophies, Khadijah was surprised by the question. She really expected a great deal of objections. But she respected his maturity and knew she could be nothing less than honest. "He loves me, I'm sure. But no, he does not love me the way I deserve. It's been a long time since we've been in love. I think he knows how unhappy I am, but he doesn't want me to be with anyone else." This time Khadijah's eyes were showing concern.

"Baby, there's something else." Not sure how to continue, she reached for Austin's hand. "I think his sister is the owner of the station you work for. She owns Radio Works. Is your station a part of Radio Works?"

Considering the glare Austin had in his eyes, Khadijah had hit the nail on the head. "Oh my goodness. Dij, I think I saw him today. Is he kinda heavy with a receding hair line?" Austin turned to her not wanting to hear the answer.

"Oh my gosh." She looked terrified. "Austin I'm afraid of what he may do if he finds out about us."

"What do you mean you're afraid? Afraid of what?" Austin's posture changed from calm and understanding to tense and hostile. Khadijah couldn't speak and Austin began overreacting.

"Oh hell no. I know damned well you're not telling me he put his hands on you. Tell me you're not saying..."

Khadijah started crying, and all Austin could do was feel her pain. He loved her, and she was sure of it, but he had to let her cry and be honest with herself. If out of the marriage was something she wanted, he could not contribute to that decision. He didn't want any future regrets that she may have to rest on his shoulders. In other words, he didn't want it thrown in his face down the road.

Austin started the car and put in his favorite Fred Hammond CD. True enough, Christian music may make the tears flow a little harder, but the reason for the tears begins to make sense. Khadijah turned up the volume on one song, reclined the seat a notch and wiped her tears away. Austin thought it was time for him to say something, but he had to make certain he used his words wisely.

"Khadijah, you are beautiful, intelligent, talented and have a kind and loving heart. Don't ever expect anything less from anyone than what you give. That includes me. Do you understand?"

She turned and looked at his expression of seriousness and knew crying wasn't the answer.

"Austin, I do understand. Being with you reminded me of that. I love you with all of my heart, but I can't include you in this mess. I need to get some control over my life and until I can do that, I don't need to be unfair to us."

Khadijah leaned closer and kissed him gently on the lips before she continued with her plea. "You told me last night that you don't ever want to lose me and baby, I feel the same about you. But belonging to someone else, we really don't have one another. I won't let it be that way. I've already known for a long time that I wasn't happy in my marriage and being with you didn't contribute to that."

Her posture was staunched before she made her claim. Austin could feel her conviction in each word that rang with finality. "I'm filing for divorce tomorrow. My girl is an attorney back in Detroit.

If I file there, I won't have to follow the laws of Texas. The wait won't be long. Now, the only thing I need from you is to know, will you wait for me?"

"I think I already answered that question." Austin smiled and winked at her. He reached to turn up the music when his cellular rang. The number came up with a 202 area code and thought he should see who was trying to reach him.

"This is Austin James." He always answered the phone that way when he thought the call could be business.

"Austin, hello. This is Mrs. Tyson. Hope I didn't interrupt you. The receptionist at the station gave me your number."

"Oh, no problem. What can I do for you?"

"I was thinking tomorrow evening would be a great time to get together for dinner. My brother and his wife would be joining us. I'd like for you to meet them. They just moved here to Dallas." Although she was asking, she was actually telling Austin that dinner tomorrow would be a good career move.

"Dinner tomorrow to meet your brother and his wife? Well…."pausing for a minute and cupping the phone with his hand, Austin whispered… "This is my boss." Khadijah was shaking her head and telling Austin no, but he couldn't decline the offer. "Mrs. Tyson that would be excellent. I'm on the road right now, if you'd like, I'll make the reservation and give you a call in the morning with the details."

"That would be excellent. Call me at 202-555-0245. I'll talk with you later."

Khadijah couldn't believe what she had just heard. She was speechless. She tried to understand, but in her mind there was no understanding.

"Dij, I had to. What you don't know is, I had a meeting today with her, and she offered me syndication. Baby, do you have any idea what that means?" Austin reached for Khadijah's hand and waited for her response.

Khadijah wanted to be happy for Austin. She just didn't know how she could handle being at the table with Austin and her husband. She put on a smile and tried to be convincing, "Baby, I'm so happy for you. Okay Bay. I'll be fine. Syndication? Wow." She reached over and kissed Austin on his lips.

When they arrived at Austin's house, Khadijah and Austin were both still a little shaken about their revelation. Khadijah knew the consequences of getting caught cheating on Chris and Austin knew his affair with Khadijah could cost him his career. They were both preoccupied with their predicaments.

Instead of rehashing the situations, they enjoyed the few hours they had together. They had agreed Khadijah would leave just after eleven so she could be home at a decent hour, so they listened to oldies and enjoyed reminiscing on their high school days.

14

𝔍he flashing light on the telephone alerted Marquis that he had a message. He assumed it couldn't be anyone of real significance, so he began undressing for his shower. As the water was pounding against his muscular back, Marquis moaned with pleasure. You can always tell how a man's day had gone by the way he reacted to the effects of a shower. Some men simply get in and wash away his hard day and others allow themselves quiet time to think while they feel the warm water beating on their tired bodies. And sometimes life is so great they simply get in that water and begin acting as if they're something they are not. You know….a singer. Marquis was guilty of the latter. He was singing quietly when he was interrupted by the sound of the ringing telephone. With his body dripping wet, Marquis lunged across the bed to say hello.

"Hello."

"Hey dawg. Whassup?"

"Yo man, where you been?" Drying off and reaching for the remote control for the television.

"I've been at work handlin' my business. You're the one chillin' in a hotel."

"Negro, please. Adrian, why are you up at this hour? I'm gonna start calling you batman. Your ass doesn't ever sleep."

"Whatever man. Where you been? I've been calling you for the last hour, and I know you got my message. I gotta tell you 'bout this female I'm working with."

"What female? You work with a lot of females. Oh, you talkin' 'bout the female project. Let me guess, she can sing her ass off but she fat as hell, ugly as hell or body just jacked up?" Marquis was resting across the king sized bed in his room flipping through channels.

"Nothing like that, man. This female is awesome. She's beautiful, body fine, and she can sing like you don't know. Man, she is everything I've been lookin' for. Marquis, man, she's smart, funny, witty, humble, and spiritual, and she's focused. I have never met anyone like her. I had to share this with someone."

Marquis sat up and muted the television to give his boy his undivided attention. He was hearing a lot more than Adrian was intending.

"Adrian man, are you hearing yourself? Are you talking about a client and her talents or are you talking about a woman who could potentially be the woman you've been hoping for? It sounds to me as if you met a woman you might wanna get with on the real."

"What? What you talkin' about?"

"What's funny, witty, humble, smart and spiritual got to do with her singing talents? What's up with that?"

"Man you're trippin'. I was just telling you about her. It ain't nothing like that. This female's gonna be the Queen of Rhythm." Adrian was putting himself in check by defending himself and his emotions.

"Yeah, if you say so. I think you see more than some, Queen of Rhythm. I think you see your queen. But that's me. I'll leave that alone until you wanna be real with it. Anyway man, I checked out the club. Man, they had this one chick who was off the chain. I'm gonna try to hook up with her before I leave. And don't say nothing to me about picking up a dancer."

"Hey, what I got to say about who you pick up? I mean hey if you

161

want to make a change from the uppity females you're used to."
Adding a few chuckles in between, he continued. "Who am I to tell
you not to? If you ask me, an occasional stop at a titty joint is what
you need. It'll get you away from the pretentious females who
hang at the jazz spots you frequent. Hey, but that's just if you ask
me. Besides, considering your pick up earlier, a couple of real
titties are what you want." Adrian couldn't resist his outburst of
laughter.

They laughed for a while about Marquis' earlier experience with
the transvestite and ended the conversation about the two other
women before admitting it was getting late, and they both had an
early day ahead of them.

Adrian was wide awake, and his only thought at the moment was
Chanel. He being the confident man that he was, he punched in the
hotel room number three times before deciding to ask the operation
to connect him to room 716. Adrian was hoping she, too, was
overly excited to the point of insomnia. And, truth be told, he was
also hoping some of her excitement was based on how she felt for
him.

Chanel answered the phone fully energized. "Hel-lo." Singing the
word, you could hear the happiness in her voice.

"Chanel, hey, this is Adrian. I was checking to see if you needed
anything before going to bed."

Chanel was confused. She couldn't help wondering why he
dropped her off and then wonder is she needed anything. Excusing
her thoughts, she responded, "Well, aren't you sweet. I was just
looking in the phone book for delivery. I feel kinda hungry."

"Why didn't you tell me? There aren't going to be many delivery
services at this hour. We could have stopped for breakfast. I didn't
think you could be hungry considering how much you were eating
at the studio."

"Ha. Ha. Ha. Got jokes, do ya?" With a girlish tone Chanel added,

"I didn't eat a lot. Did I?"

"I was just kidding. If you'd like, I'll come by and swoop you up so we can get something to eat. How about IHOP? It's probably the only decent place to get something at this hour."

"Yeah, that sounds real good. I'll be ready when you get here." Biting onto her lip and thinking about spending time with him away from the studio gave Chanel a few womanly chills.

Although calling home wasn't on the very top of her list, Chanel wanted to be a woman of her word and hold up to her promise to Doris. It was time for her and her sister to behave like sisters again. Chanel knew their mother would want them to be very close and always be there for one another.

The phone only rang once when Doris whispered into the receiver, "Hello."

In a gentle voice, Chanel began with her apology, "Hey Doris. I'm sorry for calling at this hour. I know you must be tired from working tonight, but we didn't get done in the studio until around 11:00."

"That's okay. I wanted to hear about Mr. man anyway."

Doris didn't resist listening. In fact, she was very attentive when Chanel described how handsome Adrian was and how wonderful the label had been treating her.

"Ooh Doris, he is incredible. I can't even tell you how handsome he is…. I wouldn't know where to begin." Beginning to giggle and fading into a clearing of her throat.

"So he's really fine like that?" Sitting up in the bed and clearing her throat to continue, Doris got really serious. "Okay. So the question is, can I come to Dallas? I have my own money, and I know people there so I won't need to stay with you if that's a problem. Come on NO, I really want to be there with you. Don't make me beg?"

Chanel couldn't believe what she had heard. There was actual sincerity in Doris' voice. Chanel was smiling when she okayed for Doris to visit.

They both laughed for a few minutes when Doris asked Chanel what hotel she was staying in and what part of Dallas it was in and then the surprise question was asked. "So tell me the truth NO, do you like him? I'm not asking do you want to get with him, I just want to know if you could, would you?"

"Girl, why are you asking me that? You know I can't do anything that would jeopardize this opportunity. Besides, you know where I am with my Christian walk. I am really trying to hold out for marriage." Beginning to giggle again, she let the truth out. "But since you asked, and because I'm a young woman feeling things, the answer is, oh yeah. He is gorgeous, he's sweet, funny, smart, and he has this way of looking at me that sends me to a level I have never been. I know you think I'm being crazy, but Doris, I don't want to mess this up."

"Your new name is Chanel, right? I mean hey, I'm used to Nannie Olivia, so I need to get the new name right. I wouldn't want to mess it up in front of anyone." Doris giggled for a moment, and when she continued, she had never sounded so sincere. "I know we haven't been very close over the years, but..." pausing to make sure she said the name right. "...Chanel, I want you to know, I want this to happen for you too. I don't want you to make the same mistakes I've made. I wanna be right there for you, girl. Let's do this thing right. I'm your girl. Your sister. Kewl?"

Chanel had tears in her eyes as she listened to her sisters' invitation to become close again. She lowered the handset from her ear so she could wipe her eyes. She did everything within her will to hold back her sniffle because Chanel didn't want Doris to know she was beginning to cry. To interrupt her emotional moment, she began coughing and asked her sister to hold a minute.

Returning to the conversation, she continued. "Um, excuse me. I must have swallowed wrong. Wow. Doris of course you're my girl. I want you to be there with me when I make it. Thanks sis'."

"Listen, if things are meant to be with Mr. Adrian, then they will be. Just handle your business."

"That's true. But like I said, I'm not even thinking like that. I'm gonna behave in Dallas and handle my business the right way." Chanel ended the conversation with details on where she would be staying and how to get there. Doris added a few don't worries, and you go girls and told her she would be there in a few days. Doris let Chanel know she would be staying with a friend and that she would be in touch once she got there.

Doris checked her voice mail and frowned when she didn't have any pending messages. She was hoping Marquis would have responded to the message she'd left earlier. Envy was beginning to take harbor. The mere thought of Chanel being happy with good news was getting the best of her. Plus Doris knew she had to lay the ground work before she went to Dallas. Time was of the essence if things were going to run smoothly.

Instinctively Doris began to react. She looked through her purse for the business card with the large gold embossed NFL letters. When she found it with a twenty dollar bill wrapped around it, Doris stared at it for a moment and then smiled a devious smile. "Bump it," she thought. "If I don't make this happen, who will?"

Marquis listened to his voice mail and smiled when he heard Alyssa's message. He looked at the clock and noticed forty-five minutes had passed since the message had been left and thought it was too late to return the call. Immediately after hanging up the receiver, the phone rang. Marquis thought it may have been a ring back, but was very pleased to hear her kind voice on the other end. "Hi. This is Alyssa. I hope it's not too late." Doris had changed her personality like leaves change colors in the fall.

Pleasantly surprised, Marquis began to reassure the lady. "No, not at all. In fact, I just listened to your message and decided it was too late for me to return your call. But thanks for calling back." As Marquis listened to her seductive voice he quickly reached for his manhood and held onto it, stroking it gently while he enjoyed their conversation.

"I'm glad you're awake. I was kinda skeptical on calling you back, but I thought, what the hell. I was imagining you in bed looking and smelling good and thought, the most you could do was cuss me out and call it a very short acquaintance." Doris sat patiently awaiting his response to her flirtatious comments.

"Oh, is that right? No, I wouldn't ever cuss you out for imagining those type of thoughts and then calling me. I gave you the number and at least now I know I made a good impression. So, does some good news come with this phone call? Will I see you before I leave? Maybe dinner or something fun?"

Both of them were aroused and imagining wild and erotic thoughts. Doris was hot and bothered, and she loved it so much that she began pinching her erect nipples lightly. And at the same time, Marquis was stroking his erect penis as he imagined her tantalizing body.

"That sounds really nice. I would love dinner and maybe shoot some pool if you're up to a good ol' fashioned spankin'."

If there's gonna be any spankin' going on it wouldn't be her doing it, he thought. "Spank me. Spank me." He added with a laugh.

Oh I'll spank your ass like you ain't never been spanked, the thought exploded in her head before she sighed in frustration.

Surprised by the sigh, Marquis asked, "Is everything okay?"
Having to lie to excuse her sigh, Doris quickly replied, "Yes, I'm fine. I just spilled something."

Marquis and Alyssa seemed to be hitting it off quickly. They laughed a little before Alyssa ended the conversation by telling him he needed to get some rest due to his early day of meetings. Marquis liked the fact that she remembered his agenda while in Houston and told her good night. After hanging up the phone, Doris high fived herself in the air, cursed her libido and prepared for bed.

What a Season

Instead of pulling into the garage, Jamale parked in front of his house. He and Cee-Cee held hands and stopped to kiss after the fifth step when they were startled by the screeching tires from the car up the street. When they turned, neither of them recognized the car, so they didn't think twice about it. When they approached the door, there was a small paper bag sitting on the door mat. They were both surprised by the bag, and as Jamale reached for it, Cee-Cee cautioned him before touching it. Picking it up with two fingers, Jamale dumped the contents onto the ground. Inside was a pair of red female panties that had so much perfume sprayed on them, they both choked into a mild cough. Cee-Cee stared at Jamale for an explanation, but he was clueless.

Knowing he needed to say something, Jamale began his attempt. "Baby, I don't know what this is all about. Let's not let anything interrupt our wonderful future."

It was out of character for Cee-Cee to question Jamale's sincerity, but as she looked through her squinted eyes, Cee-Cee changed her happy expression to anger. "How can you expect me to ignore this? Jamale, is there something you need to tell me?" Cee-Cee could see Jamale's disappointment, and it hurt her deeply. It didn't take her long to admit that she'd used poor judgment by questioning him. "Baby, I am so sorry."

Without resentment, Jamale made certain Cee-Cee was secure with her position in his life. "Girl, you're gonna be my wife in a few days. You don't ever have to worry or wonder where my heart is." Quieting the tense moment, Jamale injected some of his charm,

"Now come here so I can practice carrying you across the threshold."

Cee-Cee was happy for a moment when it suddenly dawned on her where she had smelled that cologne. It was Ralph Lauren Polo. Jeff used to wear it every day. She hated it then, and she hated it even more now. It reminded her of all the unhappy days when she was married to him. Cee-Cee dismissed the thought that it could be Jeff and began to admire the handsome man she would soon be marrying.

When Jamale picked her up, Cee-Cee closed her eyes and rested her head on his shoulder welcoming his strong arms. Before he could begin to step, her outburst startled him enough to stop him in his tracks. "Oh my God, this is going to be our home. I'm gonna be your wife." She pulled away from his arms and jumped to her feet. "Baby, you know carrying me across the threshold was bad luck. Now you have to kiss me for five minutes to break the spell." Without a word spoken, Jamale reached for her face and whispered that he loved her.

Before the kissing began, the phone had rung. Jamale said hello a few times when he finally gave the caller his attention. "Listen, I don't know who this is, but whoever you are, you are interrupting a wonderful moment with the woman I am marrying in a couple of days. So, if you don't have anything to say, I would appreciate it if you wouldn't call back. Have a nice life."

After hanging up on the caller, the phone rang immediately afterwards. Jamale and Cee-Cee weren't going to play any telephone games, so they agreed to turn the ringer off. Jamale had plans for his bride and wasn't going to allow the fool playing games to interfere.

When they got upstairs, there was a surprise waiting. Cee-Cee couldn't believe her eyes. She stood there with her mouth open and Jamale stood there watching her. She couldn't believe what she was seeing; there were dozens of roses around the room.

Jamale also had a picture of the reception hall he had reserved, pictures of the flowers she could choose from on such short notice and a box wrapped with a card that read, "To my wife on our wedding day."

Cee-Cee was speechless. She looked at her engagement ring and then at the man she loved and started crying. Jamale reached for her and held her in his arms when he began to speak, "Cee, I love you and Jaylen with all of my heart. You two don't ever have to worry about anything. I will always take care of you two for as long as I live."

Jamale wiped her tears and began undressing her. "Come on. Let me run a shower and let's get our day started. You can do your thing with our wedding while I'm at work."

She smiled as she finished undressing. "Okay."

15

𝒮he knocks on the door were very quiet. Chanel was expecting Adrian, so she was smiling and very deliberate when she pulled the door open. Unfortunately, Adrian wasn't smiling; in fact, he wasn't very subtle with his words to follow.

"Don't ever open a door without knowing for certain whose on the other side. I could have been your worst nightmare. Don't ever do that again. Promise me. I'm serious. Promise me."

Chanel's stance was that of a scolded child. She was so surprised that she didn't know what to say for a moment, but when she saw the sincerity in Adrian's eyes, her only appropriate response was, "I promise."

Reaching for her hands and offering a warm smile, Adrian spoke tenderly. "I apologize for being so harsh, but I don't' want anything to happen to you." With a boyish look about him, he continued, "Well, do you accept my apology?"

"Yes, but don't do it again. I was seconds from takin' you out." Chanel revealed her smirk while her eyes were rolling and head going side to side. She brushed past Adrian with lots of attitude and added, "Now, let's get something to eat."

"Oh, is that right? You got attitude?" Creeping behind her, Adrian wrapped his arms around Chanel locking her arms to her side and whispered in her right ear, "Who you say you were gonna take out? Girl, don't you know I will put you across my lap and spank you."

Stunned by his horseplay, she slowly turned her head to the right when their eyes met, and their lips were close enough to feel the warmth that escaped their mouths. The moment was very awkward, and neither of them knew how to react. When he let go, he started towards the door fumbling with the keys.

"So, do you want IHOP or do you want to stop for coffee and pastry?" Adrian pulled in his bottom lip hoping to put out the fire that was burning inside him.

Chanel watched Adrian as he paused before he spoke. She imagined what he was feeling was imitating the rushing desires she was experiencing and felt his pain, so instead of stretching the moment any further, she answered quickly. "I definitely don't want anything that will make me feel heavy; so if we can get some juice and a pastry that would be enough. I'm not really too hungry. What about yourself?"

"Juice sounds good. I know a place not too far from here where we can get some fresh juice and a great selection of freshly baked pastries."

Blinded by their awkward experience, they didn't have much to say in the car. They did, however, agree to get the juice and pastries to go. The conversation back to the hotel remained minimal. Chanel and Adrian managed a smile or two, but there was a definite feeling of uneasiness in the car.

"Adrian, would you like to come up to my suite to enjoy your juice and pastry?"

Adrian was surprised that she asked. His first thought was to say no, but his heart wasn't in sync with his mind, so he answered with a gentle, "Sure."

As they stood in the elevator, Adrian wanted to apologize, but he didn't want to make her any more uncomfortable than he knew she was. Chanel unlocked the door and entered the room. She made a sudden turn and bumped into Adrian causing him to spill most of the juice onto his shirt. Chanel rushed into the bathroom apologizing and grabbed a towel. "Ooh Adrian, I am so sorry."

Struggling to keep the rest of the juice from spilling onto his clothes, Adrian placed the cup carrier onto the table. Chanel wasn't sure if she was helping or harming when she began wiping and dabbing his shirt, hoping to keep Adrian dry.

Damn she's cute when she's nervous. If she only knew what all that rubbing was stirring up inside of me, she'd stop. Adrian's thoughts were racing through his mind. They were going so fast if he weren't careful, he'd find himself losing control of the situation. He gently stopped Chanel from her efforts to dry him and spoke tenderly, "Thank you. It'll dry, I'm sure."

The wrinkle on her brow let him know she felt bad about the spill. The last thing Adrian wanted to do was ruin the moment. He reacted quickly and began making jokes. "Damn girl, how many thumbs you got? Five?" Although the tension was relieved, his shirt was still very wet.

"Chanel, I have a tee shirt on under this. If I hurry and get out of the shirt, I could stay dry. Would you mind if I took my shirt off?"

"Not at all. I'll get a hanger so you can hang the shirt on the shower rod to dry." Slowly unbuttoning his shirt, he watched her as she thumbed through the few hangers in the closet. He smiled at her when she stuck out her bottom lip to pout after realizing the hotel hangers were designed to hang in the closet only. The last thing he wanted to do was chance the moment again by embarrassing her, so he stepped into the bathroom before she noticed his smile.

While Adrian was in the bathroom, Chanel sat on the sofa bending over removing her shoes. When she sat up, Adrian was waiting patiently in the doorway with his tee shirt on. She had never been in the presence of such a work of art. God had truly created a masterpiece. His sculptured body was beautiful, and the hair that peaked out of the neckline of his tee appeared soft and curly on his developed chest. His biceps were carved, and even the branded Greek on his left arm was sexy. He was all man and Chanel recognized she was in the presence of temptation.

"Is everything okay? Are you sure it's not too late or early, should I say, for me to be here?" Adrian wasn't sure how to read Chanel's blank stare.

"No, no. I'm fine. Why do you ask?"

Walking towards Chanel, he decided to answer openly. "I sense some uneasiness."

The gleam in her eyes was very innocent. She tried to speak through her nervousness hoping to assure Adrian. "Un, un. I'm fine. I'm glad you're here."

Adrian went along with her response, though he was sure she was uncomfortable. He had never been so tense over something so small. He was going about this thing as if he had three lucky chances, and he had already blown two of them. Cautiously he reached for their drinks. The half empty cup was hers. Before drinking from his cup, he paused as if he had a little leprechaun he could turn to for advice. Adrian wanted to do everything to make the sticky situation better. But he didn't need any lucky charm; he knew to do what any gentleman should do, by offering her his drink. "Here, have mine."

"Nooo. Keep yours. I'll drink what's left of mine."

Being persistent, Adrian offered again, this time insisting. "Please have some of mine. I won't be satisfied until I know you've had enough. Besides, if you eat that big coffee roll, your mouth is gonna be dry like sandpaper, and you're gonna wish you had some."

The ice was broken. Chanel giggled when she leaned towards the cup. Adrian held the drink while she took a couple of small swallows. She tried desperately not to look into his eyes, but how could she resist such a stare. Again they found themselves in a precarious situation. It was time to stand firm to the saying, don't start nothing and it won't be nothing, so he interrupted the moment with some comment about the time and some early appointments.

"I'm sorry. I wouldn't have had you come out so late. I wasn't that hungry." Chanel was totally oblivious to Adrian's need to be freed from his very strong and passionate desires.

"Don't worry about it. I offered because I wanted to come. It's late, so I'm gonna get my shirt and get out of here so you can get some sleep too."

The few feet to the door seemed like a mile. Adrian stopped in front of Chanel as they found themselves speechless staring compassionately at one another. Both their eyes closed as their lips began to touch.

Before they could get swallowed up in their passion, Chanel put both hands up and gently pushed some distance between them.

"I can't do this. Adrian, I am so sorry. I can't allow anything to get in the way of what I am here to accomplish. Adrian…"

Adrian hushed Chanel with his finger to her lips. "Shhh. You don't have to say another word. Chanel, you have no idea how much I respect you and your decision. I don't ever want to do anything to hurt you or your dreams. It's okay, trust me. I am not hurt, angry or disappointed. It just felt right. I hope you accept my apology if I overstepped my position."

Chanel was relieved and able to speak comfortably. "Adrian, you don't have to apologize. It did feel right. It's just the wrong time in my life. Can we put this behind us?"

"Done, baby girl. Get some rest." With his shirt in hand and hoping to cover his erection, Adrian swiftly walked towards the door. Without turning around to look at Chanel again, he wished her goodnight.

"Goodnight." Chanel leaned back on the locked door with her eyes closed and head tilted back, she cried out. "Ahhhhh. Why did I do that? A simple kiss would not have hurt anything. I should call him back, but I can't." Every ounce of her wanted Adrian. She had never felt her body crave for a man. Her thoughts ran wild, almost keeping her from drifting off to sleep.

Out of Season

Chris and Khadijah's four bedroom house was in the final stages of completion, rendering them temporary quarters at the four stars, Quantum Suites. Visiting their unfinished house became her therapy for the moment. She had to do something that would prepare her before facing Chris, so seeing some form of progress was the quick fix. Khadijah sat in front of the peach stucco house for twenty minutes reminiscing on some happier times. She tried to smile as she recalled what seemed a lifetime ago.

It was in her second year of college when Khadijah was struggling with most of her classes. Working the evening shift at the casino and trying to be a full time student was wearing her down. Chris admired Khadijah the instant he laid eyes on her. He sat next to her in their Statistics class and became very friendly with her. As their friendship developed and the studies increased, Chris noticed his friend becoming wearier each day.

One Thursday afternoon Chris had invited Khadijah to lunch when she explained her financial problems to him as he listened attentively. Surprisingly, Chris made Khadijah an offer that left her temporarily speechless. Chris offered to help with her expenses without any strings attached. For a moment, she thought he was kidding, but Chris never snickered as he usually would after making a joke. He reached for the maroon eel-skinned checkbook holder out of his jackets inside pocket. The black Mont Blanc pen glided across the paper as he wrote her a check for fifteen hundred dollars. While handing her the check and looking directly into her eyes, he continued with his offer by asking her to give up her job and apartment and move in with him.

Chris explained that he lived alone in a three bedroom condominium and would love to have some company. He also made clear that he didn't need help with the monthly expenses because they were gonna get paid with or without her being there. Khadijah felt rescued, relieved and overjoyed. She thought about Chris' families' money and acclaimed what the hell.

They lived the first year completely platonic. However, two years later they were sharing the same bed, the same dreams and the same wedding vows.

In a quiet whisper, Khadijah exhaled her thoughts, "Damn, how things have changed. I can't believe what's happened to us." She was numb. She couldn't cry or even feel sorrow as she reflected on her years with Chris. Their marriage was over and there would be nothing to stop her from filing for divorce.

While driving to the hotel, Khadijah considered the many ways she could approach the divorce with Chris. She concluded there was no good way, so her plan was a simple but direct approach. She figured towards the end of the evening would be the best time, that way she could go to sleep, and he could do whatever it was he needed to do.

Khadijah's body temperature escalated, and beads of perspiration formed above her lip as she moved toward her suite room. She was nervous as she pushed the plastic card into the slot to unlock the door. When she entered, Chris was sitting in the chair facing the door with a bottle of tequila in his hand. He was apparently drunk and judging by the amount left in the bottle, predictably very drunk.

Slurring each word, Chris shouted, "WHERE THE HELL HAVE YOU BEEN!?"

"Hmmm, I take it you're not meeting your sister for dinner?" Khadijah muttered her question hoping to evade his question, but Chris wasn't having it.

"I KNOW YOU HEARD ME! WHERE THE HELL YOU BEEN!?" Tripping over his own feet, he plunged towards the floor, grabbing for the chair to break his fall. The chair and Chris crashed into the door. As the woman from housekeeping passed, she could hear the yelling and the chair banging the door. Startled by the ruckus, she rushed to speak into her walkie-talkie. Her English was broken, but it was clear enough to understand. "Se-cur-ty. Se-cur-ty. Room-ay tree, say-ven, ocho."

Chris' drunkenness was something Khadiajah was very familiar with. She tried to ignore him by going into the bedroom of the suite and shutting the door, but that didn't stop Chris. He found his way into the bedroom, and before she could react, he grabbed Khadijah by the shoulders and slammed her onto the floor. She was stunned. This episode was different. Chris screamed in Khadijah's face repeatedly, "You fuckin' bitch....where have you been?"

Khadijah tried to push him off of her, but her strength wasn't enough and didn't allow her to move him. Exhausted by her efforts, she realized what Chis was attempting to do and Khadijah began crying.

"Chris, what are you doing?! Get off of me! Stop!" He had unzipped his pants and was going to prove to his wife that she belonged to him.

"You're me goddamn wife and you'll give it to me whenever I want it!"

"Chris!" Shouting louder and crying harder, Khadijah pleaded. "PLEASE STOP! YOU'RE DRUNK!" Before she could utter another word, the palm and then the back of his hand was slapping her face.

Startled by the knock on the door, Chris yelled to the person on the other side of the door, "GO THE HELL AWAY!" Again, more knocks, but louder. Knock! Knock! Knock!

"PLEASE HELP ME!" Khadijah began screaming when the door lock turned, and the security officer entered. Chris found perfect aim at her face again while shouting "SHUT UP!"

The door was slightly opened as the security officer spoke. "Security. Is everything okay in here?" When he pushed the door open, he saw Khadijah on the floor with Chris hung motionless over her. Chris was beginning to feel trapped.

"GET THE HELL OUT OF MY ROOM! GET FUCKIN' OUT!" Chris began yelling obscenities at the officer and attempted to go after him, but lost his balance and fell onto the floor. The middle aged security officer radioed a call to the front desk to call 911 for the police. Khadijah got up from the floor and ran into the room with the officer. Chris continued with his obscenities as the guard and Khadijah left the room.

Chris' behavior changed from anger, into a drunken plea. He got onto his knees and started crying how much he loved Khadijah. "Dij, I love you. Please don't leave me. I love you so much. I am so sorry. Please come back." Khadijah was embarrassed as she sat in the hallway with her head buried in her hands while waiting with the security guard for the police to arrive.

Not paying attention to the crowd that had started forming, Khadijah was stunned when she looked up and heard what appeared to be the entire housekeeping staff gabbing in their native tongue about what they assumed was happening. Hotel guests were standing with their heads outside of their doors two floors up, and hotel security stood around as if they could make an arrest themselves.

Khadijah was so embarrassed but thankful to God she didn't know any of the eyewitness news imitators. She concentrated on the transparent elevator as it climbed to the third floor. Everyone could see Irving's finest aboard. When the police officers arrived, their first command was to better the situation and make everyone who had no need to be there disappear.

Officer Bartlett started. "The show is over. You can go back to what you were doing." She was a short and stocky officer. It was a strong probability that she could be a dyke, but who knew. Who cared? Maybe her cocky posture and husky voice derived from the lessons of the police academy.

Officer Hernandez picked up where his partner left off. "Necesito a todo el mundo, que se vallan por favor." That was for the Hispanic speaking people who claimed they no speak-ay English.

Khadijah was rattled when the offers arrived. Her face was puffy and slightly discolored, her mascara had run down her face, and her hair looked like a bird had jumped in it and built a home. The unplanned drama had pretty much worn Khadijah out.

"Hello ma'am. I'm Officer Bartlett. Can you tell me what happened tonight?"

The scenario had all the remnants of domestic violence, but routine questioning was mandatory. Khadijah's drab and frustrated tone was evidence she wanted the questioning process to be quick. "Well, let's see. My husband is drunk and behaving like a foolish ass."

"Okay, but I need you to be more specific on what occurred." Bartlett wasn't going for the acting a drunken fool excuse tonight. It was crystal-clear he was being more than just a fool.

"Yes officer. The bottom line is, I came in, he was drunk, I wasn't participating in his argument, and so he slapped me a couple of times."

Again with the routine questioning. "So do you need medical attention?"

"No. It's not that bad. All I need to do is get an ice pack on it and get some rest."

Meanwhile, after getting a statement from the security guard, Officer Hernandez knocked on the suites door to speak with Chris. "Chris, my name is Officer Hernandez. I'm with the Irving Police

Department. I need for you to open the door so we can talk!" Holding his baton in one hand and his other hand resting on the holster, the officer waited for the door to unlock and open.

"Okay." When the door finally opened Chris looked deranged. When he saw Khadijah with Officer Bartlett he got a bad case of punk-a-sitis. He cried and pleaded hoping for some mercy. "What are you doin'? Dij, I love you, baby." Pointing to the peacekeepers, "Why you get them involved?" Chris started to push past Hernandez when both officers grabbed him and pushed him down to the floor.

"Chris, we need you to calm down. We're here to help, but you have to settle down." Bringing Chris' arms behind his back and holding his head to the floor, they cuffed his wrists.

Shouting at the officers, Chris tried to move but couldn't. "I am calm! You're hurting me! Ahhh!"

Shaking his head, Hernandez attempted to calm Chris once more. "Chris, you need to settle down before we have to arrest you."

"Okay. Okay." Pleading to Khadijah again. "Honey, tell them this is a big mistake. Tell them."

Hernandez and Bartlett helped Chris off the floor and onto his feet. He was still drunk and staggering, so they helped him onto the sofa.

Khadijah was no longer nervous or frightened, she'd become very angry. "Officer, please shut the door. I really don't want to look at him." Officer Bartlett shut the door and spoke with Khadijah in the hall outside of the suite.

"Officer Bartlett, I want him arrested. He attacked me when I came in. You can ask the security officer what he witnessed when he entered the room. Actually, you can ask him why he felt he had to enter my room and call for reinforcement."

"Ma'am, we've gotten a statement from him. Are you sure you

want to press charges?"

"What do you mean, am I sure? Yes, I'm quite sure. Do you not see my face?" Beginning to get agitated with the officer. "Listen, I know you guys must see a lot of domestic calls and find the woman beat up, and they decide they don't want to arrest the man, but I ain't one of them. I want him arrested."

"Okay. The charge will be assault. You're going to have to give a statement. Do you know where the station is?"

"No, I don't, but I can follow you down there if necessary."

"Well, that's up to you. If you'd like, you can come down in the morning and give your statement. Either way, he's coming with us and spending the night at the station."

"Okay. I'll do that then. Thank you."

Officer Bartlett knocked on the door to inform Officer Hernandez of the decision to arrest Chris. Khadijah moved aside so they could pass.

Barely able to stand, Chris screeched, "Khadijah, I can't believe you're doing this. After everything I do for you. If you do this, I swear I'm filing for divorce." Those words were music to her ears.

"Good. If you don't, I am." Khadijah turned away to apologize to the hotel staff before going into her room. She sat on the bed crying a river of tears thinking about the things happening in her life. Peace of mind began to consume her as the emptiness began to fade away. Reality was staring her in the face, and she no longer had to be away from the one person's love she deserved. A smile overcame Khadijah when she began dialing Austin's number.

Sniffling between words, she tried to focus on the happiness she found with Austin. As she poured out the words that confirmed how much she cherished their love, tears of joy were flowing. Khadijah hadn't determined how she would tell Austin about the altercation with Chris. What mattered most to her was Austin knowing how much she loved him. When he tried to interject, she stopped him. "Baby, please let me finish. Bay, Chris and I had an awful fight and…"

"Bay, stop. Where are you? I'll be there as fast as I can."

"No. I can drive. How do I get to you from Beltline Road in Irving?"

Trying to make sense of what was being said, Austin silenced the back and forth suggestions by adding words with authority. "Listen, you are in no condition to drive, especially not knowing your way around town. Just sit there and wait for me."

Her voice started crackling as she tried to insist. "Baby, please let me do this. I don't want to wait here another minute. Please baby give me directions. Please."

"Alright Dij. This is what I want you to do. Meet me at the café. At least I know you can get there without getting lost. I'm about twenty minutes away. Just sit in your car until I get to you. And make sure you lock your car doors. Oh, and sit as close to the street lamps as you can. Dij, everything is gonna be okay. I promise you that. I love you."

"Okay. I love you, too. I'll see you in a few minutes."

Austin had been waiting at the café for five minutes. He tried calling Khadijah on her cellular, but she wouldn't answer.

After circling the parking lot, Austin noticed Khadijah's car down the street pulling out of the gas station. Austin was relieved to see her. He parked and rested on the hood of his car until she got there.

When Khadijah exited her car, Austin could see the fear in her eyes. Austin went to Khadijah and wrapped his arms around her not saying a word. She began crying quietly and held onto him. Her pain was deep, and he could feel it as her body trembled in his embrace. He could see beyond her pain and wanted her to understand they were drifting together into a life of eternal happiness. He pulled away from Khadijah and raised her head up and whispered the gentle words, "Everything's gonna be fine."

Khadijah nodded her head up and down, wiped her face with the back of her hand and smiled when she released the nightmare from her head.

"That's my girl. Give your man another smile." Austin hugged her once more. "Do you wanna ride with me and leave your car here tonight?"

"I have my luggage in the trunk. I don't think it will fit in your car."

Austin loved how Khadijah considered him and what would be best for him before considering herself. "Well then, I'll leave my car and ride in yours."

"We can't leave your car here. Baby, I'll be okay to drive. I'll follow you."

"Bay, it's a car. It can be replaced. I need to know you're okay."

Khadijah's heart was melting as she listened to how much Austin cared. It had been so long since she felt such compassion. "I'm all right now that I'm with you. I'm gonna follow you home."

Austin kissed Khadijah before they got into their cars and drove to his house. When they settled in and talked for a few minutes, they agreed they would go into the details of the incident in the morning. It was late, and they were both exhausted.

16

$\mathcal{I}$t was a beautiful early Tuesday morning; Jamale was reading a few scriptures while Cee-Cee was in the shower singing her favorite song. She didn't care that she was out of tune, her day was going to be as perfect as perfect could be. Jamale paused for a moment imagining a lifetime with the woman in the shower and was elated knowing Cee-Cee was included in his future. He laughed at her singing before he began making some very important phone calls.

The phone had rung three or four times before Peter answered the phone, "Yeah. Hello."

"Hey man, this is Jamale. Your crazy brother up?"

"Yeah. He's down in the kitchen handling his business."

"Oh really? What does she look like?"

At the moment, Cee-Cee was the only woman who wasn't included as "business" to the other men and Peter knew he needed to set the record straight regarding Khadijah. "She's sweet, man. She's one of our home girls. It's a trip man, but I'm gonna let Austin tell you everything. I'm getting ready to go downstairs so give me a minute to get him away from his business.

"Business" always made the men laugh. They were like young teenagers at times, however, Jamale was on his way to becoming a fully fledged man. Jamale asked Peter to set the receiver on speakerphone because he needed to talk with both of them.

"Man, the speakerphone isn't working too clear. I'll just tell him to pick up the other line."

"Bet."

While Jamale was waiting, Cee-Cee was coming out of the bathroom. She was wearing his Greek robe and a towel wrapped around her hair. Jamale looked at her in amazement, admiring how beautiful she was and called her over to sit next to him on the bed.

"Hey man, what's up?" Austin spoke first.

"Peter, you on the line too?"

"Yeah man, I'm here."

"Kewl. Hold on a few minutes, I wanna get Adrian on the other line too."

By now, the gentlemen's curiosity has been peaked, and Peter gave Austin a what the heck is going on look before he spoke.

"Aiight. Is everything okay?"

Jamale chuckled and told the guys to hold on before switching over to the other line. Finally Adrian was connected, and Jamale began his spiel. "All ya'll there?" They each answered and then exchanged their hello's.

"Here's the deal. I need each of you to be available tomorrow night. I don't care what you brotha's got planned, cancel it. And, as difficult as this may be for one or two of you, I need you to find a lady who can do some last minute miracles and be ready to put on a gown and be beautiful."

Peter spoke up first. "You must be talkin' 'bout the other two brothers on the line, 'cause I know as well as you know, I won't have any problem getting a woman to present a miracle."

Austin added, "Dawg, I got the finest woman sitting in front of me as we speak."

Adrian was very confident when he added, "I'm not even gonna entertain the conversation. When you see what I have to offer, you both will be rethinking what you're saying. Jamale, what's up with tomorrow evening?"

"Here it is. I asked Cee-Cee to marry me, and tomorrow evening I'm gonna make this beautiful woman with whom I love, my wife."

There was a brief silence, but each of them chimed in on how happy they were. They started repeating some adage about their boy getting married.

Adrian interrupted the men and all of their expert advice on marriage and asked, "Broah, why do we have to have a lady?"

"Cee asked for your help. She really doesn't have any friends, and you know she doesn't have any family to include. What's the problem man, you need some help from Peter to find you a lady?"

"Sheeit. When you see the female that's gonna be on my arm, y'all gonna be asking me for all kinds of help."

"Yeah, believe what you must. But on the serious, y'all my broahs, you know I gots to have you standing beside me. You know, just in case I decided to run for the door, one of y'all could stop me." Cee-Cee looked at him and jokingly put up her fist as if she would knock him out. All the fellas laughed because they knew that was hardly going to happen. Jamale loved Cee-Cee.

Jamale explained that Marquis would be his best man. Only because of his job keeping him away, he spends the least amount of time with them. Neither of the men had a problem with the decision. The guys were excited for Jamale. They each agreed that they would get their tuxedos and look good as hell as soon as Jamale told them the time of the wedding. Cee-Cee nudged Jamale, "Bay, have the guys have their ladies over to Sherrie's Bridal at two o'clock if possible. Also, the women need to be over to Yolanda's shop at ten tomorrow morning so she can style our

186

hair."

Jamale smiled at Cee-Cee as she prepared for their wedding. She was gleaming with excitement. When she noticed Jamale smiling, she became silly and licked her tongue out at him. "Give me that phone." Cee-Cee made her requests to the fellas and thanked them as they congratulated her.

Jamale was very proud of his woman. He couldn't help the smile that escaped. Cee-Cee loved when Jamale smiled at her for no apparent reason. Suddenly she had the urge to taunt him with her sexuality. She removed his robe and began caressing his body when the doorbell rang. Jamale gestured for Cee-Cee to go downstairs to see who it was while he finished his conversation with the fellas.

Quickly Cee was shouting for Jamale. "Jamale! Baby, come here quick!"

Jamale hurried off the phone and shouted as he ran down the stairs. "What's wrong!?"

Cee-Cee pointed down at the sidewalk in front of the house. In red paint were the words, "FUCK YOU."

"What the hell? I don't know whose being so childish, but I know if I ever find out, I'm going to have their ass locked up. Damn! How am I going to get that bright red paint off the sidewalk before the neighbors see it?" Jamale turned to kiss Cee-Cee on the forehead before speaking. "Baby, let me make some phone calls. This is not how you are going to start your new life in your new home. I'll take care of it."

Over Seasoned

Peter and Austin laughed for a minute until they looked over at Khadijah. Peter walked over to her and gave her a hug. "You know you're like my sis'. If you ever need anything, you'd better come talk to me." Peter kissed her and signaled over to Austin to comfort her.

Khadijah's once sexy slanted eyes were no longer sexy. Fortunately, the swelling and discoloration on her jaw wasn't that bad. Had it been, Austin's anger wouldn't have been so easily contained. Each time he imagined Chris hitting Khadijah, rage would consume him. But he knew, for Khadijah's sake, he had to mask it.

"Hey beautiful. Come over here and give me some of them luscious lips of yours." Austin extended his arms until she was resting comfortably next to him. He hated seeing her look so sad. All he wanted to do was make her feel better. Austin began explaining the wedding situation and asked if she would do him the honor and walk down the aisle with him.

"Bay, I'm not sure I'll be up to it." Khadijah's eyes were puffy from crying. She was almost embarrassed to look at him.

"Baby, look at me." Cupping her face with his hands and gazing into her eyes. "You are beautiful, and everything is going to be fine. I want you walking down that aisle beside me. Consider this practice for when you are marching in our wedding."

Khadijah smiled and rested in his arms with both eyes closed.

Peter pretended not to be listening, but he couldn't help smiling thinking about his brother and Khadijah jumping the broom. Peter thought about asking Ms. Kasey to do him the honors at Jamale's and Cee's wedding, but knew that it wasn't enough time in a day to make that happen. Instead, he considered the many other options he had.

Suddenly the phone rang. Austin reached for the phone and was thrown by the man's voice. "Listen here Nigger. I'm not playing with you about my money. If I don't have it today, you won't live to see tomorrow." The caller hung up.

Austin's stone face expression had Peter concerned. Peter never considered the caller to be Franco. Peter had never given Franco his home number.

"Yo man, whassup?" Peter stared at Austin with a very concerned look, assuming something may have happened to one of their frat brothers.

"Dij, can I have some privacy with my brother?"Austin gave her a kiss and walked out of the kitchen. Peter followed him not saying a word.

Austin shut the door behind Peter. He looked down at the floor for a moment, and when he raised his head, he gave Peter a cold stare. "Man, whassup? Talk to me."

Questioning Austin with sarcasm, he asked, "Whassup? Man you tell me what's up? Man, I don't know what you're talking about. Who was that on the phone?"

Austin was very disappointed and angry with Peter, but he had too much respect for his brother to disrespect him. "I don't know who it was. But he sure had no problem threatening to kill the nigger if he didn't have his money by today."

Peter's feet were planted deeply into the carpet, almost paralyzed. The last thing he wanted was for his brother to know he had gotten into debt gambling. Peter was in control of his hobby; so he thought. He never dreamed his gambling would become an addiction, let alone a threat to his life. His problem had found its' way into his home, and although he didn't feel he owed Austin an explanation, Peter loved and respected his brother and wouldn't do anything to show otherwise.

"Austin, man I am so sorry you had to get that phone call. Man, I'm not even going to lie to you. I got in a little deeper than I could handle. I took a big hit on last night's game. I'm short on his dough until Friday. I was gonna settle up then."

"Broah, you can't avoid those type playas. They will have your ass hemmed up. Man, I'm not even gonna treat you like you're a child and lecture you about what's right and wrong. You know the difference. Man how much you short?"

"About a "G". Austin, again, I'm sorry. I know you got nothin' but love for me. I know I should have gone to you, but more importantly, I'm sorry I allowed myself to get to this point."

"Dawg, you're right. I got nothin' but love for you. Let me go to the bank and get the cash for you. Handle your business." They hugged one another and returned to the kitchen without another word said.

After the threatening phone call, Peter was very cautious when he left the house. He watched cars on his left, his right, in the front and in the rearview mirror more than he ever had. Every car that trailed Peter seemed suspicious, and he was paranoid. When he parked in the garage and entered the atrium of the Towers, Peter was finally able to breathe easily knowing his Mafia wanna-be killer wasn't following him.

There was an echoing hollowness as the rhythmic tap of shoes walked across the large sections of marble. Probably because it was past nine a.m. and most of the people were at their perspective work places. The few people still wandering the lobby were either congregating outside of the small snack shop or looking at the items for sale at the vendor stations preparing to close down shop.

To the left of the revolving door that leads to Pearl Street, stood a man who had taken ownership of that scrupulous spot three months ago. Every week his goal was to make some innocent woman the victim of his pick-up lines. What he actually was guilty of being was a pain in the ass. This particular morning his prey was the woman with the unquestionable double D's as she strolled in. "Ummm, umm, umm. Girl, can I treat you like dinner and suck you like a neck bone?"

The woman didn't take his pick-up line too kindly. She turned around in rage. "What the hell did you say?" She stood so close she could smell his sewerage mouth that had clearly missed toothpaste for decades.

Aww girl, I don't mean no harm. I just couldn't help it. I think you so fine you make onions cry."

"Nigga you need to go somewhere with them tired ass lines. And go wash your ass!" She walked away with her ass up higher in the air than it already was.

The vagrant was flattered by her attention, however negative it was. He stepped forward shouting across the lobby as she rushed away from him. "Don't you know we could make beautiful babies together?" He picked up his dirty Nike bag that sat by his feet and headed out the door. The few people in the lobby laughed at the man as they tried not to be seen by the woman who was getting hit by the insults or questionable compliments. Mr. Michael's, the security guard had just returned to his station and figured by the small talk and laughter from the guys that "Eddie the wino" had struck again. Mr. Michael's attention wasn't on Eddie; it was on the woman whose hips had turned him on daily.

One of the men noticed the other woman entering from the garage and was ready to make his move. "There she is right there." Wiping his tongue across his top lip while he admired her.

"Man you've been trying to get with that forever. She ain't tryin' to holla at you." The other man who appeared to be with him quipped.

"Yeah, but you can't blame a brotha for tryin'. I'll holla at ya later." He gave his boy a look of commitment as he walked away.

The voice of the man calling for Attorney Kasey seemed to echo throughout the building. As Peter exited the snack shop, the first voice didn't catch Peter's attention; it wasn't until Peter heard the response when he turned. There she was, the woman who thought she knew more about him than he wanted her to know. The thought of her knowing the phrase "J.A.P.A.N." was cute, but far from the truth. Yes, he was a Nupe, but he was far from just another.

Peter stood watching and waiting for Karyn Kasey to finish her conversation with the brother who obviously said nothing that interests her. Peter's sly grin grew as his thoughts of Karyn increased. Look at her. She sees me looking at her. Umph, I can only imagine the sexy thong she must have on under that suit. When I do get her, she's gonna regret all the time she wasted tryin' to run game. Peter smiled when he saw that she'd noticed him waiting off to the side. When Peter saw Karyn trying to rush the conversation with Mr. Whomever, he smirked at her subtle brush off and admired her style even more.

Damn his ass is two shots of fine, she thought. Oh, but he can't think it's that easy. Let me throw some of my flavor in his beef stew. A man's game was considered beef stew because its typical ingredients were so predictable. If you tasted one, you've tasted them all.

As she walked towards the elevator, Peter timed his steps to meet with hers. Aww yeah, come a litt'l closer to daddy, he humored himself. He smiled as he walked in front of Karyn and greeted her. She returned the gesture and pardoned herself as she continued to walk around him.

Oh no the hell she didn't, Peter's mind was going as fast as a speeding bullet. Thrown by her action he reacted quickly. "Whoa. Whoa. Hold up. Wait a minute." Rushing to step in front of her to stop her, he continued. "You not gonna be that cold are you? You saw me standing there waiting patiently for your conversation to end. I'm hoping you have at least one minute to finish our conversation you so abruptly ended yesterday." Peter had a look of innocence and was almost pathetic.

The lady had a very sassy look about her. She wore a very short hair cut that complimented her well sculptured face. Her dark chocolate skin was almost like velvet and the bronzed color lipstick she wore made her lips appear fuller than they naturally were. She wore a gray houndstooth tailored power suit with a speck of burgundy in it. Her matching leather attaché case, purse and shoes confirmed that she had it going on. But, it was her fast thinking and, whip the facts on your ass attitude that gave her the bitch of the courts reputation.

Oh, I got his ass now, she thought. She turned in somewhat of a slow motion and reached out to shake Peter's hand. "Hello. My name is Karyn Lynn Kasey." She made sure he saw the three karat diamond bracelet on her arm. "I apologize for not being able to continue this conversation, but I am due in court shortly, and I need to get on my way. So, have a nice day." Karyn started walking away when Peter grabbed hold of the situation.

Not wanting Karyn to know how deeply her words had wounded his ego, he tried to ignore the words that played tricks on his mind. Oh, hell no she didn't. Oh, but yes she did. And although begging was not something Peter would ever consider doing for a woman, he certainly sounded as if he had surrendered to doing just that. Peter whimpered softly, "Don't you have just one minute out of your busy day to spare a brother?"

Karyn smiled and gazed at Peter with her deep dark eyes. She knew he was exactly where she wanted him, which at the moment was him begging just for a little bit of her time. Karyn really didn't have any intentions on making him wait too long, but she knew a brotha as fine as Peter needed to be cooked slowly like a bad piece of meat.

Peter walked with Karyn to her elevator. He didn't care about the odd-even elevator system; he had a few minutes before he had to be on the eleventh floor. Peter was getting a minute of Ms. Kasey's time whether she thought she could spare it or not.

When the elevator arrived, Karyn pushed number fourteen and stood quietly as Peter began. "Now that you can't run from me, and you've introduced yourself, I'd like to have my turn." Peter reached out his hand and smiled. "Hi. I'm Peter James and it's a pleasure to meet you." Pushing his luck, and he knew it, he continued. "Would it be possible for us to meet for lunch this afternoon or perhaps share a victory cocktail after your day at court?" Peter couldn't control his thoughts. Or, if you'd like, we can get busy right on the judge's bench.

Their hand holding continued throughout his introduction. Peter enjoyed her expression of approval when she noticed his well manicured fingernails and the soft texture of his hands. Peter knew he had it going on, and in no time Karyn would be eating out the palms of those very hands.

It was evident she appreciated his coy way of making her time appear to be more valuable than his own, so when she smiled and answered, "Sorry, my dog has an appointment to get her nails manicured," he was thrown off. Karyn wasn't impressed.

Superman was being brought down by Karyn-the-kryptonite. Is this chick comparing my manicured nails to her dog, he wondered. Peter wasn't going to allow Karyn to believe she had it going on so strong that she could insult him. "Well, okay. Maybe we'll both have some free time to spare in the future. We're almost at your floor. I hope you have a nice day and the best in court Attorney Kasey." Peter was no longer up for the challenge. He had had enough of the chasing and figured tomorrow is another day.

The bell chimed when it reached the 14th floor. Ms. Kasey started through the door and suddenly stopped to hand Peter her business card. "You can leave your number with my secretary, and I'll get back with you. Thank you for the wish of luck and you have a nice day as well, Mr. James."

Karyn walked confidently past the receptionist who was watching every move that was going on in front of her. Betsy had seen it more times than enough; men going up and down that elevator behind Attorney Kasey. However, this time seemed slightly different. Not too many men actually got a business card with a smile.

He couldn't believe what had just happened. This was a definite first. Riding the elevator alone, Peter began talking to himself. "Damn she's difficult. I don't even know why I'm bothering with her. There ain't no way in hell she's gonna agree with my rules. But there's something about her, and I gotta know what it is."

Peter's thoughts were interrupted by the vibration of his cell phone. The phone number came up "unavailable" on the screen so Peter didn't bother to answer it, and by the time he reached the lobby floor, his phone beeped to tell him he had a voicemail. Peter listened to the caller and frowned as he pushed the number three to delete the message. This was the third call from Franco and decided not to listen to the two other unheard messages. As Peter got onto the elevator, he remembered where he had seen the dark tinted 300M from the other morning. It was Franco. Is Franco following me? His revelation was chilling. Franco had followed Peter to the Thanksgiving Tower.

Although the Steelers beat the Ravens, they'd only won by three points. They didn't cover the point spread, and Peter was out of five thousand dollars. Thank God the thousand dollars Austin gave him and the four thousand he had in his checking and savings accounts would be enough to settle his debt. He was relieved to have the money and had every intention to pay Franco at lunch. Peter was tired of feeling threatened. He listened to his voice messages again and grimaced. Two more messages. The messages he left were very clear and precise. "GET ME MY MONEY TODAY OR YOUR ASS IS FUCKED."

Peter was sure Franco the psycho wasn't joking, and the last thing Peter needed was to have some out-of-control White boy on his ass. He thought to call Franco as soon as he got to his office; however, there was a system problem in the office that had him preoccupied most of the morning.

17

 $\mathcal{W}$ hen Cee-Cee arrived home, her answering machine displayed seven messages. Cee-Cee was happy to hear her mothers' voice saying she had gotten Jamale's call about the wedding. Her mom sounded so happy and that made Cee-Cee proud.

The second, third and fourth messages weren't as pleasant. Three messages were from her ex-husband Jeff threatening to pay her a visit in the near future; each of the calls warning her not to take him lightly. On each account, Cee-Cee pressed the key that deleted unwanted messages.

Message number four was different. The sound in his voice was harsh and deadly. His warning had conviction. The terrifying sound of conviction Cee-Cee remembered hearing during each of the blows she took from his punches. "You apparently didn't understand my warnings. Nikkia don't think I'm playing with you! Jaylen is MY SON and no one will replace me! I don't give a damn what them damn divorce papers say. Remember, "Until Death Do We Part!""

Cee-Cee slid down the wall and sat on the floor in tears. She couldn't believe this was happening. After all the years apart, Jeff was trying to hold his threat that he wouldn't let her be happy with another man. She hadn't lived the Jeff nightmare for years and swore she wouldn't relive it. She was pissed that he could think calling and upsetting her home with his threats would be acceptable.

The telephone had rung three times before she got the nerve to answer it. "Listen here Jeff, you can't control my life. You need…" Before she could finish, she heard Jamale's voice.

"Baby! Bay! It's me. What's going on?"

"Bay, Jeff has called here leaving me threatening messages on the answering machine." She started crying.

"Baby please stop crying. What did he say?"

Sniffling between words, Cee-Cee attempted explaining. "He said Jaylen is his son and no one will replace him. And he said…" pausing, she remembered the Polo cologne smelling panties at Jamale's front door. She began panicking, raising her voice a few notches as she shared her breakthrough. "…Baby, the panties in the bag, I didn't tell you this, but, they had the Polo cologne that Jeff used to wear. Oh my God."

"Baby, calm down. That doesn't mean it's him. Back in the day, Polo was the cologne men wore when they thought they were a playa. Any one of the crazy women from my past could have put them there." Jamale interjected a chuckle trying to relax Cee-Cee and the situation. He wasn't worried about Jeff or his threats. "Listen, I don't want you to be home worried. You have too much to take care of today. Aren't you planning on being a beautiful bride tomorrow?" Trying to lighten up the mood.

Cee-Cee caught the hint and started smiling. "Yes I am. Thanks Baby."

"Hey, I love you. I got a few things I have to take care of, but I'll keep my cell on just in case you need to reach me."

"Okay, I'll see you later." Without warning she had a revelation."Wait a minute. I won't see you until the wedding. It's bad luck to see the bride the night before the wedding."

"Girl, you and all of your superstitions. All right, I'll see you tomorrow. Love ya!"

Cee-Cee turned the ringer off at home and turned on her cell phone. She figured if someone of any importance needed to reach her, they would know to reach her on it. She hurried to change clothes. It was close to the time to meet the women at Sherrie's.

Seasonal

Walking through the airport with her stiletto heels and hip hugger jeans, Alyssa caught the eyes of most the people she passed. She had an hour glass figure, and the jeans she wore showed just that.

Waiting at terminal B, gate 9, Alyssa waited for the ticket handler to make the announcement to prepare for boarding. Glancing at her watch, Alyssa appreciated she had twenty more minutes before departure and thought she had time to call the hotel to let Marquis know she would have to have a rain check on their date. When the voicemail came on, she left a message telling him she would be in Dallas a few days and maybe would be able to spend some time with him when he returned home.

Meanwhile, at the hotel in Houston where the conference was being held the announcement that the veterans could leave the conference early sent the room in an explosion of claps. Marquis began to gather his things, pulled his chair from the desk, and waited for the release.

Andrew and Chad tried holding a discussion outside of the conference room, but Marquis wasn't having it. He politely dismissed them and headed towards the elevator.

Marquis inserted the key to open the door to his room and immediately noticed the flashing light on the phone and made checking the messages his priority.

He sat back onto the bed and let out a laugh as he listened to the first message. "Marquis, you need to get your short ass back to Dallas tonight so you could be here for my bachelor party. I know you're trippin' right about now, but hey man, it's time. Cee and I are getting married tomorrow. I don't know how you're gonna pull it off, but you need to be here. You're gonna be my best man. Oh, by the way, that wasn't a request. It was an order. See you tonight." Marquis rested his head on the pillow and shook his head as the message ended and then went onto the next.

"Hey Marquis, this is Alyssa. I'm sorry I have to cancel. I hope you'll understand and accept a rain check. I will be in Dallas for a couple of days, so I thought we could have an evening together there. My cell number is 713-555-1629. I look forward to hearing from you. Bye."

Things could not have been more perfect. He didn't want to miss the opportunity to spend time with Alyssa, so her being in Dallas was great.

The next flight to Dallas left in two hours. That gave Marquis just enough time to pack, return the rental car and go through the massive airport security.

In Season

When Peter finally had a free moment and enough nerve, he decided to call Karyn and leave his number with her secretary. In the back of his mind, he knew Karyn was too much of a hard ass to allow her secretary to put the call through so he was prepared for the let down and good thing because he was right. After listening to the cool jazz that played during his holding period, the friendly voice returned. She was very polite when she asked if he would leave a number where he could be reached. For a moment, Peter contemplated saying no, but then he thought if he didn't, he would never be given another chance. The receptionist could feel his apprehension and Peter could imagine the smile on her face as she thought about how pathetic he must have looked earlier in the elevator as he so graciously took Karyn's business card. Nevertheless, he spouted out the number and wished her a good day.

Peter sat at his cubicle gazing into the monitor at the verbiage that only a geek with his knowledge could understand. His perplexed look caught the attention of the woman who approached his area, but Peter ignored her standing behind him. He knew exactly whom she was and had made the determination on his first day on the job that he wouldn't "do her" with his worst enemies dick. She reeked of cheap perfume covering up what appeared to be a lack of deodorant. She was disgusting and was the talk of the eleventh floor. Actually the talk may have perpetuated throughout the building.

As Peter's head began to swarm from her pungency, he sighed unusually loud hoping the woman would catch his drift, but it wasn't until his cell phone rang that she walked away. Peter didn't care to look at the caller ID, he was just happy for the unexpected interruption.

"This is Peter." That was his professional way of answering his calls.

"Hello. This is Ms. Kasey." Her voice sounded fixed and confusingly sexy.

Sitting back on the navy blue swivel chair, Peter tried not to be overly anxious. He tried to relax before he spoke, but how could he. He was in a cubicle with women on both sides of him and he was sure they would be listening to his every word. He opted for the more professional approach. "Hello Ms. Kasey. Glad you returned my call."

"I'm glad you called and left your number. I had hoped you would." Peter was stunned that Karyn was being polite. He thought his imagination was playing tricks on him when he heard sexiness in her voice, so he ousted the thought. But polite? He couldn't mistake that.

Reducing almost to a whisper, he continued. "You gave me such a hard time, I didn't know if I should. But I'm happy I did."

"Well Mr. James, I know a good thing when I see it. I just wanted you to know that sometimes I have so much on my plate that I can be a ....let's just say I can be difficult."

"Ms. Kasey, do we always have to be so formal? Personally, I prefer being called Peter."

Chuckling at Peter and imagining how sexy he must look trying to ease the formalities. "Let me start over. Hi Peter, this is Karyn. Is that better?"

"Much." If nothing else, Peter had a good understanding of women. He learned a long time ago if a woman is resistant of her own tenderness, don't add fuel to her fire by throwing it in her face. Peter wasn't going to be guilty of taunting her because she'd broken her own rule. Instead, he would help her along by telling her without actually saying the words how appreciated she was. Besides, he already knew she could be a ...well, let's just say, difficult. "This is a very pleasant surprise. I imagined how busy your days are and thought maybe to call you on the weekend, but I couldn't seem to get you off of my mind. So I took the chance."

"Well thanks. I'm happy for the chance. And you're right, my days are busy, but I was wondering if tomorrow afternoon would be a good time to get together?"

Peter's tense muscles were being soothed by Karyn's words, and she didn't even know it. For that matter, Peter didn't know his body was stressed by the stressful issues weighing down on him. The stress behind Franco's threats and the large amount of money he'd lost on the football bet. But now, the woman whom he'd been admiring and trying to give him an inch so he could take a yard was finally cooperating.

Peter didn't know what it was exactly that he'd done to get Karyn to make her next move, and frankly he didn't care. Karyn was doing the asking of Peter's time, and soon. Not like most women who try to play the make him wait game. She was asking to spend time the next day.

"Tomorrow afternoon? Ooh, well, truthfully tomorrow afternoon I've got definite plans. However, if you really want to spend some time with me tomorrow, I can make it happen. But there's a condition."

It caught Karyn by surprise that there would be a condition she'd have to accept before she could spend time with him. She didn't like it one bit and reverted back to her difficult self and responded with agitation in her voice. "A condition? What kind of condition? In fact, maybe this wasn't a very good idea after all. I'll give you a call another time."

Peter felt like he was in the seventh inning, tied score of the final game of the World Series. He had just gone from three balls and no strikes with bases loaded to strike two and two outs in a matter of seconds. He sat up in his chair, and he didn't give a damn about his nosy coworkers to his left or right. Brotha was begging. Desperately suppressing his shout, he called for her. "Karyn. Karyn. Karyn. Wait a minute. Don't hang up. Let me explain." He went through the entire spiel about the circumstances of the wedding and was floored by Karyn's next question.

"So what time do I need to meet the other women?"

"Did I hear you correctly?"

"Should I ask again?"

Clearing his throat, he answered, "No. Uh, they're meeting at the bridal shop at two today. Would it be possible for you to meet them?"

"I'll have to rearrange a few things, but I can be there. Let me grab a pen for all of the information."

When the call ended, Peter didn't care the rumormonger on his left had put her pen down and turned her radio down to listen in on Peter's conversation. Peter had hit a grand slam home run.

Extra Seasoning

The bold and shiny lavender taxi cab pulled away from the airport curb towards the exiting tollgate, driving down what Doris thought to be a lifeless interstate. She studied her surroundings thinking how different Dallas appeared compared to Houston. She couldn't believe all of the undeveloped land. Actually, she imagined there once being tumbleweed turning and blowing across the fields of grass and little Laura Ingles running to Ma and Pa in their two room cabin. It all looked so, "Little House on the Prairie."

The driver appeared to be in his thirties in age and Doris could see him admiring her pretty face through his rearview mirror. She recognized his sunken eyes and dark features that were very characteristic of people from Africa, but had no idea what part. Doris tried to guess, but she was no expert on the continent and its people.

"So handsome, where are you from? She thought she would try her luck.

"Somalia." He announced with great pride.

"Oh, okay. I wanna go there someday." Lying through her teeth and he knew it. He responded with a grunt and a smile.

"So, how long have you been in America?" Speaking slower and louder as if not only a foreigner, but a deaf and dumb foreigner. Doris really didn't care. She figured if she could finesse a man to give up their hard earned money to look at her developed tits and firm ass, certainly she could con an African cab driver who would love to get some fine Black American coochie.

"Eight year." He spoke clearly but still with bad grammar.

"Okay. And do you own this cab or are you working for a

company?"

"It tis my caab."

Good. Good, she thought. "So how far is the hotel from here and how much are you gonna charge me, handsome?"

"It tis 'bout twentee mile. But for you, beautiful lady, I only charge you forty dollar." He had learned a long time ago about American woman and their way of trying their luck. He may have been from another country, but he certainly wasn't ignorant. He knew the signs of an American woman flirting for a deal. And, as for fine Black American ass, it couldn't compare to the fine green American dollar.

Doris watched her driver as he eyed her through the mirror. She didn't want him to see how he had just slapped her in the face with his words. Instead, she watched through the window as she got closer into a less lifeless Dallas.

As they pulled up to the red carpeted entrance to the Westin hotel, Doris thought she'd try her luck once more. But she quickly learned the African brother wasn't down with any discounts.

When she exited the cab, she expected the valet attendants to stop what they were doing to carry her bags into the hotel. Concierge must have been an unfamiliar word to her. It was evident Doris hadn't centered herself on the finer things in life and didn't know how to fake the funk either.

Doris was truly impressed with the fact her sister was staying in such an exquisite hotel. But she was more impressed with herself that she had the skills to sucker her way into the lavish world attached to the Galleria.

Doris had a brainstorm of an idea and grinned with deception as she walked towards the front desk. "Hi, I'm in room 716. Chanel Rayson. I walked out this morning and left my key in the room. Would it be possible to get a replacement?"

The clerk had seen Chanel yesterday when she arrived and assumed the woman standing in front of him today was that same woman. He didn't think twice before giving Doris the key. Doris thought this would be the perfect surprise for her sister.

When she walked into the suite, she couldn't believe her sister was living so large and began to feel a bit envious. She couldn't imagine what the record company was spending on Chanel, but at the moment, she was going to enjoy every nickel of it.

Doris turned the radio on in the living room before going into the bedroom. She shut the door, took a couple of things out of her suitcase and got into the shower. "Shit. If I'm gonna pretend to be her, I'd just as well live like her. I love the way those water massagers feel."

Meanwhile, with Chanel out with the girls, Adrian thought this would be the perfect time to leave flowers in her room as an apology for last night.

Enjoying the water massaging her back, Doris didn't hear Adrian enter the living room of the suite, and because of the radio playing he didn't hear the water running in the shower or when the bathroom door opened.

Adrian placed the vase onto the coffee table so that Chanel would see the flowers as soon as she entered the room. Before getting dressed, Doris opened the bedroom door to get her purse out of the sitting room and was shocked when she saw the handsome man standing there. He was more shocked when he saw who he thought to be Chanel standing there with no clothes on.

Taking a wild guess that he was Adrian, Doris began performing. "Oh my goodness." Trying to cover herself and then hiding behind the bedroom door. Doris' mind was going a mile a minute. "Adrian, what are you doing here?" Her thoughts still running fast. Damn that Nigga is fine.

"I am so sorry. I though you would have been with Jasmine. I had no idea…"

Cutting him off, Doris shut the door and shouted through it, "Hold on. Let me get some clothes on, and I'll be right out." Doris reached for the pink silk robe with the tiny floral print. As she started for the door, she had a second thought. This was an opportunity she wasn't going to let pass. She sprayed the after bath oil onto her body and massaged it into her skin before putting on the robe. Before leaving the bedroom, she tried to relax Adrian with her apology. "Hey I'm sorry if I surprised you. I didn't know you were out there." But in her mind she knew she had just passed go and was about to collect two hundred dollars.

As Doris was turning the door knob, Adrian was turning away from her. He was embarrassed. When she stepped out, and he turned around Adrian was totally taken aback as Doris came out in a short bathrobe. It wasn't until she got closer to Adrian and spoke that really made him uneasy. "Now, what were you saying?"

Hell, being a man and all, what was he suppose to do? A beautiful woman who had occupied his thoughts the last couple of days standing in front of him half naked. He did what any man who was nervous would do, he stammered. "I…I am so, so sorry. I was just coming over to deliver these flowers. I had no idea…" And then he noticed that she wasn't showing any form of anger, embarrassment or nervousness. Adrian relaxed a bit and continued. "I didn't get much rest thinking about last night. I hope you're really okay with what happened."

"Do I look like I'm bothered? In fact…" Unsure of what happened last night, Doris reacted. She stopped her statement and reached up for his face bringing it close to hers and began kissing him. He was puzzled, but hell, he wasn't any fool. He followed his gut and went with his natural instincts. He put his arms around Doris bringing her closer to him and returned the kiss.

The kiss was very passionate, and their bodies were very close. The silky belt to her robe that was half tied loosened and Doris' body was exposed. Adrian looked down at her body and saw how beautiful she was and began kissing her neck and then her breast. Doris was sighing in pleasure and wanted more.

"Chanel, what are we doing?" When he came to grips with what was about to happen, Adrian stopped and took her by the hands and told her he wasn't going to do this. He explained how much he respected her decision last night, not to allow anything to get in the way of her dream and if waiting were something he had to do, he was willing.

Doris was pissed. She couldn't believe what had just happened. Standing in front of her was this picture perfect, fine man, with a hard dick and she wanted desperately to be pleased.

"I'm going to leave now." Adrian wasn't thinking clearly. He hadn't even wondered why she wasn't at the bridal shop. The bulge in his pants must have drained every ounce of blood from other parts of his body because Adrian's skin color had turned two shades lighter.

"NO is out of her damn mind." Doris fell back onto the bed, reached between her legs to feel her moisture and with the pillow pushed against her face she began to simulate a crying baby.

The walk to the elevator was long. Adrian turned, looking back at the door imagining the woman who had seductively captivated him. He tormented himself on the elevator ride down with a million "What ifs" rushing through his mind. When Adrian walked through the lobby, he felt all eyes were on him as if he were the dick-on-wheels-traveling-freak-show. After he got into his car, he sat for a while thinking and wondering what had just happened. He would have never imagined Chanel having a rose tattooed on her breast and a naval ring. He tried to relax his thoughts, but he was haunted by the incident, and his question took temporary ownership of his mind. "Damn! What the hell was that all about?"

18

$\mathcal{T}$he tall trees and the many plants around Marquis' loft helped to accentuate the African décor in his third floor loft of the restored old Sears building. The cucumber melon scented candles overlaid the rooms with their aroma, and the crisp sounds of Eric Benet poured from his state-of-the-art stereo system. Marquis' loft was his escape from the all too familiar funky stench of a men's locker room and the loud obscenities that flooded the room from the football players.

As he relaxed on his tiger striped chase, Marquis sipped on his dry Sapphire martini. Marquis hadn't had much time in his home over the last few months; therefore, this was a moment for him to appreciate. Marquis wasn't expecting any phone calls or visitors, and for a brief moment, his intention was to enjoy the serenity of his home and just chill. His only priority was to let his boys know he'd returned to Dallas.

Marquis listened to the phone chime as it reached the second ring. Resting comfortably in his black designer boxer briefs, he figured he'd better answer the call before he found himself getting caught up in the mood and drift off to sleep. Something he had done all too often.

Pleasantly surprised to hear her gentle voice, Marquis sat up to take another sip of his cocktail. The ambiance was perfect, and his mocha chocolate body was ready for the tenderness of a woman.

If Marquis was going to make Alyssa's stay in Dallas memorable he'd have to charm her quickly. "Hello Sweetheart. I'm glad you got my message. I didn't expect to hear from you so soon." Three hours had passed since he left his phone number on her voicemail. Alyssa's eyes widened with doubt, unsure if he were pleased or being sarcastic. She didn't care one way or another after her close encounter with Adrian, Marquis was her only candidate in Dallas, and she needed him. "Well, I didn't want to miss out on the opportunity of spending time again. So I thought I'd better be on my P's and Q's."

Their conversation started with a lot of meaningless exchange, although Marquis was happy to hear Alyssa was in Dallas. After Marquis' long couple of days in Houston, he welcomed her invitation to spend time together. He had a few hours to kill before meeting with the fellas, and he didn't have anything else planned. A few hours with Alyssa would be perfect. At the moment, however, his thoughts were occupied with her sexy body moving across the stage at Club Ladies & Gentlemen.

Marquis wasn't paying attention as his mind was on other things. However, when his mind wandered off track, he quickly navigated himself back to the conversation and began to show interest in her family. He knew it usually was a shoe-in ingredient to a successful night. Marquis had played the game many times and was very good at it. "So, tell me about your family. Do you have any brothers or sisters?"

Alyssa was frowning as if each word were painful as she spoke them. "Yes, I have a sister, but we're not very close. I guess we're just different. I let her live her life, and she lets me live mine."

Marquis' next comment was sincere and compassionate and he intended on gaining points with the sensitive man approach. It had been a guaranteed good move to his game of "get the drawz" in the past.

"You really need to get close to your sister, especially if she's the only one you have. Who's the oldest between the two of you?"

Before Alyssa could answer the question, Marquis' phone beeped in another call. It was Austin. "Alyssa, I need you to hold that thought while I answer this call. I'll be right back."

"Whassup fool?" Happy to talk with his boy.

Cynically Austin responded. "Jamale getting married, that's what's up. I called you at the hotel, but they said you checked out this morning. When you get in?"

"Less than an hour ago." Sitting up, Marquis spoke with haste. "Say man, what we gonna get into for him tonight?"

"That's what I was calling you for?"

Thinking about the plans he was making with Alyssa, he paused. "Damn. I got this female on the other line trying to get with me. Hey man, the fellas gotta do something for him."

"Ol' girl gonna have to wait. It's your job to make his last night as a bachelor righteous. You're the best man."

"Sure-you-right." Marquis had a brainstorm that hit him like a bolt of lightning. "I got a hell-of-an-idea. Let me call you back."

"Aiight."

Clicking back to his call, Marquis apologized. "Sweetheart, I am so sorry for keeping you on hold that long." He explained his situation for tonight and asked if it would offend her if she worked the party.

"I don't mind. The only problem is I didn't bring any work clothes with me. I hadn't planned on dancing while here in Dallas." Her devious thoughts began, *unless I was gonna be your freak while here. I'd dance my ass tired.*

Marquis offered to pick Alyssa up and take her shopping in the next hour. He also told her to bring her things; she could spend the night at his place. Alyssa jumped at the chance. It was an opportunity to get stuffed like a goose and she was more than willing.

While the men were planning, the ladies began pulling into the strip mall on Preston Road. Sherrie's Bridal Boutique, although smaller than the discount bridal shop next door, her business didn't suffer in revenue. In fact, the majority of her customers came from her neighborhood due to the poor quality of their assortment.

Sherrie was given a lot of opposition from her family and friends when she first proposed opening at that location, but Sherrie never second guessed her decision. She understood it would be to her advantage to have quality opposed to quantity.

Chanel, Jasmine, Khadijah and Karyn were excited as they introduced themselves in the parking lot. Seemingly, the women guessed they were the mystery ladies of the LeTreau wedding party and each lady shook hands after exchanging salutations.

Karyn began with the ice breaker. "Well, I'm a last minute date. I'm Peter's date." She started laughing, and the other ladies joined in. "What about you ladies?" Focusing on Chanel and Jasmine.

Jasmine responded with a confused look. "No. No. I'm not in the wedding. I guess I would be considered Chanel's driver."

Chanel chimed in. "Don't put it like that. I'm visiting Dallas on business and don't know my way around. I'm Chanel. I guess I'm Adrian's date." She liked the thought of being anything other than a client of Adrian's. Jasmine, on the other hand, stale expression showed that she didn't like the thought at all.

"Well, I'm Khadijah, and I belong to Austin." She placed her claim with conviction.

"I hear you gerl. Claim your man." Karyn said with sista gerl attitude. All of the ladies laughed as they headed toward the boutique.

Cee-Cee stood in the door watching the ladies as they bonded. She questioned why there were four ladies, but knew there had to be an explanation. Cee-Cee smiled and reached her hand to greet them one at a time.

"Hi. Cee-Cee Peterson."

Shaking her hand and walking past. "Hi. Karyn Kasey. Peter's date."

"Hi. Cee-Cee Peterson."

"Hi. Chanel Rayson. Adrian's date."

"Hi. Cee-Cee Peterson."

"Hi. Khadijah Hannah. Austin's woman." Stating with more attitude than the first time and looking at the ladies and smiling.

"O-kay." Cee-Cee laughed with the ladies as she reached to shake with the final woman.

By now Cee-Cee was sure the next woman was the fourth wheel because all of the men were accounted for. "Hello. Cee-Cee Peterson."

"Hello. Jasmine Ponde'le. The driver." Again the ladies laughed. The ice was broken, and the ladies were a good fit. It wasn't very often you could get a group of beautiful women together and not have some kind of drama. This was definitely different, and Sherrie stood to admire it.

"I just want to thank each of you for doing this for me. Yolanda, my matron of honor couldn't be here, but she'll meet you guys tomorrow. She's going to do your hair and make-up before the wedding." Cee-Cee tried to stay calm, but she couldn't help herself. The moment Sherrie called them over to select gowns she got silly.

"I'm gettin' married. I'm gettin' married to the finest, sexiest and most wonderful man in the world. Ahhh." She was doing a strut through the aisles of the boutique, and the ladies applauded her as she finished.

"All-righty then." Sherrie added smiling at her sista as she called them over to the bridesmaid's dresses.

The ladies thumbed through hangers of beautiful gowns while Cee-Cee pulled out a few to look closer at. But none of them had that special zing she knew she wanted. Sherrie watched the ladies knowing there wasn't any time for indecisiveness. Instinctively she stepped up and did what she had done too often. She helped the bride with her decision.

"Cee-Cee, it is going to be cream gowns with a single red rose, correct?"

The light bulb turned on above Cee-Cee's head, and Sherrie knew it. "Yes. That's it."

Sherrie pulled from behind the door the most spectacular gown that would look beautiful on each of the ladies. They were beautiful, and when they tried the gowns on, there was no doubt their "dates" would love it too.

"HEEYY!" Yolanda came through the door with a ton of excitement. "Yolanda's in da howz."

Yolanda's entrance gave the ladies a second dose of excitement that really wasn't necessary, but certainly welcomed. They went through the formalities when suddenly Yolanda turned up her nose and jokingly added, "All them educated women in their beautiful gowns...I know mine gonna be more flyy though. The matron of honors dress is supposed to be different."

Sherrie chimed in and rescued Yolanda immediately. "Gerl, you can be different. I'll add some beads and rhinestones to the nape of the dress so you can be different. Okaaaay?"

"Okay, gerl." Giving Sherrie light taps on her shoulder as she agreed.

Sherrie walked away towards her office in the back of the store smiling and shaking her head. When she returned, she had a stunning gown that required two hangers; one for the gown and the other for the long detachable train. The ladies all froze in place when they saw how elegant the gown looked while on the hanger. Judging how Cee-Cee marveled at the gown, the ladies would soon see how beautiful the dress would be on a soon to be bride.

Cee-Cee stood in disbelief. The gown Sherrie had picked out was so perfect. She had to ask. "Sherrie, how did you do it? How did you pick out the perfect gown for me?"

"Your Fiancée gave me your physical description and defined your character. He also made me promise to make you the most beautiful bride ever."

In unison, the ladies let out a harmonious "aww." Each of the ladies was captivated by the excitement in preparing for the wedding and Cee-Cee was glowing when she followed Sherrie into the bride's private fitting room.

Suddenly a cell phone rang, and each of the ladies reached for their purses. But it was Khadijah who gave the "it's for me" look that made the ladies smile in envy.

"Hello."

Austin was happy to hear the laughter in Khadijah's voice when she answered. It was obvious she had put last night's incident aside for a while. He'd thought to bring up the dinner plans with Chris and his boss, but decided it would put a damper on the mood. Instead, he announced his call was to tell her that he loved her and to see how the wedding plans were coming along. They talked for a few minutes when Austin asked if she would meet him outside the boutique in about five minutes. He wanted to drop off the garage remote control so Khadijah could let herself into the house.

"Okay." Interrupted by Cee-Cee's wedding dress debut, Khadijah ended her conversation. "Oh Cee-Cee. You are beautiful. Austin, let me call you back."

The ladies marveled at Cee-Cee. They each wanted to help select the perfect veil and shoes. She was stunning, and the tears in Cee's eyes let everyone know she was happy.

Khadijah looked out of the boutiques window and saw Austin's car pull up to the door. He started towards the shop, but before he could get to the sidewalk, Khadijah had met him outside.

"Hey Bay." She ran into his arms smiling and giving him a kiss.

"Hmmm, that was nice. I would ask for another, but the women in the window may trip."

Khadijah turned around to find the women in the window bobbing their heads up and down and giving her the thumbs up. Austin was trying not to be taken by their gestures, but he couldn't help himself. He bowed down to the ladies and thanked them as if he had just given a grand performance.

"Well I'm not gonna keep you from your fun. I'll see you when I get home." He gave Khadijah a kiss and smiled as he shook his head at the nosy ladies before he got into his car.

Khadijah was stuck on the sounds of him saying he'll see her when he got home. It sounded so official and so good to her that when she walked into the boutique she had a slight glow about her.

"Somebody looks like they're in love." Karyn started. "I didn't know Austin and Peter were brothers or twins for that matter. Girl he is gorgeous."

"No more gorgeous than Peter. But my baby is the shit." Leaning over to get a high-five from Karyn before she continued. "He is perhaps the most wonderful man any woman could ask for. I do love his sexy ass."

"Is he wonderful, gerl?"

"Yep. And let me tell you, Peter is just as wonderful. I don't know how well you know Peter, but you've got yourself a winner."

"Is that right?" Karyn thought about Peter being a winner. To her, a winner was a man who could enjoy one woman at a time. One who would look beyond her accomplishments and shortcomings and one who understood the difference between making her happy and bringing joy into her life. Most men who felt they had accomplished a lot in their lives didn't know the difference.

The LeTreau wedding party was excited. Cee-Cee came out of the dressing room with Sherrie carrying her gown and the ladies headed over to the counter with their dresses prepared to purchase them. Cee-Cee was so happy. Sherrie informed Yolanda that her gown would be ready after five and Yolanda was cool with the arrangement. Everything was smooth as silk. As the excitement started dwindling, Karyn had an idea.

"Ummm, I know you ladies don't think this is the end. Don't you think we should get together tonight for Miss Thang over there?" Pointing over at Cee-Cee. Although it was short noticed, all of the women chimed in on the idea and agreed something needed to be planned.

Smiling and loving the idea, Cee-Cee asked, "You think?" The short notice wedding was beginning to fall in line to a wedding that took months of planning.

Yolanda spoke up instantaneously, "Oh hell yeah. We need to bond before your big day. You can bet the fellas are going to." The ladies gave the, oh hell yeah look and nodded their heads with approval when Khadijah's cellular rang.

"Hi handsome."

"Hey baby. Don't mean to interrupt again. Just wanted to fill you in on some plans for tonight. I talked with a couple of the fellas, and we're gonna get together over to Marquis' for a little bachelor thing for Jamale. It shouldn't be too late."

"Oh, that's fine. The girls just planned a night of movie watching and stuff for tonight." Of course, she was giving the ladies a yeah right, believe that if you must look.

"Okay then, I'll see you tonight. Have fun and don't be getting' no movies that's gonna get you into trouble later."

They both laughed as they disconnected the phone call. Cee-Cee left her purse in the dressing room and excused herself from the room. Once she was out of the area, the other ladies agreed they needed to go shopping for gifts. Chanel informed them she was staying at the Galleria Westin, and they could shop together there. The plan was made and agreed upon.

Meanwhile, Cee-Cee was in the back room on her phone talking with Jamale. When Cee-Cee told him how the ladies wanted to get together, Jamale immediately suggested they have their gathering over to his house. He wanted Cee-Cee to feel proud of her new home and to be confident it would be as much her home as his.

"Okay ladies, here's the plan. We can all meet over to my future home tonight, at 7:30. I'll rent a couple of movies and pick-up some wine. There's a great restaurant who delivers, and we can do the ordering once we're all together at the house. Is that cool with everyone?"

Yolanda chimed in as she stood with her hands on her hips. "Yeah all of that sounds good, but I think I need to pick out the movies. You'll be trying to bring movies like, Sleepless in Seattle."

"Whatever." Cee- Cee laughed because she knew Yolanda was right. That was one of her favorite movies.

Each of the ladies looked at their watches, nodded their heads yes, and expressed some urgency so they could leave right away. They had to hurry if they wanted to get their shopping done.

Yolanda made the suggestion that she would take Jaylen and her son Avery to the mall to get their Tuxedo's fitted and all the other ladies started with any excuse they could think of to leave.

Once more, the ladies were excited. Little did they know, somehow there would be trauma in their drama.

19

*O*n evening of five men and a lady had been planned. The minor details were in the makings, and each of them owned up to a responsibility. Austin would get the Tiger shrimp platters, Peter would get the lobster tails, Adrian would get the platters of Alaskan king crab legs, Marquis would supply the entertainment and each of the men would bring a bottle of Dom Perignon to celebrate with their brother. Jamale, however, would be the only one not drinking champagne. The BG's (Bubble guts) always got the best of him afterwards. Instead, Jamale would be celebrating with an aged bottle of cognac that Jamale had been holding for the past eight years. It was a gift from his father for graduating college.

The plan was for all of the men to be at Marquis' at seven. Marquis would tell Jamale that all of them were meeting over to his place before going out for cocktails.

To begin his Best Man duties, Marquis called Jamale. "Hey man, what's up? Just checking on you. You ready for tomorrow?"

"Man, I'm feeling real good. I'm glad you got back in town. I wouldn't be able to do this without you standing by my side."

"You know I wouldn't miss this for nothing in this world. You got yourself a beautiful woman. Don't be trying to back out at the last minute."

"Dawg, Cee is everything I've…."Another call came in before he could finish. "…Marquis, hold on. I got another call coming in. Hold on."

Clicking over to the other line, Jamale answered, "Hello."
In a distinctively disguised voice, the message was clear. "Mutha Fucca!"

"What? Who is this?" The heavy breathing continued until Jamale shouted into the phone. "You need to grow up!" Jamale clicked back over to Marquis and told him about the incidents that had been occurring lately. They both assumed it was some female tripping and agreed it would end in time. They started reminiscing on the time Peter had a stalker and how she soon disappeared after she realized Peter wasn't playing the game with her. Jamale agreed to start ignoring the calls and everything else.

"So what time do you guys want to get together?"

"Meet me over to my place at 7:30 and we'll ride together. Friends don't let friends drive drunk."

"I can handle mine. You better check yourself."

Laughing. "I gotta go. I'll check you tonight."

The Seasoning

Cee-Cee was on top of the world. On the way to her apartment, she cried tears of joy as she spoke to God. The drivers to her left and right were dumbfounded as they watched her at the traffic light with her hands raised to heaven praising Him. She didn't care. Her life had changed. The years of disappointment with Jeff and now a man who adores her and wants nothing but the best for her and her son. All the years of being alone to raise Jaylen. Cee-Cee was ecstatic about the thought of becoming Mrs. Jamale LeTreau.

Driving down Forest Lane, Cee-Cee watched the young teenagers walking across the street with their jeans sagging down below their butts and their pant legs bunched up at the ankle. She couldn't help but laugh as she wondered why they hadn't figured out the jeans were bunched at the bottom because they weren't pulled up at the waist.

A dark skinned boy with his hair in cornrows held his jeans with his left hand and his girl with his right. The young girl pretended she didn't want him near her, but that was a show for the girls that walked behind them giggling. Another young man whose head was clean shaven was bopping to whatever sounds came from the headphones that were affixed to his ears. The children were in their own world. If they had worries or concerns, at the moment, no one knew about them.

Cee-Cee sat behind the yellow school bus watching the younger students who looked as if they were the junior high bunch. They looked confused and misguided, and she thought how Jaylen could be a part of that bunch if she hadn't kept him busy in so many activities away from the school and home. Cee-Cee parked the car waiting for the children to exit the bus and then a smile came over her face.

Jaylen stood out from all the other children. He wore a canary yellow fleece top and a pair of navy blue jeans with his rubber soled boots. He was handsome. As she admired him, she couldn't help but notice how he looked so much like Jeff. She blew the horn twice for Jaylen and when he saw her burgundy Accord, he smiled.

"Hey mom." Reaching over to put his book bag onto the back seat. As he buckled his seat belt he continued, "How was your day?"

"My day was exceptional. How was yours?" Smiling at the thought that her son asked.

"It was okay. I told everyone you were getting married. My teachers said congratulations."

Looking at him periodically as she focused on the traffic ahead, Cee-Cee smiled as she spoke. "That's nice. Tell them I said thank you. Honey, we haven't even talked about how you feel about me getting married."

"Mom, I'm happy. I really like Jamale. I look forward to moving into that big house. I'm ready to get away from all these knuckleheads that live at the apartments."

"Yeah, but are you okay with going to another school?"

Shooting his mom a confused look. "Are you serious? Ma, I can't wait to move. Trust me."

Cee-Cee was relieved knowing her young man was happy with the marriage and everything that came with it. They laughed for a while about her being nervous and they talked about the plans for the rest of the day. Cee-Cee dropped Jaylen off at the mailboxes towards the front of the property while she carried her bags to the apartment. When she got to the second floor at her door, there was a note hanging from the clip by her doorbell.

She rushed to turn the lock and get into the apartment because she was losing her grip on the garment bag that held her gown and veil. She hurried to her bedroom and hung the bag on the hook on the inside of her closet door. Cee-Cee sat on her full sized bed and looked around her bedroom and smiled thinking how she'll be happy to be rid of the black lacquer bedroom set she had rented to own nine years ago.

It was 3:45 p.m and Yolanda was due to be over in a little bit to take Jaylen for his tuxedo fitting. Cee-Cee wanted to take a bubble bath and relax, but she decided she would pack hers and Jaylen's overnight bag first so that when it was time to go over to "the house" she would be prepared.

As she was finishing the packing, the chimes from the doorbell and the telephone rang at the same time. Cee-Cee hurried for the door, and Jaylen reached for the phone.

"Hey girl, come on in. I'm trying to get a few things together before going over to Jamale's." Raising her hand with her pointer finger pointing upwards as if claiming victory Cee-Cee changed her statement. "I mean my house." She smiled at Yolanda waiting for some kind of expression that showed she was in agreement, but instead Yolanda gave her more than an expression, she gave her attitude.

"There you go. Claim what's yours. Don't have no shame in what your man is giving you. Gerl, you 'bout to be married." They stopped for a sisterly hug when Yolanda asked, "Where's my baby?"

"In the other room. The phone was ringing when you were ringing the doorbell. Have a seat. Jaylen will be right out." Walking towards the back room, Cee-Cee called out to Jaylen. "Jay, who's that on the phone? Yolanda's here to pick you up." When Cee-Cee got to the room, Jaylen's stance was strong and proud. He was wearing a smile she hadn't seen in a long time. He was beyond happy.

Cee-Cee was confused for a moment until Jaylen spoke. "Mom, it's my dad."

Her face turned to stone. Cee-Cee was paralyzed, speechless and aching in her heart. It was as if all of her blood had been sucked from her body, and all the air that circulated in the room was no longer there. The sound of hearing Jaylen call Jeff dad was unfamiliar, and something Cee-Cee had forgotten and dreaded.

How could he do this to me? She kept repeating in her mind. He never even wanted me to have him. The tears began to fill her eyes as the horrific memories traveled at the speed of light. Why didn't I have the abortion as he wanted me to? Then I would never have to hear from him again. The thought of aborting Jaylen made her cry. She loved her son and just thinking about it made her run to him and nestle him against her chest.

Cee-Cee cuffed the mouthpiece of the telephone hoping Jeff didn't hear any of her conversation. "Baby, let me talk to your fa....let me talk with him. Go out there with Yolanda. Oh, get whatever else you want to take with us over to Jamale's."

Taking a deep breath before getting on the phone and looking up as if looking to God, Cee-Cee spoke with confidence. "Jeff, why are you doing this? After all of these years, why now?" Not sure she wanted to know the answers, she sat on the bed slumped over trying to control her left heel from rapidly tapping the floor.

"Why now? Nikkia, I ain't never stopped. I told you a long time ago I ain't gonna let you marry no other man." Pausing as if he expected the bugles to blow after he revealed his knowledge of the marriage. "What? You didn't think I knew?" Although the question was intended as a rhetorical question for Cee-Cee, he answered it for her. "Hell yeah, I know."

Cee-Cee sat cold and numb. Speechlessness had overcome her once more. She couldn't believe what she was hearing on the night before the most precious day of her life. In a matter of hours, she would be celebrating with a room of women who were becoming special to her and all the joy she's gonna share with her future husband. And now, the one person who brought so much pain and suffering was trying to rob her of it. Cee-Cee wasn't going to allow it.

"Jeff, I don't give a damn what you know or what you think you can do to stop me from being happy. Those days have long passed. Jaylen and I are happy, and there ain't shit you can do about it." Standing in the middle of the floor with her hand in the air, palm facing forward, she continued. "Now why don't you go back to wherever you've been all these years and leave us alone!"

"Leave you alone? Jaylen is MY son! Aint no man gonna replace me. You can…" Before he could finish, Cee-Cee interrupted.

"REPLACE YOU?! REPLACE YOU?! You haven't been here to be replaced! Furthermore, you never wanted to be a father. Remember? You never even wanted me to have Jaylen. Oh, maybe you've forgotten the ass kickin' I took because I wouldn't have an abortion. Did you forget how you kicked my ass, Jeff? Jaylen has someone who loves him and wants to be the dad you never learned to be. So you and all your threats can go to hell!"

"Yeah all right bad-ass. Remember, I warned you. Don't think this is the end." Cee-Cee had had enough. She hung up and tried to compose herself before facing Jaylen, but it was too late. Jaylen was standing in the doorway with his chest high, lips tightened and eyes staring at his mother.

Cee-Cee began crying as she rushed to hold her son. "Oh baby. I am so sorry. I am so sorry."

Pulling away from his mothers embrace, Jaylen raised his head so he could make eye contact. In a soft but convicted voice he spoke, "Mom, its okay. I don't need Jeff. I have you and Jamale. I have a mother and a dad."

She couldn't help the extra tight hold she had on her son. Cee-Cee looked into the hallway and saw Yolanda watching teary eyed.

Yolanda knew she had to do something to squash the emotional moment. They had a bridal shower to go to in a couple of hours, and she didn't need the guest of honor to be disturbed. "See, that's my man. Ain't nobody gonna get him down. We got stuff to attend to. You ready man?" Yolanda reached her hand out for Jaylen and wrapped her arm around his shoulder as they headed for the front door.

Cee-Cee was exhausted. She tried to stop thinking about the conversation with Jeff, but she couldn't. He had made her do something she hadn't done in years. He had her angry and cursing just as she had when she was Mrs. Jeff Boston.

Before Cee-Cee could slip out of her clothes to prepare for the bubble bath that had filled the tub, she knew she had to call Jamale to let him know what had just happened. He was the one person on earth she had grown to trust with everything. Jamale was her best friend.

The phone had rung three times before Cee-Cee decided to hang up. She figured Jamale had to be handling something important not to answer his phone…and he was. He was on the other line making arrangements for her mother's flight into Dallas.

The bathroom was relaxing, and the steam filled the room with the soft scent of lavender from the bath beads she bought at the mall. As Cee-Cee stepped into the hot tub, she remembered the note that was on her door. She got out of the tub and tip toed over to the dresser trying to avoid getting the carpet wet.

Pulling her hair up off of her neck, Cee-Cee enjoyed the water relaxing her tired body. She dried her hands on the towel beside the tub before picking up the note. As she began to unfold it, Cee-Cee could smell the light scent of Polo cologne. Her face began to frown, and when she finally opened the note and saw Jeff's handwriting, she threw it down to the floor. Cee-Cee was tired. She closed her eyes and meditated as she thought her prayers to God.

Seasonal

Austin thought about his opportunity at the radio station and thought to cancel their plans to meet, but he understood what her brother did to Khadijah had nothing to do with Mrs. Tyson and the business they were finishing. Following through with their plans was the professional thing to do, and it was also a good career move.

"Hello Ms. Tyson. Austin James." His attempt to sound enthused was successful and she was excited hearing from him.

"Hello Austin. I was just wondering what time you'd be coming. I know you're a busy man, but I thought maybe we should meet sooner. I want you to meet my brother. I think he's someone you could become friends with."

Hell no. That will never happen, he thought as he listened to the woman who controlled his future.

"He's a great guy. You'll love him."

Austin wasn't a hypocrite. He didn't care who he was dealing with, he wasn't going to say something he didn't mean, so he ignored her comments. "Well Ms. Tyson, an early evening would be better. I have a bachelor's party for my best friend tonight. I'm about fifteen minutes from your hotel, if you'd like, we can get something light to eat downstairs at one of the hotel restaurants."

Austin was pressed for time. The dinner date with Ms. Tyson and her brother wasn't something he really wanted to do, but knew he had to. He thought about the traffic heading down interstate 35 and knowing he only had a ten minute drive to the Anatole Hotel.

"That'll be fine. I'll wake Chris up. He had a busy night last night. Married people. You know how that could be."

Busy my ass. Austin thought with anger. His ass was busy keeping Bubba off his ass, Austin humored himself with the thought and chuckled out loud. "Okay, then I'll see you in a few minutes. I'll call up to your room when I arrive."

"Okay, see you in a few minutes."

Austin was certain it had to be Ms. Tyson who got Chris out of lock-up. Khadijah hadn't given her statement before they let him out on bond. Damn, just the thought of Ms. Tyson suggesting Austin would like him and wanted to befriend him pissed him off.

Austin sat in his car outside of the busy parking lot of the Anatole thinking. That nigga hit on a sista, and she thinks that shit is cool. What kind of person is she? Better than that, what does she think of me, a Black man?

As he watched the people getting out of their cars, he wondered which one of the many people he was watching were "good" people or harbored a callous heart when it came to domestic abuse and the women who suffered from it in their interracial relationships. It was a topic he decided he would solicit the opinions and comments from his radio audience. It would be the next segment on his "Free Your Mind Show."

Austin's mind began to race, and his anxiety was high. Sweat was forming on his face, and anger was in his eyes. He wondered how he was going to sit across from this White boy and pretend nothing had happened. Austin's fury and rage was taking over. His mind was beginning to become consumed by thoughts of oppression, regression, depression and destruction. The mere thought of a White man hitting a Black queen and thinking it was excusable was really pissing him off. "I ought to go in there and kick his natural White ass," he thought out loud. Inhaling and exhaling from his nostrils caused his chest to rise as if he had just finished a workout.

Austin knew he was out of control. He wanted to turn his car on and drive off, but he had to face the idiot. But before doing so, Austin wanted to shout to Ms. Tyson what he thought about Chris, but the consequences were too much for Khadijah and his future with Radio Works.

The clock on the dashboard displayed 5:15. It was time for him to face the devil in disguise. Before leaving his car, Austin checked himself in the mirror twice. Although he looked calm, the storm in his heart and mind was in full rage. Austin knew that walking into that restaurant reflecting self control was going to be his challenge tonight but he stepped out of his car with confidence, shook off his anger and headed towards the hotel.

He stood at the Maitrade's desk for a moment waiting for a hostess. As he stood waiting, he saw Ms. Tyson and her brother sitting across the room. Look at him. Nigga. Austin's rage was starting to build again as he thought about Chris sitting, enjoying himself as if he deserved to. Austin took a deep breath as he passed the hostess and nodded to indicate he'd seen his party.

"Austin, perfect timing. We were just considering a bottle of wine. You remember my brother Chris."

"Yes." Austin's stare was chilling, but Chris wasn't paying him any attention. Sitting in the chair across from Chris, Austin started a conversation.

"So Chris, have you showed your sister the town yet?"

"Actually no. I just moved here myself. I don't know the town well enough to show myself the sites."

Interjecting, Ms. Tyson began with what may have been bragging. "Chris is a pilot. He and his lovely wife, Khadijah moved to Dallas a couple of days ago."

"Oh, is that right? So, Chris, where is the lovely wife of yours?"

Sipping on his drink before speaking, "Well, she isn't able to join us. She wasn't feeling well. Perhaps she needs to get used to the water." Guzzling the remaining parts of what was left in his glass, the waiter appeared with Chris' next drink.

"Sir. Tequila with a squeeze of lime." The waiter placed Chris' drink in front of him.

"So, Austin, are you married?" Words were beginning to slur and Ms. Tyson was looking a bit concerned.

"Actually, I just reunited with the woman who I plan on making my queen."

"Your queen? Hah! They're all wenches." Drinking his drink in one swallow.

"Excuse me?" Austin changed his relaxed posture to a stiff straight up position.

"Austin, Chris is tired. He didn't mean what he just said. Did you Chris?" Ms. Tyson was surprised by her brothers' comment, but she was more concerned with what else he may say throughout the evening.

In almost a whimper, Ms. Tyson asked, "Wine anyone?" Foolishly suggesting, hoping to divert the direction of the conversation.

Austin's blank expression answered the ridiculous and inappropriate question. Austin knew he had to gain his composer or he might jump across the table and kiss his boss's brother's ass. "No. If it's all the same, I'd like to skip the wine. I have a bachelor's party to go to this evening, and I'm sure they'll have plenty of champagne."

Agreeing with Austin as if he'd just stopped the wine order because he knew Chris didn't need anything else to drink she replied, "Yes, I agree. That's fine."

"Yeah well, I don't have any bachelor's party to go to, so I'm going to have another cocktail." Before Ms. Tyson could slip in a word, Chris' hand was in the air to gain the attention of his waiter.

"Chris you have to drive. Do you think you should have another?"

"Sis, don't you worry about me. That big pickup truck can handle anything on the road."

Austin was giving Chris the coldest stare he could give. His thoughts were getting the best of him. Just like a White cracker. Driving a slave master vehicle. If he could load the back of his truck with enough Black beaten bodies, he'd find the nearest forest to hang them. Austin knew his thoughts were unfair, but he'd become so pissed watching Chris gawk at the big butt Black woman who was passing their table.

"Wench. What I would do to all of that ass." Chris said with clenched teeth not intending to be heard.

"Excuse me, what did you say?" Austin's tone wasn't friendly as he demanded an answer. "Chris, what did you say?"

Beginning to laugh, Chris answered. "Ahh brother, don't take it so seriously. You know what I meant."

"No, actually I don't know what you meant."

Ms. Tyson was shaken by the tension and didn't want her brother to further embarrass her or himself. "Gentlemen, why don't we order now?"

Looking over at his boss who was trying to settle the tension, Austin continued, "So Chris, why you gotta call her a wench? Do you know that woman? Do you even know what a wench is?" His tone was more agitated.

"Oh, trust me, I know what a wench is" Forcing his drink down before making his next comment. "Hey man, I don't know why you're getting so upset. I'm no racist. My wife is Black."

"So, what you're saying is Black women are wenches?"

"Hey, if the shoe fits." Smiling at Austin and not knowing what hit next. Austin jumped up and connected his right fist against Chris' jaw.

"IF THE SHOE FITS? NIGGA, I OUGHT TO FUCK YOU UP FOR EVERY BLACK WOMAN YOU LOOK AT AND THINK, WENCH!!!" Austin was furious. He didn't care what jeopardy he had put his job in. He wasn't going to allow any man, particularly a White man talk about a Black woman that way and think it was acceptable.

There weren't very many people in the restaurant, but the few that were there were on their feet taking notice to what was happening at the table nearest the kitchen. The couple of Mexican workers from the kitchen had come out and tried to make sense of what was being said around them, but their English wouldn't allow it. The manager on duty was rushing towards the back to perform his managerial duties by controlling the situation. The Black women who sat two tables across looked as if they were getting ready to take a few blows at Chris for the times he thought they were wenches. It was very personal to them and they'd never seen Chris before. Some of the White guests stood with disbelief on their faces, and others looked appalled or offended that Austin would make such a scene. As for Ms. Tyson, well, she was angry and embarrassed by her brother. He was everything she'd thought he was; a racist in disguise.

She took to her feet and shouted, "Chris, get up! Have you lost your mind? After what you did last night, haven't you learned?"

Chris didn't say another word; partly because his jaw wouldn't allow it. He sat on the floor nursing his face and trying to sit up straight without falling over. Austin couldn't believe he had just put his job on the line and didn't care. He faced his boss with deliverance in his eyes. He wanted to tell her that he knew about last night, but he didn't. He didn't have to; she was already on his side.

"Ms. Tyson, I apologize for losing my cool, but enough is enough." Although he apologized, Austin didn't in any way try to excuse himself for feeling the way he did. He just wished he could have walked away from Chris' hatefulness.

Reaching for Austin's hand, Ms. Tyson appeared sad when she spoke. "Austin, you don't owe me an apology. Chris deserved what he got. Hell, I felt like belting him a couple of times." She tried to add some humor to the situation, but the smile Austin gave was very cosmetic. There was nothing humorous about what had just happened.

"I think it's time for me to leave. Again, I apologize." Austin was sure his job was on the line. It's amazing how a few minutes of thought could make a picture so clear. If only he would have had those few minutes before cocking his fist back and knocking the shit out of Chris.

"I understand. Austin, I apologize to you. I'll be talking with you in a couple of days to touch bases with you on the contract." She smiled and winked at Austin.

Austin returned the smile."Have a good night." As he walked out of the restaurant, one of the Black women thanked him as he passed their table. Austin knew he had done the right thing, if not for himself, for that woman.

20

While Cee-Cee was getting all of her last minute preparations done, the other ladies were doing their shopping at the Galleria Mall. Yolanda had picked up her dress, secured Jaylen's and Avery's tuxedo and had them waiting in Chanel's hotel room watching a movie.

Once all of the shopping was complete, Karyn suggested that Yolanda and the two boys ride with her and designated herself as the safe driver for the night. Yolanda accepted the invitation to ride along because she definitely intended on getting her drink on. Chanel and Khadijah didn't know their way around Dallas so they suggested riding together and to follow Karyn. It was a plan, the day had gone well and they were on their way to the house to finish the night.

Karyn pulled up first in her black Range Rover and parked in front of the cream stucco house. Although Karyn had a few of her own thoughts, Yolanda couldn't help herself when her thoughts escaped her. "*Dayum.* Check out his crib." Yolanda was probably more impressed with Jamale's front yard than his house. There was a circular drive in front of the house and enclosed in the drive was a small water fountain that was lit by red halogen lamps. It was beautiful and it gave the house a polished distinction. But had Yolanda looked further down the street, she would have noticed that Jamale's house was by no means the most elegant on the street.

Karyn loved Yolanda's down to earth attitude. She wondered why other sista's she'd come across couldn't be true to themselves like her. Instead, she would meet the "sophisticated women" that would rather back stab and smile in your face.
Karyn smiled at Yolanda's excitement over Jamale's house and

she believed Yolanda's excitement was deeply rooted in the fact that her friend and son would be moving in. There was no envy or jealousy with Yolanda.

Everyone was surprised by the ring on Karyn's cellular that sounded very much like the melody to Tom Joyner's theme song for his radio show. As it played, the children joined in, "...*oh, oh, oh, it's the Tom Joyner morning show.*"

Before answering her phone Karyn quieted the boys down. "Karyn Kasey."

"Hi Karyn, this is Peter. I'm just checking to see how the day went with the ladies."

"Oh, it was really nice." Karyn was doing a lot more smiling while talking with Peter and he was noticing it in her voice. "Thank you for including me. In fact, the ladies and I just arrived over to Jamale's for a shower for Cee-Cee."

"Okay. So you ladies are planning on getting into a little trouble, huh?"

"Well, trouble is as trouble does."

"I'm gonna leave that alone. I can think of a lot of trouble doing." Peter was behaving differently with Karyn than he does with other females and Jamale noticed it right away. Jamale nudged Peter to get his attention.

At a whisper Jamale asked, "Say man, who is that?"

Peter continued with their conversation and then put Jamale on the spot. "Karyn, I want you to say hello to Jamale, the groom."

Surprised by Peter's request, Jamale looked at him like he'd just gone crazy. "Hello Karyn. How are you?"
"I'm fine, thank you. Are you getting nervous yet?"

"No. Not at all. I've got the perfect woman for me. So, Peter says some really nice things about you. How did you get stuck with his crazy butt?" Jamale figured he'd return the favor for putting him on the spot. "No, seriously, he's a good brotha. If I were a woman, I'd like him too."

"Oh, did Mr. James say that I like him? Is that what he's telling his boys?" Karyn thought she'd add a little bit of her own flavor to the pot.

Stumbling with his words, Jamale continued, "No, no, that's not what I'm saying. What I'm saying is…." Peter chimed in on the conversation.

"Say man, I told you Karyn is an attorney, you don't want to battle words with her." Trying to save his boys neck or save his own butt. "Why don't you tell her to tell Cee-Cee that you love her or something."

"Karyn, Peter's over here panicking so I'd better not say any more. But listen, I need you to do me a huge favor tonight."

"*Oh-kay.*" Karyn was surprised she'd be asked to do a favor.

"I know this is going to sound bizarre, but, I need you to be a little sneaky. When the last gift is given to Cee, I need you to go into the guest powder rooms vanity drawer. You'll find a white envelope there that has her name on it. I need you to tell her it's from me and to open and read it."

With a lot of resistance and uncertainty Karyn responded. "*Oh-kay.* This isn't a "Dear John Letter" is it?"

"Please, just do it."

Peter was looking at Jamale confused and Karyn was sitting with the phone to her ear not saying a word.

"Karyn, Please do it. It'll all make sense in the end."

"If you say so. In the guest powder rooms vanity drawer?"

"Yes and Karyn, thank you."

After a few words with Peter, Karyn joined Yolanda, Chanel, Khadijah and the children on the sidewalk and headed towards the house. Peter couldn't take the suspense any longer. "Man what's up? What's the letter about?"

"I don't want to talk about it right now. You'll find out soon enough."

Peter looked at Jamale strangely for a moment while pulling into the parking lot of the bright red brick building that read, Southside. Adrian and Austin's cars were parked side by side and Marquis was parked in front of the main entrance to the lofts.

"Say man, tell the truth. Are you starting to feel a little nervous?"

"Truth? Yeah, but not because I'm marrying Cee. It's just the whole thought of a family. I have a lot of responsibility ahead of me and I don't want to mess up."

"Man, there couldn't be a better man for the job. You gonna be aiight." Peter and Jamale stood outside of Marquis' door for a minute exchanging a brotherly hug when suddenly Marquis opened the door.

"Well it's about time you two got here. The fellas and I are getting the champagne glasses out. We got the Dom chilled and the rest of the goodies for the night waiting. You know what I mean?"

A little bit anxious, Jamale answered, "Yeah, I hear ya."

"What's this? You gettin' nervous on me? It's my job as your best man to make sure nothing happens to you. Don't be getting' cold feet now."

"Nah, I'm kewl."

"Aiight then, let's do this thang."

Seasons Greetings

When the women rang the doorbell, Cee-Cee greeted them as if she had opened that door for guests many times. It came so naturally. "Hey y'all, come on in." Hugging the ladies as they entered. "Hey boys.... Jaylen, you and Avery can go into the game room and play." Giving Jaylen a big kiss on the forehead before they ran off.

"Ladies, let me show you the house." Cee-Cee couldn't help the smile on her face. She loved the fact that the women liked her future husband's style. His home was a reflection of him, and it was beautiful. As the ladies were being shown the house, Yolanda called Cee-Cee to wait a few steps behind so she could walk with her. Yolanda whispered into Cee-Cee's ear, "I am so happy for you and Jaylen. Make sure when things get tough, and they will, you think about how you're feeling about your man this very moment."

"Girl, thank you. I will. I love him so much."

"I know you do. Baby, this house is da bomb!" The ladies started laughing as they joined the other women who were admiring the master bedroom.

"Oh, we know what goes on in this room. Maybe we should get out of here." All the ladies laughed at Cee-Cee trying to look embarrassed at Karyn's comment.

The final room they visited was the formal dining room. Karyn seemed to have the most interest in that room. Jamale's wine collection was fascinating. There were wines that the name itself made the wine sound as if it tasted good. Karyn couldn't help her thoughts, Damn. How'd she get him? This brotha's got it going on. Karyn knew she was wrong for her thoughts, but she couldn't help it. Here I am with a law degree, a partner with a firm, no children, fine as hell, and she got a man like him. It just doesn't make sense to me. Karyn put the bottle of wine she was studying back in its place before returning to the other women's small huddle towards the entranceway.

Cee-Cee was happy and overjoyed. Reality was truly setting in. It dawned on her like the sun rising on a summer morning that she was getting ready to become the queen of the castle with the perfect king, and Cee-Cee loved every minute of it.

Before getting too comfortable with her revelation Cee-Cee drifted back to the situation at hand, her bachelorette party. "Hey ladies, we're gonna take this party in the den." Cee-Cee was trying to peek into the bags the ladies were carrying as they were pulling them away from her reach. "So, what's in the bags? Are they for me?" She asked with a smile.

"What you think? Hell yeah they're for you, but first...PADOW...raising the bottle of champagne Yolanda blurts out, "we gots to hit the DOM." Yolanda started waving her hands in the air and began the melody..."It's your wedding....it's your wedding..." the other ladies joined in with her as they danced towards the bar where the glasses were.

After their song and dance, Chanel began the flurry of toasts to be made. "To Cee-Cee and Jamale. May your life be filled with joy from beginning to end." The glasses were raised, and the drinking began.

"And, may you love him as strong as you do now even when Jamale gets on your nerves." Yolanda knew how to add flavor to any situation. The glasses were raised, and the drinking continued.

"May the warranty on the mattress be used to its fullest." Karyn followed suit with Yolanda. The glasses were raised, and a few "Oh hell yeahs" were added before the drinking proceeded.

Yolanda was ready for her next toast. "To Cee-Cee. I speak for all the women in the world. You gots to know when to shake 'em and know when to fake 'em."

It was Cee-Cee's turn to speak up. "Oh, won't be no fakin' going on up in here." Laughter had filled the room, and the party had started. The second bottle of champagne was finished, and the ladies were in full force.

Yolanda was feeling the effects of the Dom Perignon more than the other ladies; probably because she was doing most of the drinking and because Karyn was the designated driver. Drinking was something very new for Chanel, so she kept it at a minimum and Cee-Cee wasn't going to risk having a hangover, so she only had a glass or two. But they each did have a buzz going on.

"Well Ba-by, if you ain't plannin' on doin' any fakin', won't be no shame when you see this gift I got you." Yolanda reached into the large Macy's bag and pulled out a silver and white wrapped rectangular box. "You want me to open this for you?"

"No gerl, give me that box." Cee-Cee reached to give Yolanda a hug before taking the box.

The ladies sat at the edge of their seats waiting to see what the gift was. They were like children on Christmas morning. Each of them waited in anticipation to see the gift as if they hadn't been there when the gifts were purchased. Cee-Cee's eyes lit up when she flipped open the tissue paper inside the box. "Oh Yolanda, this is beautiful." The white chiffon gown with miniature pearls that draped the front was the most elegant sleepwear in the bridal section of the store. Cee-Cee stood to match the gown to her body admiring how breathtaking it was.

"Girl, thank you so much. I love it." Yolanda and Cee-Cee hugged for a few seconds when Chanel stood with her gift.

"I'm next. Cee-Cee, I wanted you two to have the most precious beginning together." Chanel gave Cee-Cee the box, along with a kiss on the cheek.

Cee-Cee held the red and white wrapped box for a moment trying to imagine what it could be. "Hmmm. What could this be?" She was excited about unwrapping it. After lifting the top half of the box, Cee-Cee's eyes began to fill with tears. Inside was a burgundy leather bible that was embossed in gold lettering, Jamale and Nikkia LeTreau.

Cee-Cee stood to give Chanel a hug and to thank her. "Chanel, you have no idea how perfect your gift is. Jamale and I met at church. That is where our beginning took place."

Chanel was proud of her gift. Chanel, Yolanda, Karyn and Cee-Cee had tears in their eyes. Women and champagne could amount to two things...overly sensitive and/or horny as hell. At the moment, sensitivity had taken its prominent place.

Khadijah sniffled as she held onto the silver wrapped box on her lap. She tried not to be too zealous when she passed her gift over to Cee-Cee, but she couldn't help it. The mood in the room was so loving and sentimental she knew the gift she had for Cee-Cee would fit nicely. "Ooh, Cee-Cee, I wanna be next."

Cee-Cee smiled at Khadijah as she reached for the box. Cee-Cee admired the box with such depth and shook it trying to guess what it could be before tearing the wrapping. Inside the tissue paper was a cream colored silk and knit blend throw blanket that read, The LeTreau's.....Blessed by God embroidered into it.

"Oh my God, Khadijah, this is beautiful." Leaning over to hug Khadijah.

I thought it could be something that you and Jamale passed down to your grandchildren."

"Grandchildren? Ooh gerl don't be aging me like that. Grandchildren?" Each of the ladies laughed when the revelation of grandchildren had Cee-Cee smiling and thanking Khadijah for the beautiful gesture.

"Okay ladies, it's my turn." Karyn was the most poised of the ladies. She controlled her alcohol and emotions well. Although her eyes had begun to water a couple of times, she hadn't had to wipe any tears. "Cee-Cee, although I don't know much about you, I felt this would be appropriate. I hope you like it."

"I'm sure I will, Karyn." The silver foiled wrapping paper and large silver bow was beautiful. Inside was a double 8x10 silver polished picture frame that was refined. Etched into the corners of the frame were ivy and a small floral pattern. At the bottom of each frame was an engraving. On the left, the frame read, Mr. and Mrs. LeTreau and on the right, it read, The Family.

"Karyn, this is beautiful. You have no idea how right you were. My family is very important to me." Cee-Cee admired the frame as she envisioned the photo's that would occupy each frame.

"I figured you, Jamale and Jaylen should take a nice picture together. It would be perfect for this frame.

"Thank you so much." They hugged and then invited the three other women to stand for a group hug.

Lost somewhere in the midst of the group hug, Karyn untangled herself. "Excuse me a moment while I go visit the powder room." Karyn walked off because it was time to honor Jamale's request. The journey to the vanity had Karyn drowning in apprehension. Not having the facts before presenting it to the court, which at the moment was the three intoxicated women in the next room, wasn't something she enjoyed. The element of surprise could be a snake with poisonous venom, and in this case, Karyn would be the deliverer of that snake.

When Karyn returned to the room, the ladies were engulfed in some conversation that had them laughing and falling over themselves. Karyn stood for a moment in the doorway taking in what she had witnessed in the course of an hour. Great conversation, lots of laughter, great gifts, and now it was time for Karyn to hand Cee-Cee the mystery envelope.

Karyn took the few dreaded steps and stood in front of Cee-Cee as if she controlled the switch that could destroy the world. "Cee-Cee, Jamale asked me to give this to you."

Karyn's expression showed some concern and regardless how tipsy they were, each of the women could see it. Karyn tried to add a smile, but it was obviously fake.

Puzzled, Cee-Cee asked, "What is it?"

Yolanda jumped solidifying she'd had too much to drink. "Gerl, just open it. It's from your man…" Letting out the airy sound of a burp. "…oops, excuse me. I mean your future huz-band."

"You're right. You're right. Let's see what Mr. Man has to say." Slowly Cee-Cee lifted the glued flap and removed the contents. Inside was a CD and a folded note. She looked surprised as she held onto the CD a moment thinking she should listen to it in private, but before she could put it back into the envelope, Yolanda interrupted the thought.

"No, no. You gots to play that now!"

"Oh-kay. Oh-kay. But let me read his note first." Brief, but direct, the note read: "Cee, play the CD." Beneath was a large smiley face with his initials.

Clearing her throat she put the CD into the player. With the exception of the hissing sound that came from the speakers, the room was quiet. Chanel and Karyn sat on the love seat together, and Cee-Cee, Yolanda and Khadijah sat on the sofa as they waited in anticipation for what was on the CD.

"Nikkia…" When Cee heard Jamale start with her first name, she knew the next words to follow would be serious. She sat up to prep herself for what was to come. "…We didn't plan on reciting our own vows at the wedding, but I wanted to say something to you before we exchanged them. So here it is:

243

Beginning yesterday, I fell in love with you. You have given me your unconditional love unselfishly, and I am eternally grateful. When I think of how much I love you and how much you have proven your love to me, I melt inside and wonder how I could ever compare. I don't know if I could ever measure up to your love because it seems immeasurable.

Today I offer you tangible gifts. In your jewelry box is a note paper with the combination to my safe. Inside of the safe you will find where your name has been included on the deed to our house, you as the beneficiary to all of my insurance policies, stocks, bonds and a trust fund for Jaylen for his education.

You and Jaylen are every part of my life. You two are my life, and I love you both completely. Tomorrow I offer you my eternal love. I look forward to the privilege of becoming your husband and excited about loving you for the rest of our lives. I love you Cee."

The ladies sat mesmerized and speechless. Cee-Cee couldn't move. She sat with tears until Yolanda stood to speak.

"Okay, I'm drunk, and now I'm depressed. Why I always get the men that sell boot-leg shit on the corner tryin' to get with me? Damn, get a real job." The ladies were laughing while Yolanda tried walking without falling.

"See, ya'll laughing and shit, and I'm serious. I want a man like Jamale. I mean damn, they don't have to have no great job, but damn, at least one that takes out taxes and all the other bullshit they take from your check." Yolanda lifted the sofa pillows and was looking around for something while the ladies laughed as they watched her.

"Where the hell is my coat? Take my Black ass home. I'm ready to get in my lonely bed and go to sleep. I mean if the night before the wedding is like this, shit, I can't wait to see what the wedding is going to be like. Seriously Cee..." Beginning to cry. "... I am so happy for you."

"Aww girl, come on. Let me take your drunken butt home." The other ladies began pacifying Yolanda when Khadijah agreed it was time to go home to get their rest.

The ladies gave Cee-Cee a hug goodnight and told her to get some rest too. When they left, Cee-Cee thought about going into the safe but realized there was no need. She trusted everything was just as Jamale said it would be and agreed she needed some rest.

Seasoned to taste

Meanwhile, over at Marquis' the excitement was just about to begin. "Man, wait 'till you see the entertainment I have stashed in my office. Female is off the hook. I met her while I was in Houston." The men swallowed the last of what was in their glasses and reached for another bottle. Enjoying their third bottle, Marquis told Jamale to sit on the leather chase and relax. Austin, Peter and Marquis grabbed any seat available while Adrian went to the restroom. "Adrian, hurry back, the shows 'bout to begin. Adrian shook his head to say okay before he shut the bathroom door. He hadn't heard from Chanel and wanted to check his voicemail to see if she had left a message.

Marquis dimmed the lights, turned on some music and told the groom to sit back and enjoy the show. The music started playing, and from the back room came a beautiful girl dressed like a Harem dancer. Across her face, she wore a chiffon scarf. And the two chiffon scarves off her hips revealed the diamond studded g-string that covered her pubic area. Her skin had a glistening sparkle that accented the sway in her body as she entered the room. She was beautiful and very enticing when she danced in front of Jamale.

The music selection was perfect for the occasion. "Freak me baby. Ah yeah...let me lick you up and down, 'till you say stop..." When she stood in front of Jamale, she turned her back towards him, straddled her legs and bent over reaching for the floor without bending her knees. Her hips swayed from side to side as she went into a squat position and turned facing him slowly as she began to come up caressing his calves. She moved to the center of the room and seductively stretched out onto the floor. She began to gyrate her hips while moaning at the same time and Marquis, Peter and Austin were cheering her on while Jamale sat quietly watching.

As the song progressed, she danced in front of Jamale and with two fingers she unsnapped the clip of the beaded bra to reveal her breast, but Jamale didn't show that he was impressed with her at all. Alyssa saw the other men in the room were enjoying her show, so she removed the two scarves off her hips and danced showing her half naked body that had a tattoo on her breast and a pierced naval.

While dancing, Adrian returned to the room and was flabbergasted when he saw the tattoo and navel ring on the woman he thought to be Chanel.

"CHANEL!" He yelled and startled everyone. Adrian couldn't believe what he was seeing. Surely his eyes were playing tricks on him.

Alyssa stopped dancing and turned to see Adrian. She was more surprised than he was. She stood with her hands covering her mouth, and her eyes opened wide. As he continued with his questions, she began looking back and forth between Adrian and Marquis.

"What're you doing!? What're you doing here!? Chanel, what're you doing!?"

Marquis jumped to his feet and rushed over to grab Adrian by his shoulders. "Adrian man, what are you talking about? Who the hell is Chanel?" Marquis and the others were a combination of drunk and confused which ultimately equated to tripping.

Shrugging his shoulders loose, Adrian spoke with great conviction. "Marquis, that's her. The girl I'm working with. The woman I talked with you about."

Unable to comprehend what Adrian was trying to tell him, Marquis stepped back to question Adrian. "WHAT!? Man listen, I don't have a clue what you think you know, but I met Alyssa at the club in Houston." Pointing his finger at the woman who looked scared to death. "That is not Chanel."

"Man, I am not drunk, confused or trippin'. Listen, I was with her this afternoon at the hotel. Earlier, I went into her hotel room because I thought she was out with the other ladies preparing for the wedding. I wanted to leave her flowers. When I got there, she was getting out of the shower. I caught her with nothing on. Man, I held her, and I kissed her. I saw her body. I know what I saw, and I know what I know." Pointing over to Alyssa he continued, "I saw that same rose tattoo on her breast and that same navel ring. Man, I know what Chanel looks like, and I know where I was and whom I was with." Adrian was furious. He stared at Alyssa with fiery darts in his eyes.

Marquis was angry and confused, but he couldn't help the smile that was forming on his face. He knew his boy wasn't that drunk that he would trip like this. Something very unusual was going on.

"Dawg, I am not doubting you. Something is definitely going on 'cause I'm telling you I met the female at the titty joint in Houston. But hold up, what hotel you talkin' 'bout?"

"The Galleria Westin. Hold up, let me make a phone call." Adrian called Jasmine to confirm if Chanel was with her this afternoon around noon. Alyssa knew she was busted. She was already embarrassed but to be called out in front of a room full of men and be naked, it wasn't going to happen. She ran to Marquis' office where her clothes were and began dressing.

Austin and Jamale sat on the sofa laughing at the situation and tried to figure out exactly what was going on while Peter was checking his phone messages. When Peter called into his voicemail, he heard he had eight messages and figured at least seven of them had to be from Franco. Peter had totally forgotten to meet with him to give him the money. Peter didn't even want to face the consequences that he was guaranteed to get if the money wasn't turned in by today. He had to get the money to him before the wedding. Peter punched in his password to access his messages, and he was right. Franco left a message, but before he could find out how many of the messages were from Franco, Peter disconnected from voicemail. He knew there was nothing he could do about it tonight.

"Say man, what the hell is going on up in this camp?" Hoping to forget his situation, Peter asked Jamale with a smile.

"Man, this is the funniest shit I've seen in a long time. Adrian is calling someone to find out about the female he says he was with, and ol' girl took off running into the back when Adrian pulled out his cell."

Jamale had gotten up to fix him a plate of food and started laughing as he spoke. "Man, I figured I'd get me a plate before round two began." Licking his fingers between his words he continued, "This is some funny shit. This is why I'm getting married tomorrow. Y'all can have all this drama, and I'll just sit back, and trip with y'all as you go through it."

Peter chimed in immediately to add to that comment. "Naaw dawg, this is Marquis, Adrian and Austin type drama. I got my shit together." Jamale and Peter hit knuckles together and laughed as Marquis and Austin shook their heads and drank their champagne.

Austin finished the last part of his drink and thought about Khadijah's situation and began lying to the fellas. "Naaw man, I don't have any drama goin' on. Peter knows my girl is straight."

Marquis raised his glass in the air to toast his comments before drinking. "Listen, I welcome this kind of drama. This is the kind of shit that keeps me real with the ladies. When they do stupid shit like this, I know there ain't shit that they can do to surprise me. I stay on top of the game."

Hanging up the call with Jasmine, Adrian paced the floor before he spoke. "Man, this shit is a trip. Jasmine said she was with Chanel, and I know I was in the room with her at the same time. I know damn well I'm not crazy."

Adrian headed towards the room where Alyssa was hiding, and his frat's followed. If Adrian had been drunk, he was sober now and not in any mood to play games. He wanted answers and quickly.

Marquis asked, "Adrian, what you gettin' ready to do?"

"I'm about to get some damn answers." Adrian wasn't thinking about being polite when he turned the door knob to let himself in and stood directly in front of Alyssa.

Like crashing waves on a turbulent sea, Adrian was being hit with a realization. "Hold up. Chanel told me she had a sister. What's up with you? Are you Chanel's twin sister?"

Doris stood there for a brief moment not saying anything until she heard the harshness in Adrian's voice when he repeated the question. But before she could answer, Marquis was telling Adrian to chill.

"Naaw dawg, this chick was perpetrating like her sister and tried to seduce me in her sister's room. What kind of bullshit is that?" Jamale, Austin and Peter stood in the doorway snickering.

Alyssa was calm for a moment, but when she saw the three men laughing at her, the soulful side of her slipped out. "Yeah, that's my sister, and I was gonna fuck you if you let me. Chanel damn sure ain't gonna do it. All you niggas are just alike...all you want is ass in your face. Now what? You fucked up. What are you gonna do when I tell Chanel how you were all over me in the room? I ain't got shit to hide. I was just there. She already told me she diggin' on you, so when she finds out what happened, you won't ever get that ass."

"Oh really? You ain't nothin' but an ol' two dollar hoe wantin' to mooch off your sister. I'm gonna put it to you like this....your sister's gonna be huge in a minute, and if she finds out her hoe sister hit on the man she's wantin' to get with, your ass will be left in the cold screwin' yourself on some mans stage so, if you know like I know, you'll skip your ass back to Houston and never let Chanel know your stank ass was ever here in Dallas. And be assured, if you act stupid, I'd rather lose the opportunity of getting involved with your sister than to let your good for nothin' ass mess with her success."

The men loved this. Their boy was kicking her ass with words, and she was feeling every blow. They didn't care for a minute about Alyssa's feelings. They were roaring with laughter.

"What-ever." Alyssa put her hand up in the air like a traffic guard would to stop oncoming traffic. "All you sorry niggas can kiss my Black ass."

Marquis could not believe this chick was a guest in his home. He gave her the choice to get on a plane back to Houston tonight or get a room. Whichever, Marquis didn't feel any remorse when he added, "You don't have to go home, but you gots to get the hell up outta here." The men laughed harder and longer as Alyssa reached for her bags.

It didn't take long for Doris to make a decision. She thought about her opportunities with Chanel's success and the money she wanted to enjoy. The decision was quick. She passed the men standing in the doorway and rolled her eyes. She didn't want to lose out on her chances with Chanel, so she went along with all of Adrian's demands.

To say the least, the evening was eventful. Adrian, Austin and Peter decided to spend the night at Marquis' while Marquis drove Doris to the airport. Jamale's things were already in the spare bedroom, so he took a shower and rested in bed thinking about his life with Cee-Cee and Jaylen. Although the planning of this wedding wasn't very traditional, not seeing the bride the night before certainly would be.

21

$\mathcal{L}$ooking across the way, the sunrise was incredible. It was like a huge orange ball of fire. A Texas sunrise no matter how many times you'd seen one, it was a spectacular sight.

Peter and Austin left Marquis' loft early enough to beat the traffic. Jamale and Marquis got up early to go out for breakfast, and Adrian sat in the kitchen still tripping on last night's revelation.

Cee-Cee, Jaylen and Avery waited in the den for Yolanda to arrive so they could go out for breakfast while Karyn was in the office tying up some loose ends. Khadijah was dressed waiting for Austin and Chanel was ordering room service and trying to imagine why she hadn't heard from Adrian. Meanwhile, Doris was back in Houston contemplating if she should call Chanel to tell her she wouldn't be going to Dallas and Franco was waiting at Peter's job for him to arrive.

As the morning progressed, time seemed to quicken. Everyone appeared to be getting excited with joy except Franco. The only excitement Franco was filled with was anger and fury as he sat outside waiting for Peter. And Peter not answering his calls and not showing for work didn't help the matter.

Karyn picked up Chanel to meet the ladies at Yolanda's salon to have their hair done. The storefront salon had four chairs and four ghetto-fabulous stylists that took ownership of their chairs.

Karyn was summoned to sit at the first chair by a short Hispanic woman that seemed to shuffle her feet as if she were doing the popular salsa dance. She spoke fairly good English with a slight hint of a rolling tongue. She was Puerto Rican and very proud of it. On her wall hung a Puerto Rican flag with bold letters that announced her heritage. Sides of the flag were pictures of what appeared to be famous Puerto Rican singers and bands. Above her set of warming curling irons sat a statue that looked like some religious artifact. Before she began fluffing Karyn's hair with her fingers, she called out to Yolanda. "Jolanda, she's one of the girls in the wedding, right? French roll with sassy front?"

"Yeah girl. Hook her up."

Using her hands as she spoke, she pointed to her chair. "You heard her. I have to to hook you up. So I'm gonna have to add a few tracks of hair." Not allowing time for Karyn to get a word in she continued. "My name is Chaquita, but everyone calls me Cha-Cha. How you doin' gurl? I don't have to do a lot to your hair. You take good care of your stuff. I'm just gonna fix it like the rest of the girls in the wedding."

Cha-Cha had mastered the art of gum popping. She could pop between words and Karyn was becoming very annoyed. Karyn wondered when women were going to learn how rude it was to pop gum in public.

Chanel was in chair number two. It was obvious the large dark skinned woman was not a morning person. She wore the "female with the funky attitude" very well. Her orange hair that was finger waved in an upward swirl that seemed to reach eight inches high off her head was starched stiff. Her gold front teeth were gleaming against her ruby red lipstick that was outlined with black eyeliner. And her large gold hoops that filled the three holes she had in each ear were dangling and clicking as they hit the other.

Chanel stared at the pictures the woman had covering her mirror. The three boys in the group picture had to be her sons. They looked just like her. Chanel had never seen anything like it. She wanted to laugh when she noticed the boys each had a chicken drumstick in their hands as they posed for the picture, but then she looked at the six inch nails of the woman who controlled the comb and scissors and rethought her laugh.

"Hey Miss Thang, you're doing my hair next. You better fix that funky attitude before you get up in my head. I don't wanna have to mess you up." Yolanda was playing with the woman in chair number two. The woman just ignored Yolanda and kept on with Chanel's hair.

Khadijah was seated in chair number three. She was the youngest of the women in the salon. She had one picture of her and a handsome man and two little girls and her belly sat out like she was about to explode. She was very close to dropping the next baby.

The small framed woman with the turban greeted Khadijah with a handshake. "Hi, my name is Rasheedah."

Smiling at the similarity of their names Khadijah returned the shake. "Hello. I'm Khadijah. Rasheedah? That's pretty. Do you know its meaning?"

"Yes I do. It means, Rightly Guided. Do you know what your name means?"

"No. Actually I don't. I was born at a time when parents named their children with a name that either caught people's attention or in some sick kind of way, they wanted to watch their child struggle trying to learn to spell it in kindergarten." They both laughed.

"Khadijah means, The First Wife of The Holy Prophet, Saaw." Khadijah nodded still unsure of the actual meaning but was happy with her lesson on names.

Chanel, Karyn and Cee-Cee sat watching videos on BET as they waited for Yolanda, Avery and Jaylen to get their hair done.

Meanwhile, Jamale was returning from Love Field Airport with Cee-Cee's mom. The fellas were finishing up with their last minute grooming and getting ready to get into their tuxedos. Adrian was over to Peter and Austin's and Marquis was at his loft setting up the guest room for Cee-Cee's mother.

The men looked good. When the doorbell rang, Peter looked out of the living room window before approaching the door. He saw the 300M with tinted windows parked on the corner and sweat started forming on his forehead. He couldn't avoid answering the door after the second ring. His heart was relieved when he saw the cream colored stretch limousine parked in the front of the house. The older gentleman spoke with a European accent when he announced he was there to pick up the LeTreau wedding party.

Peter, Adrian and Austin got into the car as Peter watched the 300M pull off behind them. They headed down interstate 30 towards Lamar to pick up Jamale, Marquis and Mrs. Peterson.

Yolanda, Karyn, Chanel, Avery and Jaylen were waiting for Cee-Cee to come downstairs. Cee-Cee stood at the top of the staircase like a bride from any movie scene.

"Ooh mommy. You're so beautiful." Cee-Cee smiled at her son as she slowly came down the stairs.

"Thank you baby."

The second cream colored stretched limousine was parked outside of Jamale's house waiting to pick up the rest of the wedding party.

Before the wedding party arrived at the church, the flowers were delivered. The first box of the three had four single long stem red roses. The second had five boutonnieres made with a red rose. In the final box was an incredible bouquet of miniature red and white roses for the bride.

The first car arrived with the men and Cee-Cee's mother. The men headed towards the reserved room for the groom as Mrs. Peterson walked towards the parked green Dodge Stratus. She walked faster than her legs were allowing, and her limp became more prevalent than when she started. The man in the Stratus seemed agitated when he noticed Mrs. Peterson crossing the street.

Mrs. Peterson's frail hand tapped on the glass until the window went down before she spoke. "Jeff, I wish I could be friendlier with you after all these years, but today ain't the day. My baby is about to be married, and you ain't gonna mess this up for her and Jaylen. You hear me?!" She waited at the window with her eyes focused on his face.

"Jaylen is MY son. I have rights too."

Her tiny old fist was up in front of his face waving as if she were going to sock him in his nose. "Boy, I ain't playing with you. You get yourself out of here before I have to lose my religion. You here me? Go on now." Mrs. Peterson stepped back as he started the car.

As she headed back towards the church, the second limousine drove up. The door swung open just as Mrs. Peterson crossed the street.

"Grandma!" Jaylen hurried to hug her.

"Hey baby. Turn around and let me look at you."

Karyn, Chanel, Yolanda and Avery stood by the car while Mrs. Peterson introduced herself.

Cee-Cee leaned her head outside the door of the limo and called for her maid of honor. "Yolanda?"

"Yeah girl."

"Do me a favor and check where Jamale is before I go into the church."

"Okay." Before Yolanda could step away, Marquis was walking towards the car.

"Hey ladies. You ladies look absolutely beautiful. Jamale asked me to come out to make sure you had arrived."

"Yeah right. He was making sure Cee-Cee made it." Everyone

smiled as Yolanda reached out her hand to Marquis. "Hey, I'm Yolanda."

"Good to meet you. I'm Marquis." Looking over to the next lady he added, "You must be Karyn. Peter described you very well." Karyn was blushing.

When Marquis fixed his eyes on Chanel, he couldn't believe what he was seeing. He stood speechless for a moment. It was too much to believe. She was identical to Alyssa; the woman he had enjoyed watching as her naked body swayed seductively to music.

"Hello. You must be Chanel."

"Hi. Yes, I am." Her smile was so innocent. Although she looked like her sister, it was evident they were very different.

Cee-Cee loved being in her moms arms. She couldn't resist her tears of happiness. It was the most special day of her life, and her mom was there to share it with her. When she and Jeff were married it was at the Justice of The Peace with no family or friends.

Mrs. Peterson spoke at a gentle whisper. "You stop all that crying. Come on, we have to get you ready." They walked behind the other women into the church. Marquis took Jaylen and Avery with him to see Jamale for a little coaching before the ceremony. Cee-Cee, her mother and Yolanda went into the bride's room to fit the veil onto Cee's head, and Karyn, Khadijah and Chanel were opening boxes with flowers. Just as they opened the first box, Peter cleared his throat to get the ladies attention. They each turned around simultaneously.

"Austin and Peter, I don't know 'bout y'all, but these are some of the most beautiful women I've seen in a long time." Although Adrian was generalizing with his statement, he was focused on Chanel."

Austin stared at Khadijah and walked over to her as he spoke,

"Yeah man, they are beautiful." He wrapped his arms around her waist and lightly kissed her lips.

Peter stepped a little closer to Karyn and took her hand as he agreed with his brothers. "Yes, they are beautiful. More beautiful than I could have ever imagined."

Karyn, Chanel and Khadijah loved the attention the men were giving them. Unfortunately, it wasn't the time to lavish in it. Karyn broke up the warm and fuzzy moment when she enthusiastically thanked the men. "Thank you fellas. You guys look awfully handsome yourselves, but we need to get your boutonnieres pinned onto you so we can get this wedding started. That is if you don't mind us helping you."

Each of the men bent down so the ladies could pin the flower onto their lapel. As Peter was getting pinned, he looked towards the door and saw the large White man with dark shades on. Everyone stopped to look at the man when Austin spoke up. "Hi. How can I help you?"

Without any hesitation and without a smile, he responded. "I need to see Peter."

Austin put two and two together and asked everyone to excuse him and Peter for a moment. Austin whispered to his brother while the others stood looking. "Man, tell me you paid that bookie."

"Man I got his money in my jacket. I got caught up yesterday and couldn't get to it. Give me a minute, I'll handle it."

"Okay. I'll divert everyone's attention to something else." Austin called the group over towards the stairwell and suggested they each practice their march down the aisle before the ceremony began. They agreed.

Peter reached for his inside pocket and handed the white envelope to Franco. "Here man. It's all there. I got tied up and wasn't able to get with you yesterday. I hope we're cool."

"Oh, is that what you think? I told you not to mess with my money. I also told you to have my money yesterday. I'm not gonna mess up no ones wedding so keep an eye out for me after the ceremony." Franco had his finger pointing in Peters face while he spoke. Before Peter could respond, Franco was going out the door headed for his car.

Each of the couples practiced a couple of times marching down the aisle when the pianist started playing some notes to warm up.

The sanctuary was beautiful. There were red and white candles throughout the sanctuary, and every other pew had a red or white satin bow.

Pastor Smith had arrived twenty minutes before the few guests who were invited began filling the church. The groomsmen lit the twelve candles that were positioned along the aisle as the church lights were dimmed. Jamale and Marquis took their places left of the pastor and the pianist played as Chanel and Adrian, Khadijah and Austin, Karyn and Peter marched down the aisle.

Yolanda marched in alone, but when she reached the halfway point, Marquis joined her to walk with her as she held onto his arm. Yolanda stood with pride as she watched Avery march carrying the small white satin pillow with the tiny gold wedding bands and miniature red roses.

It was time. The pianist played the traditional four chords that alerted the guests to stand to wait for the bride to make her entrance. Cee-Cee was stunning and Jamale stood smiling and waiting for his bride to join him. Jaylen walked slowly with his mother on arm. And when they arrived at the altar, Jaylen gave Jamale a big hug and whispered, "Thanks."

Jamale gazed into his bride's eyes as the pianist played the first few notes of the song Jamale had selected to sing for her. None of the guests or the wedding party knew that Jamale had planned on singing to Cee. When Jamale began singing, the ladies eyes began to water. Cee-Cee loved every word he was singing and she could feel each word as he sang from his heart as if he had written them for her.

"For you I give a lifetime of stability. Anything you want of me. Nothing is impossible. For you, there are no words or ways to show my love or all the thoughts I'm thinking of. 'Cause this life is no good alone. Since we've become one I've made a change..."

Jamale reached for Cee-Cee's hand as he finished the verses to the song. Her tears fell as she felt his hands holding onto hers tighter as the song's lyrics poured out the words that reflected how he loved her.

Yolanda handed Cee-Cee a tissue to wipe her tears. Jamale took the tissue from Cee-Cee and wiped her eyes. He winked at Cee-Cee and smiled hoping that would help her to smile.

The pastor spoke a few words about the sanctity in the union of marriage. He began with Jamale and then Cee-Cee repeated their vows. Avery handed them the rings to be placed on their fingers and then they kissed a very passionate kiss. The crowd applauded and was very happy when the announcement was made. "Ladies and Gentlemen, I present to you, Jamale and Nikkia LeTreau."

The guests stood as the bride and groom walked up the aisle. The wedding party followed until they reached the back of the church. Jamale, Jaylen and Cee-Cee continued around, back to the front alter. The rest of the party lined up to wait for the bride and groom to finish with a couple of pictures that Cee-Cee had requested from the photographer. She wanted a picture of her and Jamale and one with her, Jaylen and Jamale for the frame that Karyn had bought as a gift.

Cee-Cee, Jamale and Jaylen joined the rest of the wedding party in the foyer. Jaylen stood by Avery as Jamale and Cee-Cee went to the front of the line so they could be the last one to thank the guests for coming. There were people there that Cee-Cee had never seen, but she figured they were people Jamale worked with or knew some kind of way.

Peter, Austin and Adrian watched the familiar guest in the navy suit and couldn't imagine why she was there. Surely there was no invitation. She had no reasonable cause to be there, but she was there and making her way through the receiving line.

As she passed the three men she had shared a couple of Monday nights with, she greeted them with a smile, but the men didn't return the gesture. When she got to Peter, she lipped the words, "Like I said, my man." Peter tried to make out her words, but couldn't figure them out. Marquis was the last of the bridal party before the bride and groom, and when he saw her, he shared the same shocked expression as the three men behind him. But before he could ask questions, she had moved onto the happily married couple.

Cee-Cee extended her hand to thank the woman for coming, but the woman didn't respond. She moved another step in front of Jamale. Jamale wasn't smiling when he turned his head to greet his next guests and realized who was standing in front of him.

Cee-Cee looked surprised by Jamale's agitation, and before anyone could react, the surprise guest reached into her purse for the long nosed .38 caliber handgun. The gun was pointing at Jamale's chest, and Cee-Cee was screaming. The two shots that were fired silenced the scream and caused everyone to respond. It was horrifying, and before Jamale's body fell to the ground, his blood splattered on each of his boys faces.

Tiffany. The woman who believed she was supposed to be the special woman in Jamale's life. The woman who claimed to be Jamale's woman months after he dismissed her at Friday's. The woman who Peter classified as an ignorant fatal nut case. The woman who lived by her creed, "you got it, and I want it." The woman who didn't know the words "can't have."

Tiffany tried to run, but Peter tackled her to the ground as if she were any player with pads and helmet on the green turf of a football field. Adrian stood over his brother trying to make sense of his words while he shouted for someone to call 9-1-1. Marquis immediately began tearing open the buttons to Jamale's tuxedo and shirt hoping to apply enough pressure to Jamale's chest to stop the gushing blood from Jamale's body. Austin was trying to calm the women and children that were panicking and trying to find shelter from whatever else may happen. Cee-Cee was on her knees crying hysterically. Nothing made sense. She had the head of the man she'd just married resting on her lap as he laid motionless.

The situation wasn't good. Two close range taps to the chest by two fast moving bullets. Survival was almost unfeasible.

Some of the guests at the church were taking cover from what could have been a spree of bullets and others were watching in disbelief. The videographer was taping the event as if he would have intentions on submitting the footage to an amateur film festival. And the pastor was trying to calm the pregnant woman in the church. Curious as to what the pandemonium could be at the small church on the corner, the onlookers grew larger as the flashing lights of the emergency vehicles came swarming down the street. Cars were stopped in the middle of the road with passengers trying to get a view of what appeared to be a thriller film. The dramatic scene had all the remnants of horror. Women and children were screaming and running from the crazy person who brought fear to their lives. His blood drenched clothing and his lifeless body lay on the ground with his blood draining onto the sidewalk. All that was missing was the chilling and suspenseful music that played just as the plot thickened.

Franco waited outside the door of the church when the wedding started. He kept the door slightly opened to be sure that he kept his eyes on everything going on inside the church. He had a feeling Peter, that forever dodging nigga would try to give him the slip after the wedding.

He was the first to see her. His street sense told him that something was wrong and that the big lump in her purse was unusual. She shot Jamale with the calmness of a professional assassin, and all hell broke loose after that. The only thought on Franco's mind was that the police would think he had a part in the shooting. His street code told him he had to do something to Peter, but nothing remotely close to what the female had just done to the groom on his wedding day. Franco's common sense told him that Peter had suffered enough and that it was time for him to get the hell out of Dodge before the police arrived.

The police and paramedics arrived quickly. Tiffany looked like a mad woman when the police officers cuffed her and stood her to her feet. The hat she wore was no longer covering the hair that had become matted to her head. The make-up she used to cover the dark rings beneath her eyes was no longer there and she had spit forming in the corner of her mouth as if she were suffering with rabies. She was a site for sore eyes, and she shouted out the words that sounded demonic and surprised the officers. She began shouting, "NO MAN CAN FUCK OVER ME!" Tiffany repeatedly shouted those words louder each time as her bulging eyes turned bloodshot red.

"SHUT UP! SHUT HER UP!" Hysterically, Cee-Cee started screaming until the officer placed Tiffany into the back seat of the black and white sedan.

Jamale had lost a lot of blood while he lay on the ground. When the paramedics arrived, Jamale was unconscious. They did everything they could to keep him alive while rushing him to the hospital. Marquis, Adrian, Austin and Peter rode in the limousine to the hospital. Everyone knew Cee-Cee was a wreck and hoped the paramedics would be able to control her crying while in route to the hospital.

22

Although the emergency vehicle had its sirens blaring, red and blue flashing lights and two police cars to help them through traffic, it was rush hour traffic, and the highway was at a deadlock. The driver of the first limousine had taken a few turns differently than the ambulance driver and was able to avoid the accident that kept the ambulance creeping through the congested traffic on 75 Central Expressway. As the stretch limousine whipped around the corner towards the emergency room doors, there were people standing outside smoking, laughing and enjoying life with what appeared not a care in this world.

When the limousine stopped in front of the emergency room doors, all activity instinctively came to a halt. Cigarettes weren't being inhaled, laughing and conversations had ended, and steps were stopped in their tracks. When the onlookers saw the wedding party rushing from the car with blood stained clothing and the pain in their faces, the people moved to the side speculating what could have happened. It was clearly a wedding day horror story.

The second limousine followed the loud spastic sound from the horn that blew as the ambulance backed up to the doors. Staff nurses and doctors who had been waiting for the ambulance that carried the wounded groom rushed towards the door. There were unfamiliar terms being yelled to one another as they pulled the gurney from the ambulance up onto its legs and through the doors of the emergency room. The white sheets draped over Jamale were covered with his crimson blood and the hospital spectators stood mortified when Cee-Cee was helped from the ambulance. Her blood drenched wedding gown no longer possessed the beauty of a stunning bride, and it was Cee-Cee's crimson stained dress that intensified the chatter from the few people outside.

The eight steps towards the electric doors took an eternity, so it seemed. Cee-Cee's first attempt at doing what should have been normal wasn't. Walking was a natural motion of an everyday routine that no longer made sense. With the help of her mother's arm, Cee-Cee was able to make it past the people and into the building that would have dominion over her near future.

Austin and Adrian stopped Marquis before entering the automatic doors. Adrian remembered the last time he and Marquis had entered an emergency room doors and asked with great concern. "Bruh, how you holding up? Are you okay?"

"I'll be fine." Distressed, Marquis spoke as he turned and walked away from his brothers to join Cee-Cee.

The haunting memories of the tragic day the ambulance hurried Tyrone into the emergency room were ripping at Marquis' heart. The familiar smell of death was in the air; the unfeeling expressions of the faces of the people who were assigned to treat the injured; the sounds of heavy hearts as they beat with fear, sympathy and reality and the tragedy of death had taken harbor in Marquis' soul in the confined walls of an emergency room.

Marquis had taken on the burden of strength for the group. He felt he had earned his position having suffered the tragic loss of his brother. As he sat with the familiar weight of Cee-Cee's sorrow and the grief from Mrs. Peterson and his fraternity brother's tears on his shoulders, he was starting to weigh down. But he couldn't cry. He wouldn't cry. Marquis had yet to shed a tear.

"Baby girl, I know this is gonna be hard for you, but you're gonna have to be strong for Jamale."

Cee-Cee fell into Marquis' arms and cried, "I don't know if I can. Marquis, I can't lose him. I love him so much. I..." She began crying again causing Adrian, Austin and Peter to weep.

Cee-Cee's eyes were sad, and her heart was pleading as she spoke. "Oh God, have mercy. Marquis, I can't live without him. Please tell me he's okay. You were with him on the ground. What's going on? Marquis, please tell me he's gonna make it through this." Cee-Cee's eyes were as red as the blood that covered her hands. As she held her hands in front of her, they began trembling as much as the shrilling scream poured out from her mouth. When Cee-Cee could finally grasp the harsh reality that the blood that covered her hands was that of the man she loved, her pleading words carried like rumbling thunder. "OH GOD!"

Adrian, Austin and Peter sat with tears falling from their eyes while Marquis cradled Cee-Cee in his arms. Jamale was more than a fraternity brother, he was a brother they loved and Cee-Cee was their sister and they loved her too.

Adrian grabbed hold of Cee-Cee relieving Marquis from the suffering of trying to comfort her. As he cradled his heart broken sister in his arms, he whispered in her ear until she relaxed to the sound of his voice. "Baby girl, you have to be strong, Jamale needs all of your strength to make it through this."

Holding onto hope, Cee-Cee followed her husband as they pushed him through the electric doors. Everything going on had Cee-Cee paralyzed and deaf to the woman who was trying to get information from her. As the gurney was pushed through the doors towards the elevator that lead to surgery, Cee-Cee tried to walk, but her legs gave from under her. She fell to her knees and cried out to God. "Father, please, Father!"

Jaylen and the other wedding party members followed as Jamale was being wheeled out of the emergency room. As they entered, Jaylen saw his mother on the floor crying and praying in her blood drenched wedding gown. He ran to her and sat on the floor trying to comfort his mother in his little arms. "Momma, please don't cry. Please momma. Everything's gonna be okay." His strong words were weakened by the tears that fell from his innocent eyes. He was scared, hurt and had never seen his mother grieve before.

Everyone watched, but no one would interrupt them. Wrapped in the comforts of his young arms, she poured out her heart. "Jaylen, oh baby. My baby. I can't. I can't. I..." Cee-Cee began crying harder and louder repeating the words, "Oh God, Oh God." Cee-Cee's mother couldn't take any more. She stood her daughter and grandson to their feet and wrapped her frail arms around them and began quoting the 23rd Psalm.

Cee-Cee calmed down long enough to listen to her mother's instructions. "Baby, we have to go upstairs where Jamale is. I'm going to have Yolanda take the children home. They don't need to be here." Cee-Cee was trying to comprehend what her mother was saying, but nothing made sense.

Marquis took over holding Cee-Cee up while Yolanda agreed to take the children home. Karyn was comforting Peter; Chanel was comforting Adrian and Khadijah comforted Austin as they rode the elevator to the third floor. Unable to move, Marquis and Mrs. Peterson stood with Cee-Cee as they comforted her until the next elevator car came for them to ride up.

The signs on the wall as you exited the elevators had specific directions for the waiting rooms to the left and surgery to the right. The steel doors on the right had in bold letters above it, AUTHORIZED PERSONNEL ONLY. At that moment, Cee-Cee felt she had earned the status as an authorized person. Her husband was behind those steel doors fighting for his life.

The hollow sound of the third floor was piercing. The televisions in the separate waiting rooms seemed to echo although the volume was turned down. The few people's voices who occupied rooms seemed increased, and as the steel doors opened and shut the sound of them swinging were exaggerated.

The people who cared for Jamale sat quietly while he was being operated on. The crying from Cee-Cee and the others had reduced to spurts of outcries and uncontrollable tears streaming down their faces. The surgery had lasted three hours and when over, Jamale would be taken to recovery while the doctors came out to talk with Cee-Cee.

The slender, bald headed doctor in the green scrubs entered the waiting room, and everyone hurried to their feet. Through his black horn rimmed glasses that overshadowed his face, his tired eyes focused on Cee-Cee's wedding gown. Reactively, he walked in front of her reaching his hand out to shake hers.

"Mrs. LeTreau, hi, I'm Doctor Brumfield. I was one of your husband's surgeons." Pausing to give Cee-Cee an opportunity to speak, the doctor knew the information he had yet to share wouldn't be easy to pass forward. He held Cee-Cee's hand and looked over to Marquis as if signaling him to hold onto her before the words cut through her hopeful heart.

"Surgery went well. We were able to remove one of the bullets; however, the second one is lodged on the base of his spine. We felt it would be too much of a risk to try to remove it." Dr. Brumfield's words were sharp and painful.

Cee-Cee held onto Marquis' arm as she tried to maintain her balance. Standing had become an impossible feat. Her legs were becoming weak, and her head was beginning to feel the effects of not breathing. It was time to take a seat. Cee-Cee sat on the orange vinyl recliner chair clutching the two arms with the strongest grip she could muster.

Her eyes were weary, and her words were faint when she finally spoke. Cee-Cee was on the verge of mental exhaustion, and the doctor knew it. "I don't know what that means exactly. Right now, all I want to know is, when can I see him?"

When the doctor removed his glasses, his eyes were filled with compassion. The pressure in an operating room was no comparison to the pressure of delivering the surgery results to the loved ones in the waiting room.

Squatting down in front of Cee-Cee, Dr. Brumfield reached for her hands. He held her hands gently and spoke with a very unruffled voice; almost rehearsed.

"Mrs. LeTreau, Jamale is resting comfortably." He paused for a moment to make sure Cee-Cee was ingesting the information well enough for him to continue and she was until he finished delivering the status of Jamale's condition. "Mrs. LeTreau, your husband is in a coma. He..." Before he could finish, Cee-Cee slid onto the floor with her head buried into her hands, screaming and crying. Mrs. Peterson rushed to cradle her daughter while she rocked back and forth crying.

The news brought on an immediate reaction from each of the men. Peter fell into Karyn's arms to cry. Austin pressed his forehead against the wall and held Khadijah's hand and repeatedly slapped the wall with his other hand. Khadijah held onto Austin telling him it was going to be okay, while Adrian paced back and forth with tears streaming down his face as Chanel caressed his shoulder gently. But Marquis maintained his upright and strong posture as he listened to the doctor tell him they had done all they could do for now and walked away.

After the doctor left, a middle aged woman entered and stood in front of Peter and Karyn. She knew trying to give instructions to Cee-Cee would be hopeless at the moment.

"Mr. LeTreau will be moved to ICU down the hall in about forty-five minutes. There's a waiting room on the west side of the floor near the room he will be in. Also, there's a cafeteria on the ground floor east of the main entrance. Perhaps you should get something while you wait." She was friendly, helpful and very professional. It was obvious she had given those instructions many times.

The wait was long. As much as the ladies wanted to say the right things to make their men feel better, there were no right words. They couldn't relate to the bond these men felt. They were witnessing four strong Black men at their most vulnerable point. Helplessness had become their companion as they sat with their heads hung low and buried into their hands while exhaustion took over their hearts, minds and souls.

Austin couldn't hold on any longer. He began to cry loud enough to catch the attention of his brothers. Austin's chest was heaving up and down as he clutched his head in disbelief. Peter and Adrian went to their brother and tried to comfort him, but he was despondent. Peter and Adrian's tears fell as they held onto their brother.

"Bruh, come on. Let's go for a walk." Peter reached for his brothers' arm and led him down the hall.

As they walked towards the elevators, they could see the bed coming towards them. The pale man with the taped tube coming from his mouth was Jamale. He was no longer the dapper man in the cream tuxedo standing at the altar smiling and proud. He had become lifeless and dependent of medicines and machinery. He was at the mercy of God, and Peter and Austin knew it as they stood against the wall as Jamale passed.

The women at the nurses' station looked at the two broken men as they stood motionless in their black tuxedos. The wedding horror had spread throughout the hospital, and there was compassion and empathy from everyone who could take witness to their grief. One nurse walked from around her desk to ask the brothers if they needed anything. Their eyes spoke the words of sorrow that wished for anyone to make their nightmare go away. Peter thanked her as they walked back towards the waiting room. The nurse couldn't help the tears that filled her eyes.

When Peter and Austin returned with the others, Peter gave an expression that said to Marquis and Adrian that Austin would be okay. Peter signaled Marquis to come out into the hallway for a moment. Cee-Cee was still shedding tears and shaking her head in disbelief, so Marquis got approval from Cee-Cee's mother that it would be okay for him to leave her.
"What's up?" Marquis spoke in a whisper.

"They just took Jamale into his room. They should be calling for us to visit real soon. Do you think Cee is ready?"

"Naw, man. I think we should go in first and then Cee and her moms could go afterwards. That way they could have all the time they need."

"Okay. Maybe you should tell her that Jamale made it over here." Peter had leaned on Marquis' words of wisdom as if Marquis had graduated from the school of good judgment.

"Yeah, I'll do that." Marquis was very solemn. Although he was coherent of everything that was going on around him, he was behaving like he was completely controlled by the will of time and he only existed.

Cee-Cee's head lifted with hope when Marquis shared the news. She rested her head on her mother's shoulder and wiped her tears with the powder blue handkerchief that was given to her from her mother as one of the traditional "something borrowed, something new" gifts.

Finally, it was time. The nurse walked into the sorrow filled waiting room to tell Cee-Cee and the others that Jamale could have visitors; short visits, a few at a time.

The fellas agreed that Cee-Cee wasn't ready to go into the room. Cee-Cee also knew she wasn't ready, so she agreed they should go in first.

Their visits were one at a time. Austin went first and although he'd seen Jamale briefly in the hall, he wasn't prepared to sit with his brother and not be able to share a laugh. Austin's tears fell as fast as his heart was beating. He sat down in the chair that was on the right side of Jamale's framed bed. Austin touched Jamale's lifeless hand and began trying to hold a sensible conversation. "Hey man, you need to hurry and get up. We got a Super Bowl to watch. You know I need you to back me up when the other fellas start talking mess."

Austin paused to wipe his tears and to look up to God. Leaning a little closer to Jamale, Austin couldn't find any base in his voice. His loving words came out in hushed tones, "Hey man, I love you bruh. I'm gonna go on and let the other brothers come in and see you." Austin stood to lean close to Jamale's ear hoping to penetrate to his heart or brain to make him react. Austin cried the words, "I love you, bruh."

Marquis comforted Austin as he walked down the hall crying. Austin couldn't allow Cee-Cee to see him broken. Peter knew Austin would be taken care of by Marquis so instead of going to comfort his brother, he gained his composer and went into the room with Jamale.

Peter ran his fingers through his hair as he looked at the man he promised to love and support the day he pledged. His fraternity brother was holding onto life by machines, and Peter was angry this was happening to Jamale. He tried to hold his tears in, but he couldn't. It was all so senseless. Peter stood at the side of the bed looking at Jamale, trying to find the right words that could tell him how much he loved him and needed him to pull through this.

"Jamale, man, you know you need to open those eyes and say something." Peter was doing well with his words until suddenly his voice began to crack from the cry that needed to leave his heart. "Man, who's gonna teach me how to know love when it comes my way?" Peter put his hands to his mouth to cover the cry that escaped. He rested his head on Jamale's chest and tried to wrap his arms around him when Peter looked at Jamale's face before he spoke. "Jamale, I love you man. I love you bruh." Peter kissed Jamale on his cheek and turned to leave the room. He stopped at the door to take another look or to say something else, but he couldn't. He didn't want another image that would haunt him later.

Austin was waiting outside the room to comfort Peter when he left Jamale. The nurses watched as the men alternated walking down the hall crying. Although they had witnessed the tears of people mourning for their loved ones each day in ICU, never had the nurses experienced watching such compassion and grief as they did with the Kappa men.

Adrian had never experienced death or near death of anyone

significant in his life. His parents were still very much alive, and he had no biological brothers or sisters. Jamale and the other fellas were his brothers, and he was now being introduced to the sorrows of fate.

Adrian entered the room and stood in front of the door inhaling and exhaling a couple of times before his feet would move. He stood at the foot of the bed for a moment concentrating on each piece of machinery that surrounded the room. Before he could look down at Jamale, he heard the prayer that seemed to keep repeating in his mind. The words had Chanel's voice behind them. "Lord, you said your grace is sufficient, for your powers are made perfect in weakness…" Adrian needed His grace and powers more than ever because he had definitely become weak.

He lowered his eyes onto the outline of Jamale's feet under the white woven blanket. Adrian's eyes followed up Jamale's torso until he reached Jamale's shoulders. He couldn't go any further. Adrian closed his eyes and lowered his head allowing the tears to stream down his face and onto the floor. He tried to speak, but the words weren't coming out. Adrian walked closer to the head of the bed and found the chair. He sat for a moment when God's grace and power found him.

"Jamale, I have something beautiful to tell you. I think I'm in love with Chanel. Man, she reminds me of Cee-Cee. You know, the part about her love for God? Man, I used to trip on your story about how you met Cee, but now I know what you were feeling. It's a trip. There's something really special about her." Adrian was smiling and feeling comforted while talking to Jamale. He had forgotten for a moment the situation Jamale was in. God was doing what He'd promised.

Adrian stood to finish speaking to Jamale before saying good bye. Tears were building in his eyes once more, but he wasn't feeling weak. He leaned in closer to Jamale and told him that he loved him before kissing Jamale on the forehead and turning to leave the room.

Marquis was relieved when he somehow saw joy in Adrian's eyes. He didn't understand what had happened with Adrian in the room, but he knew it was his turn to walk through that wooden door that contained a room of unfortunate and meaningless despair.

Before Marquis could push the door, he heard footsteps coming close to him. He turned and saw Pastor Smith standing with his bible in hand. They embraced for a moment when Pastor Smith spoke. "Brother, God is the final decision maker. Take comfort in knowing Jamale knows Christ." Marquis nodded with affirmation as the pastor walked towards the waiting room.

Marquis walked into the room knowing what he had to say. He held Jamale's hand and began. "Hey bruh." Clearing his throat before continuing. "Things don't look too great right now, but you know you gotta pull through this. You have a new wife and son who are depending on you. Man, Cee-Cee is being really brave out there. She loves you so much." Marquis put his head down with his eyes closed before speaking further.

"Bruh, I'm your best man. I'm supposed to do everything for you today. I wish I knew what I could do to help you through this. When you think about it, let me know." Marquis tried to make humor and laugh, but it just wouldn't come out.

"Jamale, I love you man. I promise I'm gonna keep being your best man. I'll be looking out for you until you pull out of this. Don't worry about Cee and Jaylen…" Hitting his fist on his chest. "…I got this." Marquis squatted and put Jamale's hand into his hands and kissed it. "I love you man. Hear? I love you!" Marquis left the room and walked with Peter on his left and Austin on his right with his arms around both of them.

As the time approached for Cee-Cee to visit, Marquis asked if she needed him to go in with her, but she said no, she would have her mother go in with her. She'd stopped crying and knew she had to be strong.

It was awful. Jamale laid there in his metal framed bed, still, like a corpse. There were machines everywhere. He had monitors connected to him that seemed to register his every internal movement.

Cee-Cee couldn't help her tears. Cee-Cee leaned over Jamale and kissed his lips, whispering the words, "I love you." She sat in the chair beside him and held his hand. For a moment, every machine and monitor sounded amplified. Even the drip from the IV was loud. Cee-Cee was about to lose control but instead she took comfort in holding his hand. She held Jamale's hand tightly and began talking to him.

"Baby, don't you do this to me. I need you to hurry up and get out of here. We got a lot of things to do." Between words were sniffles as she continued. "I haven't told you how much I love you and thanked you for your wonderful wedding gift." Cee-Cee wiped her tears and tried to gain control of herself by sitting up in the chair and fixing her hair with her hand. She whispered, "Jamale, please let me know you can hear me. Try to squeeze my fingers or flutter your eyes." Cee-Cee sat for a moment hoping there would be some movement, but nothing. She repeated her instructions once more hoping there would be a reaction, but again, nothing. There was no movement from Jamale and the hope was beginning to turn to hopelessness for Cee-Cee. But she knew she couldn't give up.

She continued with what she thought would be the key to getting Jamale to respond. Taking in a deep breath and smiling, Cee-Cee began asking questions. She spoke to Jamale as if he were sitting upright and listening attentively.

"Remember the day we met and I told you my name? Remember how you asked me how I got Cee-Cee from Nikkia and I told you I'd have to tell you about it one day?" Cee-Cee smiled thinking about the day they'd met. Jamale was her knight in shining armor, and she was in love. Cee-Cee looked at her mother standing at the foot of the bed and smiled before she began the story.

"Jamale you need to try hard to let me know you can hear me. You have to move your finger, so I know you hear me. I promised I would tell you this story, and I want to know you heard it." Cee-Cee was staring at Jamale's eyes as if they were going to open to let her know he was paying attention. She was trying to be hopeful as she smiled, not giving up on the man she loved.

"Well, here it is. This is how I got my nickname. When I was born, my mother told me my dad was away on business. The day before my mom and I were able to leave the hospital, my dad made it back in town and hurried to the hospital. He was so happy the first time he saw me that he cried and was so proud of his little girl. He held me while I slept in his arms and he told my mom that my skin was so smooth and creamy. He was dreamy eyed when he looked down at me.

That same day my mom sent my aunt out shopping for this special little dress she had seen in the baby department at Neiman Marcus Department Store. The next day when it was time for us to be released from the hospital, daddy came to get us and my mom had me dressed in a little crimson colored dress. Jamale, my daddy was a Nupe too." Cee's words were beginning to fade.

"When he saw me, he nicknamed me Cee-Cee for Crimson and Cream. That's how I got the name." She began crying. She missed her daddy, and she was missing her husband's love. Her mom smiled while listening to Cee-Cee.

At first Cee-Cee thought, it was her imagination. She sat still, concentrating on her hand that held Jamale's. There, it was again. She was sure the second time. Cee-Cee felt Jamale's fingers wiggle in her hand. Unsure how to react, she called his name softly and stood to talk with him. "Jamale? Baby..." Suddenly the sound of the monitor was louder than ever. It was no longer a beep. It was a loud and long constant sound. Jamale had gone into cardiac arrest.

The doctors and nurses rushed into the room pushing Cee-Cee away from the bed. She backed away further and was speechless and numb. Cee-Cee and her mother stood in the corner of the room with her mother not understanding what was going on. She had just felt Jamale move his fingers. He was letting her know he heard her story. What the hell was going on?

The doctor tried repeatedly to revive his heart, but nothing. He punched Jamale's chest as if he were trying to break into it, but nothing. It was over. He looked over to the nurse for the time. The nurse announced the time of death and pulled the white sheet over Jamale's face. Cee-Cee stood in the corner of the room in her wedding dress with Jamale's blood covering it when the echoing sound of Cee-Cee's scream filtered through the hollow halls. "NOOOOOOOOO!!! NOOOOOOOOO!!!"

The wedding party didn't know what was going on behind those doors, but they rushed into the room as the hospital staff was exiting. When they got into the room, they saw that Jamale was gone. Cee-Cee was in the corner of the room hysterical, and her mother couldn't hold her back as she tried to get to Jamale. Peter, Austin and Adrian had to grab Cee-Cee while the women stood by the door crying.

Without warning the aching scream from down the hall surprised them and hit them like a bolt of lightning. Marquis had finally accepted the reality of the day and his scream shattered the souls of everyone on the floor. Pastor Smith ran to Marquis as he heard the words pouring from him, "GOD, WHY?"

The funeral was held five days later. It felt more like a dream than a reality for the fraternity brothers. Each were in their own world, and each found the strength to go on from the memory of their lost brother.

Marquis understood the only way he was finally able to deal with the loss of his younger brother Tyrone was by being forced to deal with the loss of his frat brother. He wanted to laugh and cry at the same time. He felt relief and grief in the same thought.

Adrian still couldn't believe how cruel life could be. He felt Jamale was just beginning his life, and it was cut short. He knew now that whatever he wanted to do in life, he had to do. He had to think not only what was best for Chanel's career, but also what was best for him and Chanel because life was too short and time was running out.

Austin was afraid of losing his brother to his gambling habit. He was also afraid of losing the woman he loved because she was married. The same woman he had lost before. He was afraid of losing a life-long dream of a job because of the woman he loved. He was afraid because the death of his friend showed him that he could lose in life, but he had to be strong. Jamale showed him it was all right to be afraid sometimes. Love would give him the strength he needed to survive.

Peter was the most shaken by his frats' death. It ran through his head a thousand times, that could have been me and not just for his gambling. Peter knew that Franco could have easily been on the other end of that gun and with him being buried now. In fact, he would have traded places with Jamale in a minute. He suddenly understood that it could have been any one of them. All of the women he and the fellas had run through and all the games over the years. What was so sad was Jamale was out of the game. He had surrendered his players' card, but Peter couldn't understand why that card had to leave with a new wife and the end of his life. It was over. No more gambling or games of any kind for him.

Cee-Cee could not find strength or understanding in her husbands' death. She was also in a dream world; the one when you wake up and the nightmare is still there. She couldn't believe that God could let this happen to her. Surely she must have done something in her life to deserve this, but she couldn't remember what.

At first she thought her ex-husband Jeff had something to do with the murder. Somehow Jeff and Tiffany had met, plotted and planned, and he had followed through with his threat, but she realized later he had nothing to do with it. And Cee-Cee couldn't understand how God could let her marry a man one day and bury him in the same week.

If it wasn't her, then it was Jamale, and the Nupes that God was evening the score with. She began to resent the frat her father and husband had been members of. What had these men been capable of doing that would make a woman murder one of them on their own wedding day? Cee-Cee would spend the rest of her life trying to figure the pain and suffering behind "Crimson and Cream."